Of Thorn and Thread

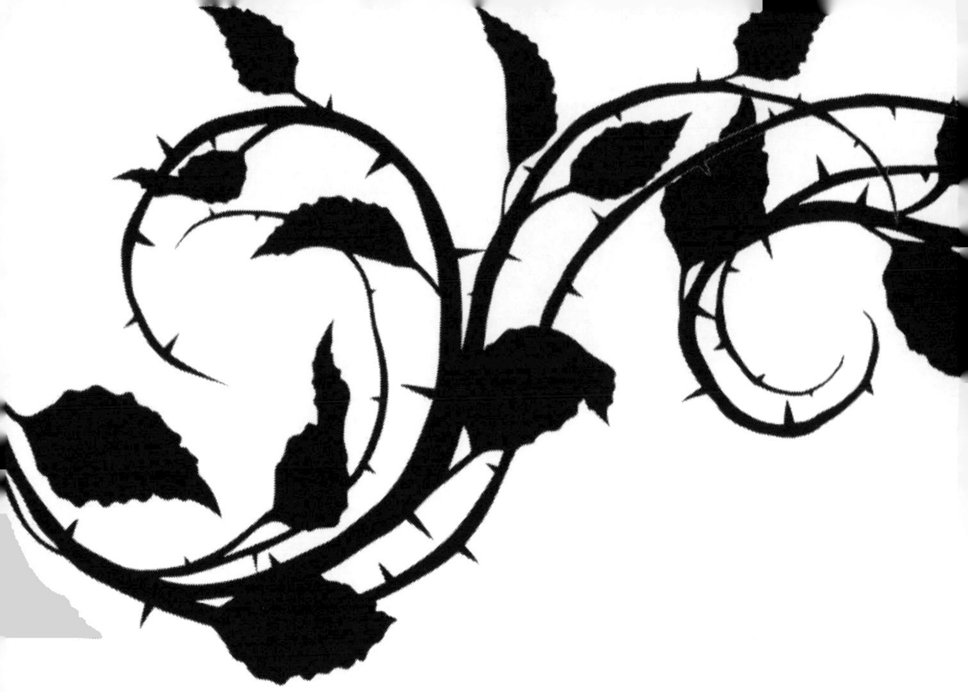

Of Thorn and Thread

CHANDA HAHN

Of Thorn and Thread

Copyright © 2020 by Chanda Hahn

Neverwood Press

Editor: A.L.D Editing

Cover Design Covers by Combs

Map Illustration by Hanna Sandvig www.bookcoverbakey.com

www.chandahahn.com

978-1950440221 (Hardcover)

978-1950440214 (Paperback)

All rights reserved.

No part of this book may be reproduced in any form or by any electronic or mechanical means, including information storage and retrieval systems, without written permission from the author, except for the use of brief quotations in a book review.

This is a work of fiction. Names, characters, places and incidents are either the product of the author's imagination or are used fictitiously, and any resemblance to actual persons, living or dead, business establishments, events or locales is entirely coincidental.

Also By Chanda Hahn

The Daughters of Eville
Of Beast and Beauty
Of Glass and Glamour
Of Sea and Song
Of Thorn and Thread

The Unfortunate Fairy Tales
UnEnchanted
Fairest
Fable
Reign
Forever

The Neverwood Chronicles
Lost Girl
Lost Boy
Lost Shadow

The Underland Duology
Underland
Underlord

The Iron Butterfly Series
The Iron Butterfly
The Steele Wolf
The Silver Siren

The Seven Kingdoms

KILN

RYA

BAIST

CANDOR

ISLA

EVILLE'S TOWER

TOWN OF NIHILL

FLORIN

SION

To those looking for their knight
in shining armor.

PROLOGUE

"What's that smell?" Harken asked, wrinkling his nose.

"Relax. It's just mold, mildew, and"—Velora closed her eyes and inhaled, breathing out the last word, savoring it—"magic."

"Magic has a smell?" Harken scratched his scruffy chin as he followed the others down the stone steps. The green mage light barely illuminated the eerie passageway.

"*Old* magic does," Velora said.

Crammed together like fish in a barrel, they navigated the narrow tunnel, ducking under roots that protruded from the ceiling. Velora picked up her skirts and kept close to Aspen, Allemar's apprentice.

Harken missed a step, the heavy pack he carried causing him to pitch forward into Allemar.

"*This* is the best you could do for acolytes?" Allemar ridiculed, rubbing his shoulder.

Aspen looked upon his master who had only a few months ago regained a human form, his soul having been trapped within a spelled dagger and then transferred into the current body in front of him. The green-gold eyes that looked at him with disdain once belonged to a guard of the Undersea. He didn't think he'd ever get used to his master's new appearance.

Aspen cleared his throat. "Harken and Dormir are the best bounty hunters. They served me well."

"I suppose one mustn't complain of a donkey if they don't want to carry the burden themselves," Allemar replied.

As the five travelers carried on, the steps leveled out, and the passageway opened up to where they could stand shoulder to shoulder.

"The smell of magic is growing stronger," Velora said, her voice barely above a whisper.

"What are we looking for again, and is it going to make me money?" Dormir asked. His hand brushed the knife clipped to his belt. "I'm tired of traveling all over this forsaken kingdom searching for some vault that's probably already been looted. There better be gold inside."

Allemar turned to confront him. "What's inside is far more valuable than gold. It's the key to bringing down the kingdom of Rya."

"No gold? Yeah, count me out," Harken said, turning on his heel and heading back up the stairs. "I've got better things to do."

"Then by all means, don't let me stop you," Allemar sneered and flicked his wrist.

Harken's head turned with a crack and he slid to the floor. Without feeling or remorse, Allemar stepped over his still warm body. "Sweet dreams."

Velora, Aspen, and Dormir stilled, watching the sorcerer with wide, fear-filled eyes.

"Anyone else care to share their unwanted opinions?" Allemar asked.

Three heads shook simultaneously.

"I thought not," Allemar said.

Forging ahead through the cave, a ball of magic lit the way ... until it stopped and circled in the air, flickering repeatedly.

"It's acting strange. Is it broken?" Velora asked.

"No," Allemar said, and his wicked smile grew wider. Velora cringed in response. "I found it." He rubbed his hands together greedily.

"Found what?" Dormir asked, not learning his lesson of his fellow hunter.

"A door. And behind it a curse that's been bound for nigh twenty years, growing in power and potency."

Allemar clapped his hands, and the light flickered once ... twice ... before growing in size and illuminating the whole underground cave, revealing the long, twisted roots of the never trees. From above, the heart of the fae court stretched from the dirt roof and intertwined with each other, reaching down to the ground creating a crooked archway. Between the arch was an iron door covered in symbols and a language long forgotten.

Allemar muttered under his breath and ran his hands along the door, brushing off dirt to reveal more symbols and sigils. With a spelled word, he trailed his finger over the door and sigils glowed faintly before disappearing again.

"What does it say?" Velora whispered to Aspen.

"It's a warning." Aspen pointed to the symbol nearest Allemar. "To anyone who opens the door. It promises death and destruction."

Velora rubbed her hands up and down her arms and shifted her weight from one foot to the other.

Allemar mumbled to himself. "Finally, I will break free that which you have bound."

His hands glowed, light bursting from his fingertips as he placed them over each one of the magic locks. Rays of green light shot from the symbols, washing over the underground cavern, creating a sickly underwater illusion.

Allemar continued to chant, his face a mask of pain. His arms trembled under the strain, his voice rising to a crescendo.

First, the tremor was barely perceivable. A mere shake, but then the earth rolled over, and the quake grew. Dust fell from the ceiling, the sketchy path beneath their feet rose as the rocks pushed forth from the ground and sinkholes opened. It was as if the earth belched out its displeasure at the dark magic being poured into it.

Aspen pulled Velora away to safety as the door continued to glow green. The pleasant aroma of magic was dispelled by the sulfurous amount of dark magic being used.

"It's not enough," Aspen whispered.

Allemar shot an ugly glare over his shoulder. "It will be." With renewed determination, Allemar returned his focus on breaking down the magical barriers. With each lock he broke, there was a repercussion in nature.

"Look!" Velora pointed as water poured down in rivulets from an underground cistern above their head. "Should we run?" she asked, as it soaked their feet.

"If you do, he'll kill you." Aspen's grip tightened on Velora in a silent warning. "Stay."

Allemar screamed. A surge of power erupted, blasting through the final magical lock, and knocking everyone from their feet and into the muddy cavern.

The door hung, broken on its hinge, and it swung outward with an ominous creak. Within the darkness, something moved and slithered about. The creaking and churning followed by an almost human groan.

Allemar got to his feet, wiping his muddy hands on his cloak. He peered into the darkness and whispered. "You're free. Go. Do what you were born to do before you were so unjustly bound."

The creaking stilled, the curse listening to the words of the sorcerer.

Dormir groaned as he sat up. Using his palms, he wiped at the mud coating his eyes, and he heard the slithering noise.

"What the—?" Dormir looked up at the broken door.

Vines shot out of the doorway, wrapped around Dormir's leg, and dragged him screaming into the darkness.

"Can we run now?" Velora asked, her body tense.

A thick fog poured out of the doorway, spilling into the cavern. Behind it, crackling thorn branches sprouted from within, growing and reaching for them.

Aspen nodded. "Run." He released her arm, and they began running back up the way they came. Slipping and sliding in the mud, the steps almost washed away.

Allemar laughed deliriously. "Yes, go! You're free."

A slippery thorn branch inched closer to Allemar's leg, and the sorcerer blasted it, turning it to ash. The rest of the prickly vines retreated and instead found a path around him, growing, and sprouting over his head.

They followed the rooted archways that grew and spread—an infectious disease killing everything in its way.

Allemar spoke aloud. "Now, I will have my revenge."

CHAPTER ONE

Blindfolded, I ran through the meadow. My breath burst in my lungs as I struggled to calm my mind and focus on the surrounding sounds. No—not the sounds. The thoughts.

She'll never find me. A burst of yellow appeared in my mind—intense joy.

I lifted my skirts to stalk my prey, but hesitated as I tried to gain my bearings.

To the left. You're about to run into the fence.

"Thanks," I whispered to Hack, our orange tabby cat. He sat on an alder tree stump watching my progress with feigned feline disinterest. But whenever I was about to walk into danger, he would mentally feed me clues. If Rhea or Maeve knew I used Hack to cheat during the test, they would never let me live it down.

I adjusted my course and the soft swish of grass under my shoes turned into the crunch of dried pine needles. I was leaving the field and heading into the woods.

Oh, stars. She's coming. Wall. Brick wall. Big brick wall. Huge!

I held back a laugh.

It was Rhea. I could tell by her meager attempt to visualize a mental wall to keep me out of her thoughts. It was useless.

Just thinking about a brick wall didn't create a mental barrier, despite what many believed.

I paused and tried to focus on where she was. Reading thoughts didn't give me a direct clue to where my sisters were hiding, but sometimes they let an emotion slip, or a thought would give them away.

Ouch! Stupid thorns.

And like that, I was off. I knew where Rhea was. Carefully, with my hands out in front of me, I headed toward the garden wall and the blackberry bushes on the edge of the woods.

"Rheanon. You can come out." I waited with the blindfold on and heard her whisper a cuss under her breath.

"That's not fair!" she whined, as she struggled to get out of the thicket. "Ouch. Stink. Ow."

"Maybe that will teach you to pick your hiding spots better," Lorn called out.

"Whatever," Rhea snapped and marched over to the stone fence next to Lorn to await the outcome of the game.

Lorn, our elven friend from the north, had put this exercise together for me. Normally, I would hunt everyone using my gifts, but this time he wanted to challenge me, and he took away my sight. "One down, two to go," he called out.

Okay. I could do this. It was just Maeve and Honor left. Honor would be impossible to find since she'd been training at hiding and stealth for years. I'd better focus on Maeve. Her mind was never quiet, but rumbled like a quiet storm.

I didn't always need to read emotions or thoughts. Sometimes nature or the wildlife itself would help give me clues.

Ack! Scram! Scat! Intruder!

A local squirrel became fussy, and I heard it chattering loudly. I knew it had to be my sister, Maeve, in her raven form.

She was lurking in the nearby tree by the noise the squirrel was making. A burst of dark red exploded my mind.

Anger.

Yep. That was Maeve. I carefully followed the sound of the squirrel as it ran up the trunk of a maple tree to protect its nest from the normally predatory bird. He didn't know it was really a human girl.

"Found you, Maeve!" I placed my hand on the tree, the bark rough under my fingertips.

A brush of wind whipped past my face as Maeve tried to show off. The magic in the air left a tingling sensation on my skin as she shifted back into her human self. Even with a blindfold on, I could imagine her dark hair, glowering green eyes, and the permanent frown on her face.

"I did better this time," she said. "If it weren't for the tattletale." A burst of red filled my mind again as Maeve directed her anger at the squirrel.

I laughed and listened as Maeve headed back to join Rhea and Lorn. Which left Honor, the toughest.

Any help? I mentally asked Hack.

Got food? he replied.

I sent him an image of the shepherd's pie that I knew was cooking in the kitchen stove.

No green things.

Hack didn't like peas.

Deal.

In the well.

I tried to hide my amusement as I headed toward the well, slowing when wind rocked the wooden handle, and it groaned. I was getting close.

Honor was the hardest for me to read and rarely did I ever get a glimpse of her thoughts or feelings. The well had a wood covering over it and I felt along the top for the edge to slide it off. I couldn't imagine Honor climbing down inside the well, trapping herself in the dark. But then again, I didn't really know her, for she was gone more than she was home.

A flash of mustard color knocked me back, and I dropped the cover back over the well with a thud.

Help!

A feeling of pain washed over me, and I grasped the edge of the well for support.

Help! The call came again. It was fainter this time. Weaker. I ripped the blindfold off and spun in a circle, searching for the call. The sun temporarily blinded me as my eyes struggled to adjust to the light, but I couldn't stop. I picked up my skirts and ran into the woods.

"Aura," Lorn called after me. "Where are you going?"

Running wildly, I was following the scattered images that came my way from a stranger in need. A blur of black flew past my shoulder and I knew Maeve was with me. I wasn't alone. I slowed when I heard nothing and panicked. What if I was too late?

A flash of light behind my eyelids knocked me to my knees, and more images filled my head. A tree hit by lighting and a moss-covered stone.

"The old hickory tree," I said aloud. Maeve flew ahead, and I followed the pain. Flashes of white appeared in my mind, and with each flash a wave of pain followed it. It was enough to halt my steps. The dizziness came, followed by nausea. I scrambled for a bush and emptied my stomach, throwing up what little I had for lunch.

I held back my own cries as I stumbled deeper into the forest, and paused when I came to the tree, struck by lightning.

"Aura!" Lorn burst through the woods and caught me as I was about to fall over.

"Somewhere around here, I think," I whispered and pointed toward the thickets. "Just past the moss-covered stone."

"Stay here." He helped me lean against the tree, and he pulled out his knife. Honor appeared out of thin air at his side. Her hair braided, the edges of her dress wet. Her face deadly calm. She *had* been in the well. I could imagine her back pressed against the side, her legs leveraged on the wall and the tips of her skirt dangling in the water. That would take incredible strength and control. Lorn and Honor headed into the forest in search of the cry for help.

I tried to gather my emotions and block out the pain, but it was almost impossible. I inhaled as I grasped my side.

"It hurts so bad," I whimpered. Based on the location of my phantom pains, whoever was calling was severely wounded.

Mother Eville's voice was in my head, chastising me. Telling me to block off the caller to protect myself. But if I did that, then I couldn't find them. It was a two-way line of communication. If I couldn't feel them, then I couldn't hear them.

The pain ebbed away, and I found enough strength to stand and follow Honor and Lorn.

I have failed.

I turned and fell over a warm body.

"I'm so sorry," I cried out. Quickly, I sat back on my heels and looked at the poor golden-furred creature. On closer examination, the fur was the collar of a red cloak. I carefully rolled the person over and saw a man in a golden helm, his chin showing a few days of dark stubble. His uniform with golden trim was foreign. I didn't recognize it as one of our neighboring kingdoms.

The red uniform hid his wound, and I only knew where it was because of my pain. I lifted his tunic, exposing the makeshift bandage that had soaked through. I pulled back the cloth to reveal a deep gash, and infected yellow pus spilled out.

I leaned down and gave it a passing sniff. There was a hint of magic about his wounds that prevented them from healing despite dressing the injury.

I closed my eyes and focused.

Lorn. Here . . .

My head throbbed. It was easier for me to pick out the thoughts of others than to send my own, which was usually only successful when amplified by fear.

We're coming, Aurora.

Kraa! Kraa! Maeve called out my location to help Lorn and Honor find me.

"Maeve, fly home. Tell mother we have a medical situation. Have Rhea mill linseed and bezoar. I will do my best to get him home in one piece." Maeve turned to fly south as fast as she could.

I pulled the helm off to reveal a young man with sun-blond hair. His green eyes fluttered open. The pain I saw within them drew me in. I clasped his hand. "I can't heal you until we draw out whatever magic is preventing your wound from healing. But I can take your pain away if you let me."

He nodded. His head rolled back, and his breathing became ragged.

My hands trembled as I put my hands on his temples, unsure if I could do it on such a large scale. As a child, this was an easy feat when one of my sisters fell or scraped their leg. I would draw away the pain and share it with them.

I reached into his mind and picked away. Pain was mental, and therefore in my wheelhouse, but magic always came with a price. It's a give and take. To take his mental pain away, it needed to go somewhere else—me.

I cried out, not expecting the intense gut-wrenching anguish. I almost threw up. My mouth gaped open, but I refused to let go. I would take his pain. I had to.

The copper tinge of blood filled my mouth as I accidentally bit my tongue.

The stranger's breathing relaxed, but I wouldn't let go.

"Aura. We're here." Lorn found me. He kneeled and lifted the stranger into a sitting position, breaking my mental hold. I gasped as it was like being slapped in the face with a hammer, but I regained control. I was still grasping for the link, like racing after the string on a kite through the grass.

I struggled for the connection, and then caught it.

Honor helped lift the stranger across Lorn's back. Elves were stronger than most men, and faster. Lorn took off running, the stranger a red blur on his back as he raced for our home.

Honor reached for my shoulder.

"Don't touch me!" I backed away. Tears poured down my face as I grappled with the man's pain.

"Aura, you can't take all the pain."

"I can," I snapped. "I must. If I hadn't been so weak, then Meri wouldn't have . . . she wouldn't have . . ." My head dropped, and then I collapsed to my knees. Tears pooled in my eyes and snot ran down my nose. "It's my fault. If I hadn't been so afraid of the pain from those men's thoughts, Meri wouldn't have had to defend me. She wouldn't have accidentally killed Armon and run away."

"That was her decision," Honor said coolly. "We all must

be held accountable for our own actions. You can only atone for your own." She looked down on me, and I felt small and weak in her eyes.

"I'm not strong like you," I whispered.

"No, you're not," Honor stated truthfully, never one to sugarcoat her feelings. "But you're good." I saw a flicker of sadness, then she looked away, and I wondered what she was hiding. "Come, I will escort you home."

"I don't need a babysitter," I muttered, pushing myself to my feet.

"I never suggested otherwise." Honor's hand rested on the handle of her short sword, her eyes scanning the woods. "We don't know what made those wounds, or what kind of danger he may be in."

I sighed. She was guarding me, and as we walked back to the house, I was grateful for the added protection. With the mental shape I was in, I wasn't sure if I could fight off an attack.

The trek home was silent and weary. Honor was on high alert, and she tiptoed through the woods. I followed, focusing on putting one foot in front of the other while my mind replayed the events.

Who was that man? Where was he from? And last, was he dangerous?

CHAPTER TWO

By the time we made it home, dusk had settled, and our tower had become a dark and ominous outline on the horizon. Our home, once an abandoned guard structure, had been expanded over the years and now included a main house and work room. My sisters—seven in all—each adopted by Lady Eville, lived in the top three floors of the tower, and our adoptive mother trained us in the way of magic and vengeance.

Bug, our donkey, stood by the front entrance, his enormous head protruding through the doorframe as he spied the goings-on inside. Honor awkwardly stepped around him and didn't even give him a second glance. I placed my hand on Bug's side and felt a shiver ripple through his hindquarters.

He backed out of the doorway and gave me a forlorn look.

"That bad, huh?"

Bad. His tail flicked, and he moved back to watch the commotion. Taking a deep breath, I prepared myself and headed inside. Our mahogany dining table had been hastily cleared off to make room for the stranger. The shepherd's pie knocked to the floor along with our freshly baked bread. Hack was under the table, making sure the scraps didn't go to waste, his face buried in the potatoes as he greedily licked up the food. He didn't even seem to mind the green things.

Mother Eville looked foreboding in a black high neck

gown, her hair braided into a soft crown around her head. Her dark brows knit into a line of worry, her face grim. Even with her sleeves rolled up and her hands covered in blood, she was a magnificent beauty. One that had made six princes argue over her hand in marriage. That was before she saw how cold and cruel their hearts truly were, and she vowed retribution upon them.

Ever since, she swore off love and focused on revenge, only helping those she deemed worthy of her time. Lorn was holding the injured man's shoulders down to keep him from moving while Mother worked. Honor moved to his feet and assisted her mentor, Lorn. Rhea was absent, and Maeve was pacing in the back of the room.

The man moaned softly as my mother poked and prodded his stomach. "There's something inside. I can't remove it with what I have here, and we have little time. Maeve, I need you."

"Got it." My sister's eyes gleamed as she shifted into a crow and hopped onto the man's chest. Her head tilted side to side as she studied the wound area. Her bird-like eyes searching for what our human eyes couldn't see. The crow had a shorter and thinner beak over the larger raven, perfect for being a pair of tweezers in emergencies.

Maeve's dark head bobbed and struck, coming up with a sharp object between her beak. She promptly dropped it into her mother's palm. Her head tilted, and she studied the wound. She flapped her wings, flew to the middle of the room, and shifted.

"Gross," she fumed, wiping the blood from around her mouth.

Mother Eville ignored her and studied the sliver. "It's a thorn. With it removed, we should be able to withdraw the poison and heal him." She tossed the tip into a ceramic bowl.

The door to the workroom slammed open as Rhea rushed inside, a mortar and pestle cupped in her hands.

"I ground up the linseed and bezoar as Aura instructed." Rhea set the bowl down on the table.

With deft fingers, Mother took boiling water from the kettle on the stove and poured it over the crushed linseed. She quickly stirred it together into a hot paste. "Hand me that linen."

Rhea took the clean linen from the shelf and watched as Mother spread the poultice across the linen. After testing the temperature against her own skin, she packed it against the man's wounds. "The bezoar should work against the poison while the linseed will draw out the infection."

"You haven't lost your touch," Lorn said.

"I had an excellent teacher," she said and glanced away. She looked across the room and our eyes met. "You did well, Aura."

"Is there nothing else you can do?" I asked helplessly, staring at the man who hadn't moved or opened his eyes since they brought him to the house.

Mother shook her head. "No, and I won't until I know who he is and why he was in our woods." She glanced toward the fireplace and our crystal protection wards. None of them had gone off, but he was also found beyond our ward boundaries. "What did you learn, Aura?" She moved to the basin and scrubbed her hands clean of the blood.

I swallowed. "Not much. His pain was palpable and distracting. I wasn't able to get anything else from him."

"Pity." She turned to Lorn. "What do you think?"

Lorn's silver eyes carefully looked over the man's clothing. "He looks to be from the northern kingdom of Rya, but they haven't traveled this far south since the last gathering of kings when you ceremoniously made a fool of them. The journey is treacherous and not for the faint of heart. He must be a man of great determination to make it this far while wounded."

Mother dried her hands on a tea towel and frowned. "It's as I thought. The mirror has shown me nothing but fog over Rya for the last few weeks. This means there's trouble brewing." From the hidden pocket within the folds of her skirt, she pulled a dagger and placed it under the sleeping man's throat, scraping dangerously close to his Adam's apple. "Make no mistake, if he is here to harm us, I *will* kill him."

Lorn placed a gentle hand on my mother's wrist, pulling the dagger away from his neck. "Lorelai, it won't come to that." He carefully took the blade from her and placed it out of reach on the windowsill. "Because I will kill him before he touches any of you."

Her hand shook, and she nodded. Turning to us, she pointed up the stairs toward our rooms. "You, all of you, go to your rooms and stay there. Lorn and I will watch over him until he wakes, and we can question him thoroughly."

"But what if you need us?" Maeve argued.

"We won't," she said firmly.

None of us budged. We stood in place, all defying her. Until Honor flicked her braid over her shoulder in annoyance and handed Lorn three more daggers she unloaded from hidden pockets in her clothes. She marched up the stairs first and turned to glare at us. "You heard Mother; move!" Honor snapped.

Startled by the command, Maeve ran up the stairs first, pushing against Honor, knocking her into the wall. Rhea followed second. I passed Honor on the steps and she hesitated, staring at the man on the table. She was having second thoughts about leaving.

"Honor," I said softly. "Let's give them some privacy."

She watched Lorn as he placed his hands on Mother's shoulders and whispered into her ear.

"Oh," Honor said, realizing for the first time what I had always known. Lorn had feelings for our mother. I was always the first to know everything about everyone. I couldn't pry into the vault that was my mother's mind, but I knew Lorn's feelings. I headed up the stairs and Honor took up the rear, making sure that we were all heading to our floors. Rhea and Maeve stopped on the second floor and headed into their room, while the stairs narrowed and I headed further up into the tower, to the empty and dreary third floor.

I stepped into the round room and stared at the empty mattresses that belonged to Eden and Rosalie. Their bedding had been rolled up and stowed away what felt like ages ago. It was almost two years since Rosalie had left to marry Prince Xander, and they now had a wonderful daughter named Violet. Eden had found happiness with Dorian in Candor, and we had recently received a missive announcing the wedding of my sister, Meri.

All of them had gone on grand adventures, and the one time I attempted to, I messed up. Many months ago, I faltered when cornered by thugs in town. Unable to defend myself, I cried out for help and Meri had come to my rescue. She inadvertently killed a man, Armon, while protecting me. She ran away, and I attempted to follow.

Sighing, I flopped back onto my bed, fingering the pink needlework flowers on my bedding. It was a disaster. I dragged my pillow over my head as I tried to drown out the memories. I had begged my sisters to let me follow Meri. Knowing my limitations with travel and large crowds, Rhea had given me her three corded magical bracelet that took her six months to make. It would allow me to travel through a mirror exactly two times.

I used the bracelet and traveled through the mirror to Isla and arrived just in time to stop my sister's curse from taking hold and killing her. By reading her mind, I could garner the knowledge to save her from the sea witch, but to do so, I would have to kill the one person she loved—the Prince of Isla.

I flung the pillow to the floor and held up my hand, studying the lines along my palm, envisioning the feel of the dagger. I had tried to do it, to stab him, but as an empath I couldn't hurt someone. In the end, it was someone else who made the sacrifice. A guard of the Undersea named Vasili. He took his own life to save Meri's. Another death that weighed heavy on my conscience.

My fingers trembled. I blinked, and my vision blurred with my tears. It was my fault that Meri had a bounty on her head and had to run away, which led to her getting cursed. If I were brave like Honor or Rosalie, I would have thought to sacrifice *myself* and save her.

I laid my head on the pillow and watched the moonlight stream through my open window. I just hoped that the stranger sleeping on our kitchen table wouldn't suffer the bad luck that seemed to follow me.

~

I couldn't sleep. Slipping out of bed, I grabbed a robe and tied it around my waist. Tiptoeing down the stairs, I hung back in the stairwell and listened to Lorn and Mother speaking in hushed voices.

"I don't like it, Lorelai," Lorn whispered. "There should be no reason for someone from Rya to be so close to your home. He could put you and your daughters in danger."

"I don't either. But we're hardly in danger. My daughters and I can handle ourselves quite well."

"Not Aura," Lorn muttered. "Ever since the accidental murder of the village boy, she's been unstable. I know she tries to hide it, but that incident did more damage to her than she will admit."

"She's fine," Mother admonished.

"No, she's not. She's still unable to shield herself properly. If she doesn't soon learn to control her powers, she will become a danger to herself and the girls."

My teeth clenched, and I tried to control my anger and deny it. But Lorn was right.

"Well, I will just train her harder," Mother said.

"The kind of training she needs can't be done here. I should take her with me and train her the way I do Honor."

"No," she said vehemently. "Not Aura."

I felt a moment of affirmation, that my mother stuck up for me, but the feelings quickly dissipated as she continued. "She's not like her sisters. She won't survive your training, Lorn. As much as I tried to train them to be ruthless and use their anger as armor to protect them from the hate of the world, Aura is as pure as the snow."

"Her empathy is her weakness," Lorn argued. "Remember, I'm the one that conducts their tests and chose their course of training. Maybe I made a mistake."

"I disagree. Her empathy *is* her strength. But she is hiding under a cloud of insecurities ever since she came back from Isla. She's safer here at home."

"You can't protect her forever," Lorn said.

"Not forever; just a little longer."

"Lorelai, you need to tell her about her mother. What if that man is here because he knows what you did?"

"Stop, Lorn." The pain was clear in my mother's voice. "I can't tell her yet."

Mother. A word that I only associated with the woman standing before me, one who looked nothing like me. My real mother, just a figment of my imagination, a sentence in a story of my life. I knew about my birth mother.

She had died. Mother Eville found me abandoned in the woods and raised me here. In Nihill, the town whose name literally meant nothing.

I peeked around the corner and watched my normally stern mother, her raven-colored hair cascading down her back, become choked up with emotion. Lorn stepped forward and wrapped his hands around her waist. She leaned into his chest for comfort and wiped the tears from her eyes. A few moments later, she pulled away uncomfortably.

There was no way to deny that Lorn and my mother were in love, but for some reason, they put up a front and hid it from us.

I debated sneaking back upstairs, but I heard a groan and froze my foot in the air.

"He's waking up," Lorn said.

I heard fumbling and leaned forward to see Lorn pull a knife and keep it below the dining table, out of sight.

Mother stepped forward and leaned over the man. She pressed a finger to his forehead. "*Somnus.*"

The man blinked and his head dropped back to the table as he fell under her sleeping spell.

"You should have let me question him," Lorn muttered.

"No, not tonight. I have no desire to hear anything he has to say. As soon as he is well, I want him gone from our lands."

"What if he's come here for help? What if he is looking for the missing heir?"

"If he is, then he will have to look elsewhere. You know as well as I do, that nothing good ever comes out of the kingdom of Rya."

CHAPTER THREE

When I came down the next morning, the stranger was gone. The table was empty and set for breakfast. All signs of last night's medical emergency had disappeared with the rays from the morning sun.

Mother flitted around the kitchen, like a butterfly too afraid to land or stay in one position for long. The smell of cinnamon bread filled the air, and I knew she must have requested the special baked treat from Clove, our brownie. Clove cleaned our home during the night, stoked the fires, and made sure that there was always fresh baked bread every morning. In return, she lived under our floorboards during the day because brownie's eyes were very sensitive to the light.

Thumping came from behind me as Maeve bounded down the steps. She skidded to a halt and blurted out what I was too shy to ask. "Where's the stiff?"

I gasped at her insult.

Mother's brows furrowed. "He's not a stiff. We've moved him to the barn. Lorn is guarding him."

"What does he want?" Maeve asked.

"It's none of your business," she chastised. "Once he's better, he'll be on his way."

Maeve plopped down on her chair and sighed dramatically until she saw the cinnamon bread, and her mood improved.

Rhea and Honor came down next. Rhea was deep in thought, scribbling in her journal, and Honor cast a wary look around the room. As soon as Honor saw Lorn's absence from the kitchen, she excused herself to go out to the barn to be with him.

"How come she gets to go out there, but not us?" Maeve pouted.

Mother gave a cross look. "Because Honor's training is under Lorn's purview, and she is the *only* one I'll allow near the stranger."

Rhea's quill scratched along the page in her journal as she answered, "That's because Honor secretly knows how to kill someone in a hundred different ways."

"Not true," Maeve countered.

Rhea paused her writing and looked up. "'Tis."

"Aura?" Maeve looked to me for confirmation.

"I . . . uh. I don't know. I can't read Honor," I lied. "Nor do I want to," I added under my breath.

Maeve scooted her chair closer to mine and cupped her hand around her mouth and whispered conspiratorially. "Well, you probably already know all the details about the man in our barn. So spill."

Under normal circumstances, I would say yes. A person's thoughts would be so loud and unguarded that I could easily pluck their deepest secrets from them, but the stranger's were eerily silent. Even growing up in a household full of eight women, it was a constant buzz of incoming feelings, thoughts, and bursts of colors from their emotions. But over the years, I learned slowly to filter them out at will. Except for Mother's. I often would try to read her mind, and for my trouble would end up with a migraine. Lorn always knew when I was reading his thoughts or targeting him. He would grin and purposely think of odd images or thoughts as silent jokes until I stopped trying and avoided him on purpose.

Mother sat down at the table and cleared her throat. "Let us give thanks."

We bowed our head and prayed over our meal. I kept my eyes open, and Rhea recited our blessing. Mother was staring out the window toward the barn. She swallowed, and I got a flash of blue paired with her expression. Worry.

I took a slice of bread, dropped it on my chipped plate, and picked up the butter knife. "Maybe you wouldn't worry so much," I gazed at my mother knowingly, "if you let me near him. You know I could figure out *why* he's here."

"No," she said sharply. "You will do no such thing."

"Why not?" Maeve argued. "I think it's a marvelous idea. Let Aura at him and she'll crack his mind like a walnut. She'll figure out where he's from, his favorite food, and *if* he has any dastardly plans to kill us." Her lip curled into a mischievous smile.

I dropped my knife, and it clattered on the plate. Rhea frowned. Her quill stilled, and she looked over at our mother warily. Maeve was always challenging our mother, poking her. Seeing if she could get her to show her teeth, and this morning was the same.

Our mother looked at Maeve and one solemn eyebrow rose as we waited for the repercussion. "There's no need to trouble Aura. She's already been through enough. If the stranger poses any threat, I will see to it he is taken care of." Mother glanced at me and quickly averted her eyes.

In that split second, I caught what she was trying to hide.

I inhaled. "You're going to erase his memory."

Mother's head snapped toward me, and her eyes narrowed for a second.

I was right.

"It doesn't matter *why* he's here. You're afraid. Afraid of who he is and where he comes from, and because of that you're willing to erase his memory for no reason."

Her mouth pinched, and her voice rose with anger. "Rya is the worst of the kingdoms. They deserve whatever is coming to them. In fact, I hope they fall into war, or better yet, a plague."

"Why?" I asked. "Why do you hate that kingdom so vehemently? Does this have to do with the missing heir to Rya?"

"Where did you hear that?" she said coolly.

"I overheard you and Lorn discussing the missing heir last night. And all this time I thought the king and queen were barren."

"It's a rumor. There is no heir."

I stared at her; my eyes narrowed as I tried to dig for the truth, but I was masterfully blocked by her power.

Mother swallowed, wiped her mouth with the cloth napkin, and pushed the chair away from the table. "I'm feeling unwell. I think I will lie down for a spell."

My fingers clenched painfully around the butter knife as I watched her retreat across the room.

"You shouldn't have provoked her," Rhea spoke up. "Now when she comes back, she'll make sure our lessons are twice as hard."

Maeve grinned. "Bring it on."

"I overheard Lorn and Mother talking about the heir of Rya last night."

"There's no heir," Rhea said.

"Or that's what they want you to think," Maeve chimed in. "And the heir, at this very moment, is secretly plotting to overthrow the king and queen. I bet it will end with a beheading."

"Gross!" Rhea shook her head and went back to her book.

We ate breakfast under a cloud of heavy silence. After I cleared the table, I gathered an apple and some of Clove's cinnamon bread. I wrapped them in a kerchief, tucked it in my skirt pocket, and headed into the workroom.

The workroom was our drying room for her herbs, and where we worked on our potions and draughts. The scent of cedar, lavender, and bergamot filled my nose, and I smiled as I passed the table. From the rafters were bundles of dried herbs, and along the walls were baskets filled with more herbs. Most of the town believed we filled our workroom with bat wings and eye of newt or cyclops' eyelashes. But we didn't store those here. We locked them up in the cellar.

I passed through the workroom, opened the back door, and stepped into the lean-to that was Rhea's forge, where she practiced in alchemy and metallurgy. The fire had been cold for some days, and there were scraps of metal lying about. She must be in between projects right now. I thought back to the traveling bracelet she made and knew that one day Rhea would be famous through the known kingdoms for her magical artifacts.

I headed toward the stable, slowing down to scatter feed for the chickens. Seven scraggly hens came running toward me, squawking in greedy glee. The dried corn fell from my fingers, and before it hit the ground, a pixie swung past and stole a few kernels mid-air.

The androgenous pixie, no bigger than a monarch butterfly, with green hued skin and mischievous eyes, gave me a wave before taking a bite.

"Dah!" a gruff voice called out, as shuffling came from behind me.

I spun and laughed as Sneezewort, the hob, who tended our gardens and animals came running between us with an old broom. Sneezewort was short of stature with a round, rosy-tinged nose and long ears that tucked under his moss and twig hat. He only came up to my hip, but was loyal as they come to our family. Sneezewort used his broom as a sword and challenged the pixie as she came back to steal more feed from the chickens.

"Scram, you pesky pixie," Sneezewort growled and swung the broom. The pixie easily dodged and came up behind him, pulling his moss hat over his eyes. "Eiyee," he screamed. "The beastie blinded me." He wildly swung the broom with even more vengeance.

"Ow," I cried as Sneezewort smacked me in the shoulder. I pulled his hat back and took the broom from his hand.

"Oh, thank the stars, Miss Aura," Sneezewort grumbled. "I thought for sure I was a goner there."

"All is fine." I gave him a pat on the shoulder and heard the pixie's mental cry of glee. She swept toward us, and I flung out the broom at the last second. The pixie flew right into the bristles and became entangled. A splash of pixie curse words decorated the air along with bubbles of red as she directed her thoughts at me.

"Here you go, Sneezewort." I handed the trapped pixie to him. "Maybe since she is so hungry and is determined to steal, she would like to stay for *dinner?*" I winked.

Sneezewort blinked at me a few times before he caught my meaning. "Oh, yes." He licked his freckled lips and rubbed his stomach through his brown shirt. "It's been ages since I cooked you up your favorite pixie pie!"

"Eek!" The pixie screamed and begged for her life, promising to never steal from the Evilles again. She said a bunch more, but I grew tired and let Sneezewort take her to the far fields for release.

I dumped the rest of the feed in a pile on the ground, not really caring if pixies stole food or not. I just didn't care for the way they were treating our family hob. Sneezewort deserved better.

I watched the barn with interest. Honor and Lorn were standing just outside, speaking in low voices. Biting my lip, I debated my options. I wanted to talk to the stranger, and the more Mother warned me away, the more I realized there was a reason.

Window is unlatched, a bored tone reached me.

Hack was coming around the stable, rubbing his back against the cedar corner.

"I can't crawl in that way. They'll hear me."

True. You are pretty useless when it comes to stealth. Unlike me. He sat and licked his paws, flexing his claws.

I rolled my eyes. "Then what do you suggest?"

Hack put his paw down and he closed his eyes into half slits. *A distraction.*

It wasn't a bad idea. Hack was smart. I leaned in close. "Quick, run after Sneezewort. He's about to release a pixie. Have him bring it back here and—"

Hack purred, and I could hear his eagerness. *Yess, Yess pixies are good.*

"No eating!" I wagged my finger at him.

His tail flicked in anger and he looked away as if ignoring me.

"Hack," I ground out his name in warning.

He turned, flicked his tail, and bounded off through the field. I hung back in the stable's shadow and waited. It wasn't long before I heard a loud cry.

"Eiyeee!" the pixie screamed as Hack chased it toward Honor and Lorn. Sneezewort was right on both of their tails with his broom, hooting and hollering, swatting both Hack and the pixie.

The commotion startled Honor and Lorn as they tried to catch Hack and save the pixie. I used the opportunity to slide the window open and hop up, the sill digging into my stomach as I went in headfirst. Gravity took hold, and I slid the rest of the way in, landing in a heap on the floor.

Quickly, I righted myself and looked around the stable. Bug was out in the field, and only Jasper, our horse, was in his stall. The other stall held the stranger. I peeked over the door and saw him on Lorn's cot. Lorn usually stayed in the stable whenever he came to visit.

I opened the door and slipped inside, taking the stool next to the makeshift bed. The stranger was still asleep. His coloring looked better and his breathing was even. All signs he was recovering with mother's treatment. I didn't know how long I would have before they discovered me, so I sat and listened.

Nothing. I got nothing from him. No aura, no images, no stray thoughts.

I frowned and tentatively reached for his hand, holding it within my own.

I grimaced and waited for the onslaught of feelings to come, but again I was met with silence. Maybe it was because he was asleep? Yes, that had to be it. But even during dreams, I could sometimes catch glimpses. I was about to release his hand when I looked up into his green eyes and faltered.

The stranger was awake. He studied me, and then glanced at my hand clasped around his. I quickly dropped it.

"I'm sorry," I whispered. "I shouldn't have touched you without your permission."

He said nothing, but stared at me strangely. "Who are you?"

"I'm Aura, and you're in our barn."

"Our?"

"My family's," I said, carefully not revealing more. "Who are *you*?" I returned the question.

"I'm no one of importance," he said defensively.

I could feel the lie.

"Well, *no one*. Why were you found wandering in the woods? What happened to you?"

"I'm on an important quest," he sighed and closed his eyes, dismissing me. "And I must be on my way at once. I have no time to spare for your idle chatter."

I was aghast. I'd never before been dismissed by anyone, and with such apathy. I patted my white blonde hair and knew that it was still perfectly plaited despite my tumble through the window. Many men had complimented me on my fair skin and pale eyes that looked lilac or gray depending on my mood. I wasn't tall and graceful, like Rosalie, or beautiful like Eden. I looked like a thin will-o'-the-wisp compared to them, but I wasn't horrid.

But this hurt.

"Hard to do when you don't have a horse and you're injured. How did you get injured?"

"I was attacked a week ago. As for my horse, I don't know. I was feverish and must have fallen off my mount, and he ran away. I implore you to please lend me another horse and help me on my way."

"You're awfully rude for someone close to death. If it weren't for me, you would have perished."

Those enchanting eyes opened and looked me over from head to toe, reaching his own conclusion on who I was. "Then

I'm grateful for your assistance. But unless you can tell me how to reach the home of Lady Eville, I have no time for young, lovesick girls."

He was a jerk. A horrid, vain jerk. No wonder my mother hated the kingdom of Rya. Especially if this is the breed of men they produced.

"I am no young, lovesick girl," I spouted, pulling the kerchief out and shoving the bread and apple into his chest. "I thought you might be hungry since I wasn't sure when you last ate. But maybe you would prefer if we dropped you out in the wilderness and let you forage for yourself, you pompous wad."

He didn't even seem the least disturbed by my show of anger. One golden eyebrow rose and then it dropped. He sat up and the blanket slid down his midsection, revealing strong tan muscles. I looked away, staring at a rusty nail in the wall.

I swallowed.

"See," he chuffed. "The pious maiden who hopes to woo the injured soldier."

"You're a soldier?" I asked. "Then what business do you have here?"

His pinched lips didn't affirm or deny. "My business is my own, and that of Lady Eville." He stood up and gathered his leather armor that had been piled in a corner. "If you would be so kind as to lend me a horse and help me on my way, I will be forever grateful."

"That's where you're wrong," I snapped. "I'm not kind." I grabbed his satchel and stormed toward the door. He wobbled after me, his hand going to his bandaged side as he gasped in pain. I slid the barn door open, relieved to see that Honor and Lorn weren't around.

"Miss, miss," he called after me as I quickened my pace. "My things."

I walked across the bridge, my feet echoing along the wooden boards. Beneath me, the rumble of Traygar the troll's breathing soothed me, knowing that he was guarding us still. I turned when I reached the other side of the bridge and watched as the stranger followed me, pulling on his overshirt, his boots tucked over his arm, his sword hastily slung across his back.

With a satisfying grin, I tossed his satchel into the mud on the other side of the bridge, past our second ward.

"There you go. You're on your way." I dusted off my hands and flung my braid across my shoulder. "Go that way." I pointed toward the town of Nihill.

He slowed next to me and gave me a curious look. "You're an odd girl."

Odd? I hated being called odd. I was always the odd one.

It took every ounce of my being to not curse him right there. No, wait a minute. Maybe I would. I came up next to the man, gave him a pat on the shoulder and whispered.

"*Confundus.*"

He blinked and looked at me in surprise, as if he were seeing me for the first time.

"Lady Eville lives far beyond the town. Go that way." I pointed before turning and walking across the bridge, my braid swinging with each of my happy steps, glad that I had gotten rid of the problem with a spell. If lucky, he'd go into town and forget the very reason he came here.

When I got to the other side of the bridge, I turned and waggled my fingers at him. He looked down at his belongings and began a slow tread into town.

By the time I reached the barn, Lorn and Honor were running out of it in alarm.

"Where'd he go?" Lorn asked. "What happened?"

"I sent him on his way," I said innocently. "He was looking for someone."

"Who?" Lorn said.

I rolled my eyes. "Who do you think? But it seems like no one wanted him here, and you were terrified of us interacting with him. So I took care of it. A spell and a packed lunch, and he's off. He'll wander until he forgets what he was looking for and head home."

Lorn looked across the bridge toward town. "I have a feeling he won't easily forget, despite how powerful your magic is."

"He will," I said confidently. "Now, who's hungry?"

CHAPTER FOUR

I thought Mother and Lorn would be angry with me because I made the strange man disappear without telling them, but they seemed wary, yet relieved. Three days went by and the stranger didn't return to our doorstep. Mother spent her time in our sitting room, scrying the kingdom of Rya through the large black mirror that hung on the wall, but instead of a moving picture, it showed only fog.

Even hitting the side of the mirror didn't clear the image. Rhea had gone to her workshop and come back with two long rods she attached to the mirror and claimed they boosted the magic within it.

"They look ugly," Maeve whined. She waved her fingers over her forehead. "Like bug antennae."

"Well, it may look dumb, but it will work."

"I'll believe it when I see it," Maeve flopped in the chair and hung her leg over the arm.

"Ladies, don't slouch," Mother chastised from her high-back chair.

Maeve pulled her leg down, properly tucked her dress around her thighs, and folded her hands in her lap. "I never said I wanted to be a lady."

"Of course, you want to be a lady. What else do you want to aspire to be?"

"A dragon." Maeve cackled, and her eyes glittered dangerously.

"Not in the house," Mother warned. "Plus, you haven't passed your shifting tests yet to transform into anything larger than a swan. And you, Aura, need to work on your shielding."

I stilled like a prey animal sensing the predator about to strike. I knew what was coming.

"So you will go into town today to get our supplies," Mother continued.

I winced. "You know I'm not exactly welcome in town."

"Then you better work on your mental shielding while you're there." It was an order, not a casual suggestion as she made it seem.

"Yes, Mother."

I went to the iron hook by the door and grabbed my dark brown cape and waited for her to present me with the list of items. My hand shook as I took the parchment, but I tried to hide my nervousness.

Rhea brought me the basket and gave me a wry smile. "It'll be fine. You'll see."

"I just wish I could have spelled the entire town and made them forget."

"We can't do that. It's against our code. Too many repercussions, and eventually someone would remember."

"I know." I sighed.

I took the empty basket and headed into town, my fears weighing the basket down unnaturally until my arms hurt.

I crossed the bridge and followed the path down the hill, focusing on shielding myself. Working through all the exercises Lorn had taught me. But with each step I took, my reserve faltered. This was punishment of the worst kind. I hated large crowds, I hated cities, and I hated being around people.

Nihill sat in the middle of nowhere. A godforsaken cesspool filled with lowlifes and thieves. Eventually, over the years, it grew and garnered enough population where they finally elected a mayor. But no kingdom claimed us. We neither gave allegiance to Candor, Baist, or Sion, nor their neighboring kingdoms. We were forgotten, and no one cared about our taxes. Except for the mayor. But even with the installment of taxes, the roads or sewers were often neglected.

I tucked my hair into my hood. Thankfully, I didn't have Meri's deep red locks, for she always drew attention with her unusual hair color. I focused on keeping my head low. With a wave of my hand, I used glamour and made my clean dress appear darker in shade and color. A few more stains and tears appeared to deceive the viewer.

As soon as the glamour took hold, I could feel the ache behind my eyes as I held the spell in check. Over time, I would get a throbbing headache. It would be even worse if I tried to change my face or body. Eden could easily become someone else if she had a personal item of theirs.

I felt a small pang of jealousy at her glamour gift, but it quickly dissipated as my yearning for my sister took its place. I missed them so much. As soon as I crossed into town, the darkness flashed in my conscience.

Burst of gray signifying gloom and despair, followed by angry flashes of red for anger. The auras were overpowering. My steps slowed, and I sought shelter against the corner of a building as the townspeople's deepest innermost thoughts reached me.

He's such a deadbeat husband. Why am I even married to him?

She never does anything around the house.

Peter broke my new toy. I hate him.

If I can sell all of my vegetables today, I will have enough money to buy medicine.

I wish that new dress were on sale.

Fresh fish, my foot. This has already gone rank.

Yellow, red, gray flashed in my mind like fireworks and I tried to blink them away and focus on putting one foot in front of the other. Taking a deep breath, I headed into the marketplace.

As I passed the butcher's shop, I tried to hurry my steps, hoping to not catch the attention of the butcher's son. Clutching the paper in front of me like a lifeline, I headed into the first store.

My head ached as I bartered with the merchant for linen.

"Three copper coins, that is my final price," the merchant said firmly.

I shook my head as I picked up his hesitancy. "I will give you two coppers." My head was throbbing, but I knew he would go lower.

"Aw fine, take it, but it is highway robbery." The merchant packaged the linen for me, and I added it to my basket. It was for a new apron for Mother. Three more stores followed similar deals. I kept my head down, listened to their thoughts, and negotiated lower prices.

An old arthritic woman sat on a trade blanket near the square. Her skin wrinkled like raisins, her mouth square and hollow from lack of teeth, but her face radiated with kindness. Her aura was a bright yellow and soothing. I didn't have much money, but I wanted to help her out as much as I could. I took a few coins and handed them to the women.

"Bless you, child. Here, let me give you something in return."

"Oh, it's fine."

"A word of advice, then. When you are afraid, remember the first light will protect you." She clapped her hands in merriment and rocked back and forth.

"How odd . . ." I shrugged it off and looked at my list and frowned. I was so focused on my own thoughts that I didn't see the hooded man approach me until it was too late.

He pulled me through a doorway into an abandoned building.

"You lied to me!" Strong hands gripped my upper arms painfully and flung me further into the room. "You've had me walking in circles for days."

I blinked in the darkened room as my eyes struggled to adjust. Holes in the thatch roof let in beams of light as the man walked near me. I recognized the man from Rya.

"I don't know what you're talking about," I lied and tried to move around him toward the door, but he blocked my path.

"I saw you come into town, and as soon as I did, I remembered. Everything. I remembered why I'm here. My quest, my purpose. You stole that from me," he yelled. "when you took my memories."

I trembled before the mountain of a man, but I didn't deny his accusations.

He paused in front of me, his voice low and threatening. "And now I demand that you take me to Lady Eville."

"No," I said firmly. "I won't endanger my family again."

His brows furrowed. "What do you mean again? Who are you?"

"I am Aurora Eville, daughter of Lady Eville. It was I who found you in the woods, and my mother and sisters tended to you. You have already graced the presence of our household, and she has refused to see you further."

His handsome face paled. He immediately thrust his arm

in front of his heart and kneeled before me. "I'm so sorry, milady. My name is Liam Falcane. I come seeking aid on behalf of the kingdom of Rya. There has been a blight that has attacked our home and all that live within it. My armies have been fighting against it for weeks, but we cannot make any headway. There is talk that your household may be our only hope in finding the answer to banishing the blight."

"I'm sorry, that is none of my concern, for I am only a *lovesick girl*," I repeated his words back and pushed past him. Surprisingly, he let me leave. I covered my hair and hurried to complete the last item on my list. Now, more than ever, I wanted to retreat to the safety of our home and away from the pious knight.

Unfolding the crumpled note, I scanned the list and sighed.

There was only one more item left, and I dreaded going there, but it was the only place for miles unless we wanted to butcher our own meat, and we didn't have any animals other than fowl. I entered the rundown butcher shop and covered my nose from the smell. Tobias was the one manning the counter, and I trembled at the sight of him. He was one of the men that attacked me, tried to get under my skirt, and my sister had killed his friend while defending me.

It's fine. I told myself. Just keep my head down. I came in and slid the paper across the counter. Tobias wiped his bloody hands on his apron and looked at the slip. His greasy hair hadn't been washed in weeks, and his acne had only gotten worse since I last saw him.

"We just butchered a cow today. It's fresh," Tobias said.

It was a lie.

What a pretty thin. I would love to see what's under her hood. Forget the hood. I wonder what's under her skirt.

I stumbled into the counter as Tobias' crude thoughts assaulted me.

"How about pork?" I said, keeping my head low.

"Yeah, I got pork. What cut?"

"Shoulder," I whispered.

"What? Speak up, wench."

"Shoulder," I said louder.

He pulled down brown paper and leaned over the counter. "You seem familiar. Have we met before?"

I shook my head.

"Now, if you want, I can throw in some of that beef for a discount if you want to help me out a bit."

Crude images flashed in my mind of the things he wanted to do to me.

I was going to throw up.

I tossed the coins onto the table and grabbed the package before he had even finished wrapping it and ran outside. I rushed around the corner and put the basket on the ground, and leaned over, my hands on my knees as I tried to focus on breathing. I pulled my hood down and after a few deep breaths. I felt better, but a shadow fell over me, and a dark aura made me terrified.

I stood up.

"I knew I recognized you." Tobias held the butcher's knife in front of him. "You and your red-haired sister killed Armon. You're one of the Eville girls."

"I didn't kill anyone," I snapped. "What happened was an accident, but if you don't leave me alone, I can't guarantee your safety."

Tobias' face turned ugly. "I'm not afraid of you. I remember that you were a coward, a crybaby. But now, there's no one to protect you." He grabbed my braid and yanked me down an alley between his shop and the next.

I screamed as he pulled on my braid. "Let go!"

"Not until I get revenge for Armon," he breathed into my neck. His breath smelled of death and rot.

He slammed me into the wall. My head cracked against the stucco, and piercing pain radiated out of my skull. The knife appeared at my throat and the edge pushed against my jugular. Dèjá vu all over again. Tobias reached for my skirt, and I heard a tear as he ripped it away.

Fear paralyzed me, and all the spells and attacks I knew rushed out of my mind. I became helpless against the numbing fear.

"I will teach you what it means to bow down to a man. When I'm done, you'll be screaming my name."

Tears filled my eyes, and my vision was blurry as mother's words came back. "You need to protect your mind." This was a lesson I didn't want to learn.

No one would come for me. Meri couldn't save me now. I was alone.

No. I wasn't alone because *I* was enough.

I tampered my fear, dug deep into the pit of my soul, and turned to look into Tobias' lust-filled eyes. "You're wrong, Tobias," I whispered, feeling the blade nick my throat. "When I'm done with you, you'll be screaming my name."

I reached out and prepared to cast a spell.

A shadow fell over us. Tobias was flung backward and knocked into the ground, a flash of steel, and Liam had his sword pointed at Tobias' throat.

"You piece of trash," Liam growled. He carefully used his sword and drew a line of blood that matched the one Tobias gave me. A bloody red necklace. "How dare you lay a hand on a lady?"

"I won't touch her again," he cried out. His fat, blubbering face produced fake tears.

"I didn't need your help," I said sourly. "I was fine."

Liam grabbed Tobias by his collar and held him up to the wall while he addressed me. "You were about to be accosted."

"I had a handle on it," I said, putting my fists on my hips. My foot tapped angrily, showing my displeasure.

Tobias had other plans. *I will teach this jerk a lesson,* he thought.

"He won't stop." I pointed toward Tobias.

Tobias ducked and tried to get away. Liam punched Tobias in the face. Blood spurted from his lip, but the man glared wickedly. He went limp.

As soon as he turns his back, I'll kill him.

Liam thought Tobias had learned his lesson, dropped him on the ground, and turned his back to face me.

I sighed. "Don't turn your back."

Tobias grabbed the hidden knife out of his boot pocket and charged. Liam spun to defend himself, but he didn't have to. I stepped between the two men and reached for Tobias' head. I brushed my fingers across his brow as he ran past.

"*Compassio.*"

I released all of my fear and emotion from the day of the attack months ago—back into him. I let him feel what I felt. Let him have a taste of my empathy magic and then some.

"What's going on?" Tobias stumbled backward. The knife fell from his hands. A milky film covered his eyes as I took him back to each person he ever beat up or abused. He relived every moment, but from the victim's perspective.

"Stop!" Tobias cried out. "Don't touch me." He backed

into a corner and covered his head. Cowering on his knees, he sobbed and ran his hands along the ground. He would be blind until the vision wore off, and hopefully by then, he would know what it was like to be the victim, and therefore no longer be a predator.

But I doubted it.

"What just happened?" Liam said in disbelief.

I couldn't answer. I stumbled out of the alley as I was also forced to relive the same nightmares simultaneously. There were so many. I collapsed on the ground, pressed my forehead into my knees and cried.

CHAPTER FIVE

A hand patted my back awkwardly, and I rolled my head to the left and stared at Liam. He sat next to me on the ground and held a handkerchief out to me.

"Here."

I didn't want his fake sympathy.

"Go away," I said. "I don't need a heroic-ridden knight to rescue me."

"Well, actually, you were right. You didn't need my help. You handled yourself quite well. Although, your tactics were a little unorthodox. You could have taken him out well before I arrived if you had the right kind of training."

I couldn't believe him. He was insulting me all over again.

Liam sighed, and his hand lifted from my back. "But it seems that *this* heroic knight needs you."

I snorted. Grabbed his handkerchief, thoroughly blew my nose, and handed it back to him. He took it and stared at it in disgust.

"Well maybe you shouldn't offer it to a lady if you don't expect her to use it," I snapped.

I stood up, wiped off my skirts and searched around the area for my basket. The basket was crushed, but most of the items were salvageable. I kneeled in the dirt to put the items back in.

"Here." He handed me the packaged linen. I took it without looking at him. I reached for the bag of flour and our hands collided as he picked it up. I pulled my hand back, and he looked up into my eyes, noticing their pale color.

He gasped; the flour fell from his hands and back onto the ground.

I shook my head and pushed him away when he tried to help.

"Leave me," I said.

"I can't. For I need your help." He followed close behind.

"We've given you all the help that we can. You must go." I pointed down the road.

"You don't understand. It's life or death."

"Not my problem."

He stopped in his tracks. His shoulders dropped. "You're right. It's not your problem, but mine and mine alone." His voice dripped with pain and his turmoil.

I slowed and looked upon his aura. So pure and filled with righteousness . . . and then pain. Something terrible had befallen him and his people, and I was letting the rude way he treated me on our first meeting define my opinion of him. Did we not daily deal with the same stigma and mistreatment by the townspeople?

I sighed and turned back to him. Brushing my hair out of my face. "But my mother has *no* desire to help your kingdom —ever."

His aura darkened with pain and despair. I had to leave before guilt persuaded me to do something stupid. Like help him.

"I'm sorry, I really wish there were a way for me to help," I called out, as I gathered my skirts and quickly departed. I knew without looking back that he watched my hasty retreat. "But there's really nothing I can do."

∽

The way was blocked.

Fog surrounded me. So dense I could barely see more than an arm's length in front. Threatening growls and snapping of dried branches made me jump. I spun in a circle and could hear a laughter echo around me, taunting me. I tried to move through the fog, but branches and thorns snagged my clothes. Clouds moved away from the moon, and in the distance I saw the forlorn castle. My goal. The fog closed in, swallowing me.

I woke up.

Sweat beaded across my brow and my hands were clammy. I rubbed my forehead and tried to make sense of the dream. Except I knew it wasn't my dream. It was someone else's dream that merged into mine. But whose?

I tossed and turned in my bed most of the night. But there was a heaviness in the air—guilt. I flung off my blanket and tiptoed down the stairs into the main room. A low fire was burning in the stone fireplace, and I saw the small dust pile swept into the corner, and the quivering form of Clove as she hid in the shadow of our bookcase.

"It's just me, Clove," I whispered, as I set about the kitchen gathering herbs before stepping into my mother's workroom to pilfer a white candle. When I had everything I needed, I moved to the front door and headed into the night.

It was a full moon, and I decided tonight would be a perfect night to clear my thoughts and head. Leaving my boots behind, the grass felt chill beneath my bare feet. The wind pulled at my nightdress, and my braid had come partially loose from all of my tossing and turning. I headed into the woods behind our house into a small clearing of circular stones. A fairy circle.

Sometimes we would sit out here when we were supposed to be practicing our spells, and instead we'd lay out and stare at the stars and tell stories to escape. Maeve always leaned toward the horror stories, Honor loved adventure, and I loved the princess stories.

Tonight, I was seeking a different kind of escape. One from my own mind and thoughts. Here in the fairy circle I could rest undisturbed, and maybe even practice weaving a sleeping spell on myself.

I snapped my fingers and the enchanted candle lit, creating a circle of light to chase away the shadows and fears. The lavender and mint I crumbled together and sprinkled on the ground before curling up in the velvet like grass. For fairy circles were made of magic, and they were very pleasing to sleep or dance barefoot in. Looking around, I placed the ward crystal near my head. It didn't flicker in warning, signaling there was no danger to me.

Mother didn't approve of me sleeping outside under the stars, but here is where it was quietest. Away from the constant roaming thoughts of a house full of women. Where the only thoughts that plagued me were my own.

With the tip of my finger, I traced a symbol in the air for sleep and wove a simple sleeping spell over myself. The symbol glowed, rose into the air and burst, releasing a golden net of sparkles that fell like dust over my body. It coated my hair and nose, and as I breathed it in, I felt drowsy. It wasn't safe to do in the confines of the tower where a stray wind could cause my spell to drift and affect my sisters. My eyes grew heavy, and I yawned, sprawling out on the ground, tucking my hands under my head. The white prickly branches of trees seemed to reach for me, the moon grew to the size of the sky as the night became muffled and I fell asleep.

CHAPTER SIX

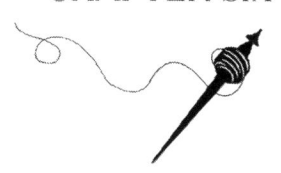

The steady bobbing rhythm jarred my fuzzy head. I blinked and sunlight pierced my eyes. I shuddered at the pain and quickly closed them. A hardness pressed against my cheek and I tried to search with my senses. I was moving on a horse and cradled in the arms of someone. Against the pain, I tried to spy through lowered lashes and saw only the golden crest on the leather armor.

As we passed under the shade of a group of trees, I opened my eyes fully and tried to speak, but choked on the cloth in my mouth.

"Mmmff," I growled angrily through the gag.

The sun cast my captor into shadow. He used the reins to spur the horse faster. I cried out as the change in speed jarred me, and thought for sure that I would plummet to the ground to my death. His left arm tightened around my waist.

"Don't worry, I won't let you fall." *You're too important.*

Without thinking, it became fight or flight. I kicked up with my leg and struck the hand holding the reins, forcing all of my weight on the one arm, and flung myself backwards off of the horse, bringing my kidnapper with me.

"Whoa!" he cried, as he wrapped his body around me as we crashed into the earth.

Pain radiated outward from my hip, light flashed in my

eyes, and I looked up as the probably stolen horse took off running through the woods. Using my bound hands, I pulled the gag from my mouth and quickly worked at the knots around my wrists with my teeth until I was free. I turned to run, but glanced at my captor and froze. I recognized him.

It was Liam, and he wasn't moving.

I should run as far as I could away from him, but something told me not to. I couldn't leave him alone in the woods—injured. Slowly, I made my way back to Liam and pushed against his chest with my foot. He groaned, and I saw blood pool in the grass.

I cursed. My foolishness had probably reopened the stitches. Feeling a sense of obligation, I stayed by his side and waited for him to wake up. Thankfully, his thoughts were silent.

A candle mark passed before Liam stirred. He groaned and sat up. I moved a safe distance away and watched him warily. Liam brought his hand up and wiped the dirt away from his face. He reached for his side and he sucked in his breath in pain.

He scanned the woods with those alert eyes and met my angry ones. His gaze quickly shied away. Feeling a cool breeze against my skin, I glanced down and let out a cry as I ducked into some bushes. I was in my very sheer nightdress.

"How dare you kidnap me," I yelled, huddled behind the bushes, crossing my arms over my chest. I realized mud covered my feet, and my hair was a tangled mess from riding on a horse.

"I'm sorry, but you left me no choice." Liam groaned.

"I demand that you take me home."

I heard the clearing of a throat and looked up as Liam stood over me, his red cloak in his hands. I should have heard the scuffle of his boots on gravel as he was coming near, or heard his thoughts. How was it he was silent? How could a man not be thinking anything when standing next to a near-naked woman?

"Here." He stared at an old ash tree, and when I wouldn't take the cloak, he dropped it on my head and turned to give me his back.

"This doesn't make up for what you did," I grumbled, wrapping the warm cloak around my shoulders. It smelled faintly of leather and oil from his armor, a not unpleasant smell. "You can turn around now."

He sighed and rubbed his brow. "I'm sorry, for it goes against everything I stand for, but you gave me the idea yourself."

"I did not," I said heatedly.

His eyes narrowed. "You did. You all but said your mother refuses to help my kingdom, but you wished you could aid me. So, I took you up on your word."

"In no way or language does that mean kidnap me. And how did you get past our wards?"

"What wards?"

"The wards on our land that warn of imposing threats."

"I guess there's your answer."

"What?"

"I pose no threat to you, or the wards would have gone off."

Liam was right. The crystal ward by my head should have alerted me. Maybe it was defective because none of our guardians were stirred from their slumber. "But still, you will be sorry when my mother finds out that you've kidnapped me."

"Borrowed." He grinned, dusting his hands off. "I fully intend to return you, after you help me."

I looked around at the forest and at my bare feet, then over to Liam. His side was still bleeding, and I was worried because it seemed to be on the opposite side of the injury we tended. It was a fresh wound. But other than the sword on his hip, the leather armor he was wearing, and his money pouch, he didn't have any belongings and our horse was long gone. I glanced up at the sun that was disappearing behind dark clouds and estimated it was a few candle marks past noon. We could have traveled quite a long distance if we left in the middle of the night. We could be halfway to Candor by now, too far for me to make it back home by foot.

I grimaced. "So, um. Who's going to save us now?"

Liam took stock of our own situation. "It's fine. All we have to do is keep heading that way." He pointed and grinned.

"North," I repeated dumbly. The air became colder, and the wind picked up, blowing at the hem of my dress.

"Toward Rya," he said.

I sighed and looked back the way we came, toward home.

Liam saw my hesitation, and he came and kneeled in front of me. His fist pressed over his heart.

"I don't say please. Ever. But I'm begging you. Please help me in saving my home from the blight that has afflicted the land." A flash of white appeared in my mind, signaling honesty.

Liam sounded so noble, so pure in his trust and commitment, and he said exactly what he was thinking. That it made it easy to put my trust in him. But on the other hand, if my mother found out, she would kill me.

I sighed. "Okay."

Liam blinked and seemed surprised at my answer. "Really?"

"Yes," I groaned. "But if I come home cursed or dead, I will come back and haunt you."

Liam came to me and bowed. "You won't regret this."

A sudden clash of thunder made me jump in surprise. The downfall of rain that came pouring down after had me scrambling for the nearest outcropping of trees.

I glared at him, the rain dripping from my hair and down my neck. I shivered from the chill. "I already do."

CHAPTER SEVEN

We traveled through the woods, my barefooted pace slower than Liam's. Each time I stepped on a twig I muffled my cry to hide my pain. There was nothing to be done. I was the one that had scared off our horse. I had Liam's cloak, so at least I was drier than him. He walked with his head held high against the pouring rain that showed no sign of stopping.

We hadn't crossed another person, path, or trail, and I had all but given up on ever being warm again. Then we came to a river, and I balked at crossing. With the onslaught of the rain, the current had picked up speed, and it was impossible to tell how deep it really was. I scanned the banks, looking for a footbridge or shallower area to cross.

Liam went to the water's edge and turned to face me, his hands extended.

"Allow me." He smiled reassuringly. *It's my duty to help her. Nothing more.*

His thoughts caught me by surprise. He had been so silent that I thought maybe he was broken. But it was the seriousness of his thoughts that irked me.

"No," I snapped. "I can do it myself." I gathered my nightdress and lifted it above my knees, exposing my soft pale skin. My cheeks warmed in embarrassment, but it was this or allow him to carry me across the river.

No, this was an acceptable alternative.

The rain still pelted my face as I stepped into the water. The cold water stung my feet, but the pain ebbed as the water soothed the cuts on my soles. I took a few tentative steps and was fairly certain the water wouldn't reach higher than my knees. Liam didn't take off his boots but waded into the water with me.

Each step I took with a purpose, testing the rocks beneath me for stability, but I slipped on moss and almost went down. I flung out my arms to balance myself and my nightdress dropped into the water. I gritted my teeth in frustration.

"Stupid," I muttered. Liam's hand reached for mine and I swatted it away. "I got it." As I continued, I took a step. The river deepened unexpectedly, I lost my balance and slipped under the water. A biting cold slapped my face as water surged into my nose and mouth. I came up sputtering. I stretched, my feet found purchase on the riverbed and I stood, the water reaching my chest.

I pushed my hair out of my face and without warning, Liam scooped me up in his arms. He carried me the rest of the way across the river and up the embankment.

My teeth chattered loudly as I pressed against his chest. "You can put me down. I can walk."

"No." His jaw muscle tensed, showing his irritation.

"I insist," I said.

"Then I will have to deny your request." *She's too slow. We need to find shelter before we get sick.*

I had another retort coming, but it fell on my lips. I hung my head in shame. It wasn't my fault I didn't have shoes or proper attire. But I wasn't purposely holding him back. I went limp and decided to let him carry me. I would just think of him like a pack mule.

A *stubborn* pack mule.

I held back a wry smile and shivered. The cloak, fully soaked with water, didn't help me stay warm. We walked for a while, and I was trying to hold back my shivering.

I need to find shelter soon.

As exhausted as I was, Liam was right. I closed my eyes and listened to the surrounding animals. All of them curled up for the night, safe from the storm.

"Up ahead, to the left of the evergreen tree," I whispered. "There's a small cave where we can find refuge."

"How do you know this?"

"I just do," I said irritably, and I was never the irritable one. When we made it to the shelter, he put me down. My feet almost gave out from under me as the pins and needles raced back, bringing feeling. The cuts scraped anew. I limped forward, my hands reaching out into the darkness.

"Wait. What if there are animals in there?" Liam unsheathed his sword.

"There's not." I made my way in and sat down, out of the wind, curling my knees up to my chest, the cloak gathering around me like a red cocoon. He followed me as his eyes adjusted and saw that it was fifteen feet deep but a little more than ten feet across.

"You are one of the most reckless women I've ever met," Liam chastised when nothing appeared to eat me. He sheathed his sword and headed toward the back to explore. I sighed and pressed my forehead to my knees and concentrated on trying to not freeze to death.

A clatter of wood dropped in front of me, and I jumped. Liam had found enough dry material in the cave to make a fire, but he reached for his pack and groaned. "My flint and steel were in the horse's saddlebags."

"Stand back," I said.

He didn't move, but leaned back on his heels and searched the cave. "Maybe I can find a piece of flint in here."

"I got it." Still, he didn't hear me. "Okay, if you go up in flames, not my problem."

I reached out my hand toward the kindling under the logs.

"*Fiergo.*"

The kindling burst into flames, Liam fell backwards with a yelp. "You could have warned me," he cried.

"I did," I said smugly, taking off his cloak. I spread it out so it would dry faster. Then I move closer to the fire, so it would dry my nightdress that was now plastered to every curve of my body.

She's nothing but skin and bones.

I sucked in a breath. My lips pinched together in anger and I turned to give him my back. There's no way I would let his comments affect me. *Oh stars. They did.* I could feel the pain of rejection hit me and I wiped at the corner of my eyes as tears threatened to spill forth. I didn't have experience with men, other than Lorn and the lecherous men of the village. Liam was the only normal person I've met, and his opinions of me were hurtful.

I heard the rustle of rocks and dirt as he settled in close to the fire. The slap of buckles being undone echoed, and I knew he was removing his sword and boots.

"How did you do that with the fire?" he asked.

"Magic. You kidnapped a sorceress, after all."

"I just didn't expect you to summon fire."

"I can't," I said stiffly. "That's about the limit of my power over fire. It's not my natural affinity."

"There are affinities?"

The fire cast an orange glow that danced across the cave

wall. Absently, I traced my finger along the shadows as I explained. "There are many kinds of magic. Farmers are strong in earth magic; blacksmiths have an affinity for fire. But most people are not strong enough to sense magic or control it. I was tested at a young age by Lorn and given my course of study. Lighting a fire is a basic spell, even most fae can do it. I can light a candle, lanterns and start small fires, but calling down a firestorm is beyond my training or abilities."

"What can you do?" he asked. I heard the worry in his voice. "I saw what you did to the man in the village. What kind of magic was that?" *Maybe I made a mistake, and she isn't strong enough to help me.*

I gritted my teeth, and I glared over my shoulder at him. "You saw it. I can light a fire."

Oh heaven, I'm in trouble. I should take her back now. She will not be able to help me at all. My troops are a week's ride away still, but to take her back would delay my quest even more.

"Shut up," I snapped, squeezing my eyes closed.

"I didn't say anything," Liam said in confusion.

I covered my mouth when I realized I spoke in reaction to his thoughts. "Sorry, I was talking to myself."

What an odd girl.

I pressed my forehead to the cave wall and wanted to disappear through it. The cold stone felt comforting against the embarrassment flaming my skin. In fact, the heat from the fire was almost becoming uncomfortable. I curled on my side, my back to the fire and Liam, ignoring the hunger pain in my belly and the sweat that pooled across my skin from the heat.

I occupied my time concentrating on the sounds of the rain outside. Slowly counting and listening to the even breaths of Liam. When they deepened, signaling he was sleeping, I rolled over and stared at his handsome face. The dying embers flickered across his skin, accentuating his dark eyelashes and the five o'clock shadow across his jaw. I wanted to reach out and brush his hair out of his eyes, but held myself in check.

This was my chance and I would not waste it. I carefully got to my feet. He was closer than I thought. Even though there was plenty of room to spread out, Liam placed himself only a foot away, which made escaping even more difficult. I wanted to take the cloak with me, but it was tangled under his feet.

With the cloak out of the question, I would just leave with what I had on me. Gathering my courage, I tiptoed to the cave entrance and woefully stared out into the rain. It meant getting wet again, but it also would make it harder for him to track me. There was no use staying when he thought so little of me.

I stepped out of the cave and turned in the direction that I thought was Rya.

~

I was thoroughly and truly lost. I shook my fist at the sky and declared war. If only it wasn't raining and I could see the stars, then I could navigate my way easily. But everything looked the same. I swore I even passed the same downed trunk multiple times. And the thoughts that were coming from the forest creatures were scattered and unhelpful.

Intruder.

Intruder.

Run.

My plodding through the storm only scared them.

"Yes, yes. I know," I muttered. "I'm the intruder." I sneezed and stumbled in the dark, landing in a puddle. "Oh, just great." Here I was, a fearsome sorceress—sitting in a puddle. I was so wrapped up in my own woes that I didn't hear the approaching horses.

"Well, isn't this a sight for sore eyes," a gravelly voice called out. "I think I found a mud swallow." A lantern swung my way, and I blinked, blinded by the light. When my eyes adjusted, I saw that I had stumbled close to a road, and a transport had pulled up. The driver, a man with a graying beard and kind eyes, held up his lantern to illuminate the area. I glanced at the banner hung under the door and lit up in delight when I saw Candor.

"Are you going to Candor?" I asked. If I made it there, I would at least get some clothes from my sister.

"That's what it says." The driver tossed his thumb toward the banner. "But do you have fare?"

I reached for my purse and remembered I had nothing except my night dress. Heat rose to my cheeks.

"I don't at the moment. But I can pay you once we reach my relatives in the capital city of Thressia."

He rubbed his chin and looked me over, and I studied him warily.

Sheesh, she probably doesn't have any money. But the missus would throttle me if she heard I left a poor child out in the rain.

He was on the fence, so I put on the most pathetic face I could. "I swear, that misfortune has only set me back at the moment. I can and will pay for my fare."

"Oh, come on." The driver hopped down from his box and helped me up into his transport wagon. I did the best I could to wring out my nightdress, but it was all but ruined. I wasn't sure how I was going to present myself at the palace. Would they even let me in the front door, or would they turn me away?

It felt good to be out of the rain, and I leaned my head

against the sideboard. I heard the snap of the reins as the transport moved forward.

"Halt!" a loud voice shouted, and the horses came to a stop. The sudden stop forced me off the bench and I slid onto the floor.

"What is going on?" I shouted out at the driver.

"Another passenger."

"But we didn't go anywhere."

The door opened, and a dark figure jumped into the transport. Liam turned to me, his face wide-eyed with worry. When he saw me sitting on the bench, I caught his look of relief. He leaned out the door and spoke to the driver. "I'll pay for our fare as long as we are going north."

"As you wish. Can we go, or are more of you going to pop out of the woods?"

"No, you may proceed." Liam slammed the door and moved to the bench across from me. His long legs bumped mine, and I shuffled to adjust my nightdress and turn sideways. I waited for the accusations to start, followed by the condemnation. Instead, he leaned his head back, closed his eyes and ignored me.

His silence unnerved me, audibly and mentally. Surely, he would have some thoughts or reprimands, but he left me a blank slate. I wasn't even picking up an aura. Instead, I was left to stew in my own internal dialogue of assumptions, which left me tossing and turning, trying to get comfortable on the bench seat.

But no matter how I positioned myself, I was chilled to the bone, and my nightdress became uncomfortably cold. His green eyes opened, and he sighed in annoyance.

Ah ha! I thought, as he finally revealed his feelings. He *is* frustrated with me.

Liam stood, claimed the seat next to me, and pulled me in close. Lifting his arm, draping the cloak over the two of us.

I gasped and scooted away, but he pulled my elbow until I fell against his side, my cheek resting against his chest. He turned to sit sideways in the transport and held me close, his left arm resting comfortably on my arm.

Frozen stiff, I dared not move or breath.

"Relax," he muttered sleepily. "It's my duty to keep you safe. And if that means keeping you warm and alive until we reach Rya, then so be it. I will be your blanket. Don't worry, your virtue is safe with me."

I would have struggled more if I hadn't seen the flash of white signaling truth with his words.

"Why did you follow me?" I asked.

"Shh." He pressed his finger to my lips. "I'm tired. I spent all night tracking you. Less talk. More sleep."

I shifted, and my right elbow poked him. I heard a mental groan of pain and my eyes widened as I remembered the gash in his side. Carefully, I reached down with my hand and felt the wound. Using magic, I eased his pain.

I heard his sigh of relief, and I gritted my teeth and let my own tears of empathy fall. It hurt so much, and he had been hiding it from me. This wasn't the same wound my mother had bandaged. It was a new one that I would question later. I took as much pain as I could handle until I heard Liam fall into a deep sleep.

CHAPTER EIGHT

The sun brushed along my eyelids, tickling them awake. I was warm, comfortable, and I didn't want to move. I nuzzled my pillow that smelled like leather and woods . . . then my pillow moved.

Oh. My arm's asleep.

My eyes flew open, and I lifted my head to glance into Liam's solemn green eyes. He didn't smile, just gave me a curious look. Embarrassed, I pulled his cloak over my head and hid. Then my body shook. No, I wasn't shaking. Liam was vibrating with silent laughter. I peeked out from under the cloak, and this time his stoic expression broke, and the corners of his lips lifted into a smile.

I relaxed, sat up, and the cloak fell from my shoulders, and immediately I felt exposed. I turned, giving him my back as I wiped the sleep from my eyes. I was aghast at how much mud and dirt coated my nightdress and my feet.

Carefully, I undid my long hair and tried to comb through the mass of tangles with my fingers.

It's like moonlight.

My fingers paused in their detangling as I listened. I must have misheard. He wouldn't have complimented me. I glanced over my shoulder and Liam was staring out the window intently. I let out a long breath and went back to doing the best to make my hair presentable. My hair was down to my waist and all I could do was put it back into a braid. Once finished, I moved to the other side of the transport and wrapped my arms around myself.

Liam glanced over at me.

So pathetic.

That one hurt. I turned away to stare out the window.

Liam leaned forward, and I flinched thinking he was going to touch me. He gave me an odd look and rapped on the roof. The transport pulled over and Liam stepped out. He spoke in low tones with the driver, and I used the distraction to wipe at my face.

I was not pathetic. I was a woman, and I could take care of myself. Liam hopped back in and we were on our way again. He seemed fine with the lack of talking, so I obliged him by ignoring him. Which went against every single fiber of my being. I was the chatty one, I could hardly keep a secret, and I loved pulling conversations from my sister's thoughts.

It wasn't the same with Liam. He had a strong mental wall, and he hid his emotions and thoughts well. When a thought did escape his mental grasp, it jarred me or made me uncomfortable, like getting pricked by a cactus.

The transport's wheels bounced over gravel, but soon the road turned to brick, and the horses' hooves clipped gracefully along. I leaned forward and looked out the window and worried.

We were heading into a small city.

"What city is this?" I asked warily.

"It's Hinsburg."

"I don't understand. I don't want to stop in Hinsburg. I asked to go to Thressia." My voice rose, as did my panic. The closer we came to the city, the louder the thoughts of the people became. First like gnats that annoyed me, then the pressure became greater, like a constant buzz. I grimaced and covered my ears as if to keep out the thoughts, but they only became more painful. The population was far greater than Nihill.

The pain became unbearable, and I ground my teeth.

"Aura, what's the matter?"

I struggled to breathe as I heard the cries of the children that were hungry. A woman being beaten by her husband. A lost child, a thief accosting an old woman. It wasn't the few hundred of my town, but thousands of people.

"Aura." Liam grasped my elbow.

Lorn was right. I wasn't strong enough. I shouldn't have left home. "I'm fine," I groaned, trying to retreat further into my mind to block them out.

"No, you're not."

"I am." I shook and sweat beaded across my brow. The transport stopped in front of a shop, but I dared not leave. I collapsed on my bench seat and buried my head in the thin padded cushion.

"Tell me what's going on?" Liam begged. Flashes of blue signaled his worry.

"There's too many. It's too overwhelming. I can't shut them out," I cried.

He reached for me, but I pushed him away. I couldn't stand to be touched when overcome with an empathetic state. My sisters learned that lesson long ago, and usually would tuck me in with a blanket and give me tea. "Don't touch me," I commanded.

"No," he growled and pulled me into a hug. His arms wrapped around me, and he pressed my forehead into his chest. I waited for the onslaught of his emotions to hit me like a hammer coupled with the thousand-voice orchestra of the city, but they were slowly fading away.

I stopped struggling. Somehow Liam was canceling out my empathy. The ringing in my ears disappeared. I listened to the sound of his breathing, even and calm. He was an anchor in a storm of mental anguish.

"How d'you do that?" I breathed out.

"Do what?" His soulful eyes searched my face.

"Make the voices stop?"

"I don't know. I don't even know what was happening to you. My only thought was to protect you." He pulled back and brushed a stray hair from my face.

And that's when I saw how beautiful and bright he was. Blinding white with his need to protect. It was his own magic that showed up and protected me. He became a shield when I needed it most.

"Your magic is beautiful," I whispered.

He frowned and shook his head. "I don't have magic."

"You're wrong. You have defensive magic. By touching me, you shielded me and made"—I waved my hand in the air dismissively—"the bad stuff disappear. You do have powerful magic. Untrained, but strong. I think it's your determination of will, that desire to protect, that strengthens your magic."

He cleared his throat and looked away. "That's what I swore to do. Protect you until you get to Rya."

I nodded and turned in my seat to glance out the window to see where we stopped. It was a dress shop. My brows furrowed, and I looked at Liam in confusion. "What are we doing?"

"Getting you clothes. I don't assume you want to continue traveling to Rya in your nightgown."

My cheeks burned. "No."

"Then let's go." He pulled away and stepped out of the transport. He extended his hand to help me down. When he released my hand, the buzzing of the voices returned. He took his red cloak and wrapped it around my shoulders, covering my dirty dress. Thankfully, his own thoughts were shielded as we stepped through the door into *Cora's Fine Clothing*.

A chipper woman with red curls piled on her head and wearing a striped-green high-collared dress greeted us.

"Greetings, and welcome to my shop. I'm Cora, and what can we get you today?" She flashed her teeth at Liam while her lust flashed into my mind.

Oh yes, this is a pleasant surprise. What a hot slice of man pie.

I held back a chuckle. I instantly knew when Cora dragged her eyes away from Liam and saw me.

Eh, what's this? She can't possibly be wanting a dress from my collection. I'll be the laughingstock of the town. Is she his lover?

I sucked in my breath.

"I'd like a dress for my—" Liam began.

"Sister," I interrupted. "Nothing too fancy. Just sensible, since I lost my trunks during our travel."

Cora's smile brightened like the stars. *Oh, that's what I thought. There's no way a handsome man like that would ever be seen with that sickly-looking thistle.* "I'm sure, I have something that would be to her taste in my back room. Let me get it." Cora waved a polished nail through the green curtains. She disappeared into the back.

"Brother?" Liam uttered.

"Yes, well, I don't have a ring on my finger, and without it, it would look like I'm your lover by the state of my undress. So this is the best course of action." Heat rose to my cheeks as I tried to explain. "Plus, she fancies you."

"What? No, she doesn't."

"Yes, she does. She thinks you are a hot slice of man pie."

"She said no such thing," Liam scoffed, and he shuffled away from me. I could tell that the revelation of her liking him unsettled his usual stoic self.

"But I don't think I'm welcome here," I whispered.

"Nonsense, this is a dress shop, and you need a dress. Why wouldn't you be welcome?"

"It's not that simple. She has a certain clientele, and I don't fit the mold."

"That's ridiculous. There are plenty of pretty dresses here."

I was about to explain further when Cora waltzed out of the back room with a simple brown shift dress and wrap belt. My hopes dropped at seeing the boring earth tone dress that was very similar to the ones I already owned. There goes getting something beautiful and different.

"How's this for your sister?" Cora held up the dress to her own petite frame. "It is sturdy fabric, can be worn for multiple days without showing wear and dirt from travel."

My hands clenched, digging into the red cloak. "It's fine—" I began.

"It's hideous," Liam spoke up.

"I assure you, this is well within a reasonable range for your sister."

"Madam, don't let her current state of travel fool you, for she may look like a piece of coal"—I shot Liam a disgusted look, but he was too far into his rant to stop—"but under that layer of dirt is a precious gem."

My mouth dropped open and so did Cora's. She stuttered,

"M-maybe, if you give me a price range, I can have something made up and delivered to you."

Liam walked over to the dress in the window, a long-sleeved sky-blue dress with a matching riding cloak. "We'll take this one."

"But sir, that's very expensive."

"And throw in riding boots, silk stockings, and any underthings she may need."

Liam reached into his belt and pulled out enough gold to pay for the dress and then some, tossing it on the counter. By Cora's internal dialogue, I knew he vastly overpaid. She bobbed her head and quickly undressed the stuffed mannequin in the window.

"That's far too extravagant," I exclaimed. "I'm fine with the simple brown one—really." I rubbed my temples to keep away the buzzing that was coming from the townspeoples' thoughts.

Liam walked over to me and leaned down. "You tried hard to hide your disappointment from me, but it was clear as day. I wasn't going to see you in that plain brown thing." He reached out and lifted my chin so I looked into his serious eyes. "Not when you deserve so much more."

I looked away, and as soon as contact lessened the pain came back. I winced.

"Will you tell me what's going on?" he asked.

I shook my head. "You will despise me when you find out. Think that I'm weak. I can't stand for that to happen."

He sighed. "I can sense you're in pain, and being near me lessons it, correct? Because of—" he hesitated. "My magic."

I nodded.

Liam frowned as if he still didn't believe. "I still don't

understand, but I will do anything to keep that look from your pale eyes."

"What look?"

"The one where it looks like someone killed your favorite pet."

I snorted. "I don't look like that."

He grinned. "You have a way of seeming so small and pathetic that my instincts kick in and I want nothing more than to protect you." A flurry of images came at me.

I blushed and fidgeted with his cloak, and then I gasped as I saw his thoughts. "You went back and beat up the other man who accosted me. You found out from Tobias and went after Clive. That's how you injured yourself here." I pointed to the wound that had slowly stopped bleeding.

"Who told you?" Liam's hand covered his side.

"I can't believe you did that," I retorted. "You didn't have the right to challenge them to a duel, no less."

"I never mentioned a duel." His brows furrowed.

I clamped my lips shut. Cora came out of the back room with a chemise, corset, stockings, and boots.

"Here you are," she sang out in a cheerful voice.

"She will change here and wear them out," Liam stated.

"Certainly, come into the fitting area, dear." Cora gestured to a silk screen panel for me to change behind.

I stepped behind the screen and was about to pull off my nightgown when I glanced at my dirty fingernails and hands. It was a shame to ruin a perfectly clean dress by putting my dirty body in it. I hesitated to change without getting a bath, and then I heard the door jingle as it opened and closed.

Liam had left, and the assault of thoughts came barraging at me.

Like putting lipstick on a pig. Nothing she does will help her sickly, sewer rat figure. *I had that gown put on display to catch Nicolette De Tourel's eye during her morning walk. Now, I have nothing thanks to this scrawny thistle.*

I crumpled to the ground and held the clothes in my lap. Once, I had thought of my magic as a gift. One that allowed me to spy on my sisters in good fun, but that was in the safety of our own home. Anywhere beyond our front door, and it became a curse. A debilitating curse that could freeze anyone like the children's rhyme; sticks and stones will break your bones, but words can never hurt me. That wasn't the same for thoughts. Those were like poison that ate away at my soul and self-esteem. With my guard down, the horrid and mean could send me into a dark spiral.

The door jingled, and I heard a mumble that sounded like my name. I tried to answer, but my limbs felt like lead. Liam rushed behind the screen and saw me crumpled on the ground, the dress untouched.

"What's wrong?" he asked.

"I don't deserve this," I said under a shuddering breath. "I'm not worth it. I'm a sickly thistle."

Liam turned and glared at Cora. "Did you say that to her?"

"I-I did no such thing," she said unconvincingly.

"The truth," he roared.

"I would never say such a thing to my customers' faces," Cora hedged.

Liam put things together. "Let me guess, you didn't say it, but you thought it?"

Cora paled.

"You also *thought* I was a hot slice of man pie too," he intoned.

Cora blushed and stammered. "What? I-I don't know. H-how?"

Liam looked over at me and reached to help me stand. "I think I understand now." He gathered our purchases and headed for the door. He stopped at the counter where he had placed the gold coins and plucked two back. "That's for your rudeness toward my sister, and your uncouth thoughts toward me."

Cora's mouth dropped open, and we left. The door slamming behind us.

Liam helped me into the waiting transport, my new clothes bunched haphazardly and discarded on the opposite bench. He didn't even attempt to sit across from me, but immediately pulled me close to his side and wrapped an arm over my shoulder.

"Does this help?" he asked.

I nodded.

He rapped on the ceiling and told the driver to head out of town, and fast. The horses took off, and soon Hinsburg was just a speck of dust on the horizon. I pulled away from Liam and moved to the seat next to my rumpled clothes.

He crossed his arms and legs and looked at me through narrowed eyes. "So you read people's minds," he stated.

I swallowed and looked at my folded hands, noticing the dirt under my thumb nail. I tucked it into my fist to make it disappear. "No, I hear their thoughts. They pop into my mind whether I want them to or not."

"The day in the woods when I thought I was dying. I heard someone in my head." Liam sighed and looked up. "It was you. Wasn't it?"

"I was in the field playing a game with my sisters when I heard your mental cry for help. You were too far gone to even speak, but you showed me where you were by images." I pointed to my temple.

"I didn't remember at first because I thought it was delirium. But it's coming back to me. You did something else to me too. It happened again last night while you touched my side. You took away my pain. How? What are you?"

I licked my dry lips, my hands trembled as I nervously explained my power. I was truthful and vulnerable with him. "I'm an Empath. I can take on your pain as my own."

Liam's mind shut down like a gate. The iciness I felt emanating from him made me shudder. His eyes became cold, his nostrils flared, and his voice rose angrily. "You will never do that to me again, do you hear?"

I flinched at his tone and waited for his anger to roil through me, but he quickly tampered it down, and I felt nothing. I matched his anger with my own.

"I will do no such thing," I argued. "If I have the power to ease someone's pain, then I will do it. I was given this curse or gift, whatever you want to call it, and I alone will dictate how I use it. You have no say over me."

Liam's hands balled into twin fists. "You are in my care, and I say otherwise."

"I can handle myself," I snapped.

He pointed an accusatory finger at the back of the transport toward Hinsburg. "You couldn't handle being in a small city. Even in your own hometown one man easily overwhelmed you. We're heading into a war, and I come to a house full of mages and sorceresses looking for someone to help turn the tide and save a kingdom, and I pick the weakest one," he snapped.

"You're right." I turned my head and stared at the passing countryside. The lush green land filled with sights I had never even seen before. Only once had I traveled outside of Nihill, and it was a disaster. I would not tell him that. Maeve would disappear for days on end and she flew and explored, but not me. I was always forbidden to leave our town but was the one forced to go into Nihill for supplies to test my shielding limits. I guess if I had done better handling our small town and became stronger, Mother would have let me travel farther. "There's no denying that I'm the weakest of my sisters." I turned back to Liam and glared at him. "But I'm the only one you've got. So deal with it."

"The pale flower has thorns," he chuckled. *There may be some hope after all.*

CHAPTER NINE

As we rode through the countryside, the land changed from hills to rolling green meadows filled with wildflowers. It was idyllic, peaceful, and I couldn't stop staring out the window at the beauty of the landscape. Liam handed me a wrapped pastry that he had purchased in town, and I ate it slowly savoring every bite. After a few candle marks, the transport pulled over at a lake to rest and water the horses. I used the time to clean the dirt from my arms, legs, and face before finding a copse of bushes to hide behind while I changed into clean clothes.

Unbelievably the blue dress fit. It was a little loose around the shoulders, but the skirt didn't need hemming. The new boots squeezed my toes. As I dressed, I had to pinch myself to see if this was real or not. I felt like a different person. I was turning and trying to admire myself in the reflection of the moving water.

Watching the wind ripple across the lake was soothing. The water flickered and a flash of light followed, signaling a spell. Getting to my knees, I leaned forward and touched my finger into the water to answer. When the ripple passed, Maeve's reflection grinned up at me.

"Somebody's in trouble," Maeve sing-songed. "I'm so jealous of you right now. I can't believe that you would run off like that. I mean, it's expected of me, but not you. You're the *good* one. Then you've ignored my calls."

"I, uh, didn't run away exactly," I hedged. "The stranger that came to our house . . . kidnapped me."

"What?" Maeve's brows furrowed. "That *man* kidnapped you? I'm going to roast him alive."

"No, don't. It's fine. I want to be here."

"Really?" One dark eyebrow raised.

"Yes, I want to help him."

"Mother is furious."

"I'm sure." I sighed.

"No really, she's so angry that she's at a loss for words. She hasn't yelled at me in days, and believe me, I've been especially annoying of late."

"Trying to distract her, are you?" I knew Maeve was covering for me.

Maeve winked, but then her sure smile faltered. "I asked to come after you, but she won't let us leave the tower."

"Why not?"

Maeve shook her head. "It has something to do with what she has foreseen."

"What is it?" I asked fearfully, knowing that Mother must have had a vision of my future.

With the darkness of the lake, I couldn't tell where Maeve was in the tower, and had to assume she was hiding in the workroom. Her voice lowered to a whisper. "She said a daughter will fall."

"Fall? Are you sure?"

"That's what she said, and you know that when she gets these visions. They're almost always correct. You need to come home now," she pleaded.

"I can't. I'm needed here."

"You can't help anyone if you're dead," Maeve snapped.

I glared at Maeve. "Exactly, so I want to help as many people while I can."

Maeve gasped and covered her mouth in remorse. "I'm so sorry, I didn't mean it like that."

"Bye, Maeve." I thrust my hand into the water, scattering the reflection and thus ending our conversation. I leaned back on my heels as the ripples faded.

"Ahem," Liam coughed. *Oh, please let her be decent.*

I held back a grin and called out to the worried Liam. "It's fine. I'm *decent*."

He came around the bushes, a sheepish look on his face. "You heard that, huh?"

I smiled. "As if you said it out loud."

"Is it true?" Liam asked. "What your sister said about your mother's vision. That you're going to fall—as in die?"

"It's rude to eavesdrop," I said. I stood and dusted off my hands. "Everyone dies." I turned to walk past him, wanting to end the conversation. This wasn't a topic I liked to discuss.

Liam didn't like my nonchalant attitude, and he cut me off, stepping in front of me. "Aura, did you know that this could happen?"

"No, not exactly. I guess now I know why. Now we can be prepared."

"And you're okay with that?" Liam seemed confused by my reaction.

"It doesn't mean that it is going to come true or happen to me," I said. "Mother's visions can have many meanings. You must trust me on this."

Liam stood there, his golden hair wet, his chin a little red from a clean shave. He must have used the time to freshen up. His wrinkled shirt sported a bloodstain, but his dark cloak would cover it. I frowned. He should have bought clothes for himself.

He stood there awkwardly, fidgeting with a bundle in his hands. He stepped forward and held it out. "This is for you."

"What is it?" I asked.

He grinned in boyish delight. "Ah ha! So I haven't spoiled the surprise for you."

"No, you do really well at shielding your thoughts. You're a natural."

"Okay, let me try something," Liam closed his eyes and let down his shield.

I saw the inside of Cora's shop and watched as I headed behind a screen. Seeing myself from someone else's perspective really did a number on me. Did I really look so small and childlike? No wonder he felt a need to protect me. I didn't even resemble an adult woman, but rather someone of twelve. When I disappeared, Liam left the building and headed into the next shop a few doors down. Inside, he agonized over picking out a comb, ribbon, and hair pins from a young woman who tried to flirt with him. He was oblivious to her attempts.

She wrapped them in white paper with a blue ribbon, and he scooped it up and hurried back toward the dress shop. Did his steps seem hurried? When he entered, he glanced at the screen and saw a crumple of dresses and my bare foot sticking out along the floor.

I felt his panic as he rushed toward me.

I blinked as the vision stopped.

"What just happened?" I asked. "Never before has someone shared such a long memory with me. I would get glimpses and images, but not an actual memory. I was there. I could smell and hear."

Liam stepped forward and held up the white package with

the blue ribbon. "Did it ruin the surprise by seeing it through my eyes? I think you saw more than I wanted."

I shook my head. "No, I think it made it even more special." I took the package and slipped the ribbon off of it, tucking it into my pocket, and I gently unfolded the paper. His memory was false, for this was not a simple comb, but a pearl one, and the ribbons were brighter than his own memories.

"Thank you, I love it."

Liam bowed his head, the protector mask back in place. "I'm glad you approve of the gift." He stepped back, giving me space, and turned to head up the hill toward the transport.

He was so funny because he was stiff and formal when he remembered his duty, but then he would slip and treat me as a friend.

I undid my braid and ran the comb through my hair, expertly braiding and using the ribbons to tie it up off my neck. When I came back up the transport, our driver, Fadal, gave me an approving nod. I grinned and stopped by the steps. I turned toward Liam waiting to see his expression.

He stood by the open door, his hand reaching for me to step up into the transport.

I gave a twirl. "What do you think?" I gushed excitedly.

Liam barely glanced at me. "You look presentable."

Presentable? I would have settled for nice, or lovely. I wasn't expecting beautiful. But presentable seemed plain. My smile fell. He was back to being aloof again. I let out a breath of frustration and gathered my skirt to get into the transport, ignoring his outstretched hand. I scooted to the far corner and waited for him to enter and take the seat opposite of me.

"We should reach the capital city of Thressia by nightfall. You said you have family in town. Do you think they could afford to lend us a horse and shelter us for the night? I've been gone far too long, and I haven't heard an update from my troops. Even if they let me sleep in the barn, I would repay them handsomely."

Liam must be remembering where we kept him when he came to my house. He must think all of my family was poor. I kept my face neutral. "Oh, I think they could spare a horse or two."

∼

When we came into the city, it was the largest I'd ever seen. Brick houses squashed together, one on top of another. Hundreds of years of heritage rebranded and rebuilt over old structures. It gave the streets a very eclectic look, and I loved it. Or rather, I loved what I saw before I had to drop the shade and stare at the lining on the seat across from me. I glanced out the window once or twice and did my best to hide my discomfort by clenching my jaw so hard it hurt. I was proud that I didn't curl up into a ball and cry. I was determined to prove to Liam that I was stronger than he thought. I had to be strong. A particularly brutal image came to me, and I let out a gasp.

In a flash, Liam was across the seat and pulled me into his lap, both arms wrapped around me, and instantly the assault stopped.

"Thank you," I sighed in relief.

"Anytime," he whispered and nuzzled my head.

We pulled up to the gates, and I stared at the royal palace through the iron fence. Three story white brick with hundreds of windows overlooking the courtyard and fountain. A gold sun on a blue banner hung on either side of the grand entrance. I leaned out the window and spoke to the guards.

"Can you please let Eden know that her favorite sister, Aura, is here."

I moved to sit back in the seat across from Liam, but he wouldn't have it. He pulled on my arm, tucked into his side again. Our hips touching, his arm draped over the back of the bench. Heat flushed through my cheeks, my heart thrummed in my chest, and I sat up straight.

"Relax, just think of me as your armor bearer. A big shield. It's hardly a big deal for me to stick close to you if it protects you."

"I just don't want anyone to get the wrong idea." I blushed.

"And what idea is that?"

"Never mind." The heat from my cheeks quickly faded.

Liam leaned forward to look out the window. "Your sister works at the palace? I wonder if she knows my old friend, Dorian? It's a shame what happened with the royal family. I wonder how Dorian is taking it, being the new king."

The gates opened, and I could feel the anticipation running through me at seeing Eden. I had missed so much and had only watched their wedding ceremony through the enchanted mirror. It wasn't the best thing to have all the Eville sorceresses congregating in one kingdom. It might cause a war.

The transport pulled up in front of the manor doors and royal guards lined both sides of the runner that came down the stairs onto the drive. Liam helped me out of the transport and kept one hand on my elbow, shielding me.

The doors swung open and a tall dark-haired man in a white jacket and blue sash bounded down the stairs and slowed in front of us, his hand on his decorated sword.

"Dorian," Liam spoke up in delight. "It's good to see you, friend."

Dorian ignored him, his eyes going to Liam's hand on my

elbow. "How is it *you're* here?" Dorian asked suspiciously, walking around the two of us.

"I'm passing through. My traveling companion is visiting her family, and we hope to be on our way," Liam answered.

"Silence." Dorian waved his hand, cutting off Liam. "I'm not talking to you." He pointed to me. "How are *you* standing here? Answer me, or I will kill you without a second thought."

Liam reacted. He thrust me behind his back and drew his sword. "You will not lay a hand on her. I'm honor bound, and I will defend Aura with my life, even if that means against you, my friend."

I laughed a loud, hearty laugh. Dorian chuckled until his laughter became higher-pitched and more like a giggle.

"Relax, Liam." I pushed his sword arm down and stepped around him.

"What should I tell Mother?" Dorian asked. "She's been calling our mirror nonstop. In case you showed up here."

"Mother?" Liam looked baffled.

"Tell her I'm fine. That I will come home soon."

Dorian's head turned to inspect Liam. "And who are *you*, and what are you doing with my sister?"

"Sister?" Liam grabbed my elbow and pulled me into his side. "Aura, this is not Dorian. We must go. Something's wrong here."

I glanced at Dorian. "Should we tell him?"

Dorian pouted, an unbecoming face on a male. "Must we? This is so much fun."

"Eden, there you are, my love." A second Dorian came out of the palace and stood next to the other Dorian. He sighed when confronting the laughing feminine version of himself who had uncharacteristically thrust out a hip. "I will never get used to this."

"I had to, darling. I heard that Aura was here, and I know with her gift that she can't possibly come to Thressia. I thought she must be an imposter."

"Couldn't you have chosen the glamour of an old woman or a guard? Derek, even. It's been a while since you tortured him," Dorian said.

"Aura, what's going on?" Liam asked.

I smiled and pointed to the perky Dorian who was now arguing with the non-smiling Dorian. "Liam, I would like you to meet my sister, Eden, Queen of Candor."

He looked up just in time to see Eden's glamour fade and shift. My beautiful blonde-haired sister stood before me in a dress of deep navy, a silver crown upon her perfect brow.

"Ah," Eden screamed and threw her hands around me. "I have so much to tell you, Aura."

And then the barrage of images and thoughts came at me. I had learned a long time ago to sort through Eden's mind.

"So being queen isn't as bad as you thought. He still calls you sparrow despite your attempts at blackmail. You should really stop with the glamouring of the house elves into giant dogs. He is going to find out, eventually." I clapped my hands together. "Really? Oh, I can't wait to be an aunt again."

"What?" Dorian turned to give an accusing look at Eden. "Wife, are you keeping something from me?"

"Aura, I hadn't told him yet." Eden covered her mouth and looked at her husband.

"Oops." I cringed.

"You sure know how to spoil a surprise." Eden laughed and wrapped her hands around Dorian.

"Really?" Dorian asked in disbelief. "Truly?"

Eden nodded. "I wasn't sure myself, but if Aura says so, it must be true."

I nodded, feeling the little pops of happiness and contentment coming from Eden's child.

"I love you." Dorian nuzzled her and leaned in for a kiss.

Liam laughed. "So this is what it's like to see Aura in action."

Eden's eyes shone with glee. "She really is magnificent. But it's no use keeping secrets around her. She will always suss them out, so it's always better to be truthful with her."

Liam's laughter halted, the smile fell from his eyes and he straightened his shoulders.

After Dorian and Eden finished kissing and celebrating the news, they ushered us inside. We passed through the main foyer and headed into a private sitting room decorated in blue and gold, with white vases filled with fresh flowers. A house-elf appeared from out of nowhere with a tray of food. I picked up from Eden's thoughts that the house-elves were traveling by secret compartments and dumbwaiters within the walls of the palace.

I didn't care for decorum and immediately helped myself to the finger foods, careful to avoid all of my pregnant sister's favorite ones. I reached for a pastry roll, pulled back, and chose a mini cucumber sandwich Eden hated.

Eden sighed and picked up the pastry and put it on my plate. "Here, you don't have to always think of others first. There is plenty for everyone, and I can always ask the servants to make more."

Eden turned and warned Liam. "You have to watch her. She is self-sacrificing to the core, even to the detriment of her own health. It's her greatest strength and weakness."

Liam looked at me, his eyes softened. "I'm beginning to see that."

I blushed.

Dorian turned to address Liam. "Is it true, the reports I'm getting from the north?"

"Yes, a blight has erupted and is spreading across the kingdom. It starts as a dark fog that moves from town to town. The fog blocks out the sun and makes it eternally night. Under the cover of darkness, creatures are roaming the lands. Giants, ogres, and trolls are outside their territory, and don't seem in a hurry to return. It seems wherever the fog goes, trouble follows."

I reached for a teacup and poured myself some tea. It had hints of lavender from the aroma, and I knew Eden had set out my favorite on purpose. Sitting back, I tried to listen in and follow the politics to learn more about the blight. Liam had been very secretive and initially told me the blight was a dark, ethereal fog. Now, I was learning the consequences of that blight on the kingdom itself.

"Just last week, the fog reached the town of Greenshire and many of the townspeople exhibited unusual symptoms, paranoia being the most common. Not to mention their crops stopped growing and their water system became tainted. They had to abandon everything and move farther south while a pack of cù sìth have claimed the land as their own now."

Dorian nodded. "The cù sìth's bark is worse than their bite."

Liam winced and gestured. "I don't know about that. I barely escaped my encounter with one alive. I can't say the same for the beast."

My head snapped up as they spoke of the legendary fae dogs. Large bull-size hounds with fur like grass. To hear one bark three times meant certain death. That Liam had survived an attack by one was no small feat.

"We've exhausted all of our resources, and the hedge

witches and seers all say the same thing. It's a vengeful curse. We don't know who else to turn to, so I sought the House of Eville."

Eden snorted. "Oh, now we are the House of Eville, are we? A few of the daughters marry up and suddenly we carry more prestige, whereas two years ago, most would have considered my *family* the blight on the seven kingdoms."

Her harsh words brought color to Liam's cheeks. "I admit, years ago, I would have agreed. Many have been blinded by prejudice, but I'm not." His eyes fell across me and I felt a heat rise to my cheeks. "To save a kingdom, I can see the value in aligning with a common enemy."

The rosy feelings I'd had moments before dropped, and so did my teacup as it clattered against the plate.

Eden looked over at me, her lips pinched in anger. She saw my hands shaking and read the situation. "Aura, I think this has been a trying day. I can only imagine how mentally exhausted you are by being in Thressia. Let's get you settled for the night."

Liam and Dorian stood as we exited. Liam made to follow me, but Eden used her newfound royal authority and froze him with a sharp look. I stood in the hallway as she went back inside. I could hear their hushed voices as they argued.

"If you know what's good for you, you'd stay far away from her," Eden challenged.

"I don't understand. She's hurting. I can tell. I can protect her from those feelings."

"You're the one causing her pain right now, you dumb oaf," Eden snapped. I could almost imagine what was happening as if I were in the room. Eden probably jabbed her finger into Liam's chest.

"Eden." Dorian's voice grew louder. "I think this is your maternal instinct kicking in. Aura's an adult."

"None of you understand like I do. Aura's life *is* pain. Constant *empathetic* pain. Her smiles and endless chatter are just a facade to hide what she is feeling. I've spent years studying her, trying to protect her from the one thing she always wanted."

"No, don't," I whispered, knowing Eden couldn't hear me on the other side of the door.

"She can't have a normal relationship. Can you imagine what it would be like to hear everyone's innermost, darkest, and deepest thoughts all the time? It would destroy a sane person."

"You don't know that," Liam said.

"I do. Mother has researched. All empaths have either gone crazy or committed suicide at an early age. For her to have any hope of living a long life, it will have to be one of loneliness and away from people. Crowds, cities, and even this curse that is brewing could be the death of her. As she grows older, her power grows stronger, and most don't live long past twenty or so winters."

"My only desire is to protect her," Liam repeated.

"But who will protect her from you?"

CHAPTER TEN

"You shouldn't have said that," I chastised Eden as she came back into the hall.

She smoothed her hands down her dress and straightened her crown. "Yeah, well, blame it on the hormones." Eden led me up the stairs to a guest suite filled with beautiful ornate furniture covered in the sun crests.

"It feels unreal," I said.

Eden waved her hand and glamoured the fleur-de-lis wallpaper to became stone walls, the four-poster bed changed into my simple bed in the tower.

"Oh, wait. I remember." She flicked her wrist, and the blanket turned into a pink spread with ruffles.

Eden loved to spoil me by using glamour on my few meager possessions.

"It's home," I said, softly. "Well, not exactly, because you're not there."

Eden moved to sit on my bed, her hand resting on her belly protectively. "I want to know what Liam is to you?"

"A friend," I said.

"Nothing more?" she asked.

I blushed. "No. I don't think he thinks of me in that way."

She sighed. "I'm sorry for what I said earlier. I shouldn't

have gone off like that. It's just that he doesn't see what he's doing to you. Those careless comments wound you deeply."

"It's actually not as bad as you think. I can't read his thoughts."

"What?"

"It's true. Most of the time I have no clue what he's thinking. He has shield magic, and he's a natural. Only rarely do I get a glimpse of what he's thinking. But Eden, more than that." I reached and clasped her hands between mine. "When he's near me, I can't hear *them*. He blocks out their cries." Even as we spoke, I heard the hum of thoughts from the hundreds of house-elves four floors below.

She blinked, and her hand went to her mouth. "Oh dear, then everything I said was—"

"The truth," I finished for her. "Don't worry, I've known for a long time. Mother explained it to me. It's why I'm constantly being tested and pushed, but it's also why she shelters me so much. My empathy gifts have grown stronger, but not my control over them. I know I only have a few more sane years left. So I want to enjoy them. I can already feel the hints of madness beginning to linger in the corners of my mind. I just don't to talk about it."

"Oh, Aura. I didn't know." Eden wrapped me in a hug. *I should have been a better sister. I should never have teased her when she was younger.*

"Stop. Stop!" I pulled away. "Stop feeling guilty and sorry for me. I've accepted it. So should you. And at least let me try to help Liam. I would like to do one truly noble thing in my life before I go find my own lonely tower and become a crazy cat lady."

"But what if Liam—" she began.

"No," I said adamantly and rubbed my temples. The pain

became unbearable. "We are friends, and nothing more. He's my anchor in the chaos, but he doesn't think of me like that. He's too noble to his cause. Plus, he said it in there. I'm his enemy. Once we've banished the blight on Rya, then his duty as my protector is over."

"He's a jerk."

"He's right." I laid back on the bed and closed my eyes.

"What do you hope to accomplish by going to Rya?" Eden kneeled on the bed and stroked the back of my hair to sooth my headache.

"I don't know. I'll do whatever I can. Mother refused to even help them, which made me even more determined to help. I think if he didn't abduct me, I would have gone north on my own," I said.

"You know she hates Rya, don't you?"

"It's something about my real mother, I think."

We spoke for a few more minutes, but I couldn't hide the pain that was becoming unbearable. The voices, I needed them to stop. I curled up in a ball and pressed my hands over my ears.

"I will have Liam put in the next room. Hopefully, he will be close enough to work his magic, but not too close."

I snorted but gave her an affirming nod. "It will be," I lied. Eden left, and I focused on shielding myself. First closing off the most brutal of thoughts and sins, then the hunger pangs. It was like a leaky roof, and every time I plugged a hole, the rain would pour in another. I couldn't keep out the shower of thoughts, but maybe I could stop the worst ones.

I tossed and turned, frustrated at my abilities. A few candle marks must have passed, and I was fighting a losing battle. I stared at the open balcony and knew it would be so easy to just jump and end it all. Then there would be silence.

"No!" What kind of thoughts were those? I rolled over and bit my pillow and released a muffled scream. The pain released a mental shock wave.

I heard a loud thud from the next room, followed by running footsteps. My bedroom door burst open and Liam was there, standing over my bed. He scooped me up in his arms and cradled me like a child.

"Shh, it's alright. I'm here."

My cheek pressed into his bare shoulder, my tears running down his skin. He was only wearing his breeches, and the bandage around his wound. I tried to pull away, but his grip on me tightened. "Don't fight me. Don't fight this."

And I didn't. I relaxed in his arms, my head dropping onto his chest. He set me back down on my bed and tucked me under the covers. Then gently he laid on top of them and tucked his arm under my head. His other one cradled his own.

"Don't do it," he warned.

"Do what?" I whispered, my hair tickling my nose. I was curled on my side facing away from him, his arm under my neck.

"What I saw."

I stilled. He picked up my thoughts of jumping off a balcony. Only my closest family members were in tune enough with me to pick up my thoughts, and here he was after only knowing him a few days picking up on mine. I refused to answer.

"Promise me that won't ever happen to you."

I tried to play it off. "I don't know what you're talking about."

"Aura." His voice lowered in warning, but I feigned ignorance.

I looked out to the balcony and shivered, thinking of my

mother's warning about my fall. Was it tied to me going crazy? I buried my head further into Liam's shoulder.

Just enjoying the silence that Liam's presence brought. I could feel my eyelids growing heavy. I heard the door open and soft footfalls draw close to my bed. Liam shifted to look at the intruder in the room.

"You felt it too?" Eden whispered.

He nodded.

"I was on the other side of the palace and it was like getting slapped in the face. Dorian is still sleeping like a baby. Oblivious. So it seems you *are* connected to my sister in some odd way."

Silence followed, and I could hear Eden wondering if I was asleep. She was deciding if she was going to allow Liam to stay near me.

"If you do anything to her other than shield her, I will curse you and you'll be walking out of here with goat's legs," Eden hissed.

"You have my word as a knight."

"I don't agree with this, but you're the only one that can help her. In fact, I will speak with Dorian and we will get you on your way at first light. It will be best if you stay away from the major roads. I expect you to protect her at every turn."

"I will," he promised.

"That means her heart as well."

"I understand."

∽

When I awoke, Liam was sleeping in a chair next to my bed. His arm stretched out awkwardly, hand resting on the top of my head to keep contact. His head drooped sideways, and I heard the soft snores. He must have waited until I was asleep before moving to the chair and giving us a proper distance. The sun wasn't even up yet, and at home I would already be up doing chores.

I sat up and his hand fell from my head. Liam woke, his green eyes locking onto mine.

Not good. She looks like she's about ready to crumble. I didn't help her at all.

I blinked and pulled the blanket up to my chin. "Don't worry, I won't break. And yes, you helped last night."

"Sorry," Liam mumbled. "I wasn't thinking. It wasn't what it sounded like."

"Actually, you *were* thinking. That's the problem. Often, our thoughts are more truthful than our lips." I stood up, wrapping the blanket around my body. "Thank you for watching over me last night. But I think I can handle getting dressed without a nanny."

"All right." He stood, his arms reaching for the sky, the muscles stretching across his chest. He ran his hands through his hair to wake himself up and then headed for the door, stopping within the doorway. "I'm right next door if you need me."

"I won't."

"But if you do."

"Go," I snapped irritably. "I won't do anything stupid in the next candle mark, but after that I make no promises." I shrugged.

Eden must have had someone watching for us to stir because servants instantly set upon us and ushered me to a bathing room, where there was a hot tub waiting for me. I thoroughly washed my hair and scrubbed my body and fingers raw. Using soap on the cuts on my feet.

Eden had found very simpleminded servants, for their

thoughts were silent. They held up various dresses, but I pointed to one similar in style that Liam had bought me in red, the color of his cloak. I picked out one extra traveling dress and a pair of boys pants and a long-sleeve blouse. It was daring and exciting, but I could get it all into a pack. We were traveling light and swift, so they supplied me with the basic essentials.

A knock came to my door as I sat at the vanity and finished pulling back the sides of my hair into two braids that fell down my back.

"Enter."

Liam swooped in and hovered over my chair. "How are you feeling? Was I gone too long?"

"I'm fine."

"Liar." He pointed to my forehead. "This right here scrunches up when you are trying to fight off the pain."

I swatted at his hand. "I hate to leave my sister so soon, but the sooner we leave the better I'll feel."

Dorian knocked, and since the door was already open, he let himself in. "I wanted to make sure you're properly outfitted."

"I am, and thank you." I stood showing off, letting the red dress swirl, and then pointed to my full pack on the bed.

"Nonsense, a lady is never properly dressed without a weapon." He snapped his fingers and in came a servant, their arms full of weapons and swords, and he spread them out on my bed. "Choose one to serve you well."

Liam grumbled. "She doesn't need a weapon, she has me."

"And that's precisely why she needs a weapon." Dorian picked up a sheathed knife. "This one has a thigh strap that hides under your skirt, or we have one that you can tuck into your bodice, or how about a push knife?"

My cheeks flushed red. "I'm not comfortable with

weapons." Reflecting back on when I attempted to and failed to take a life to save my sister.

"You fool," Liam teased Dorian. "You expect an empath to hurt someone? You might as well ask them to stab themselves."

Dorian glowered, his voice lowering. "Yet, you are taking my sister-in-law into dangerous territory unarmed. She may not want to injure someone, but she can learn to defend herself." He reached for a tube with a golden emblem on the side and tossed it to me. I was surprised and let it clatter to the floor before scrambling to pick it up.

"Press the button." He pointed to the gold plate. I did, and it slid out into a long staff. "Portable, and great for keeping animals and people"—he shot Liam a look—"at bay."

I tested the weight of it in my hands and felt it hum. Someone with potent magic forged the weapon, and I felt grounded when I held it. "I love it." I grinned at Dorian.

"I had a feeling you would."

Liam frowned, his arms crossed, and he glowered. I couldn't get a read on why he was upset at Dorian's gift. I pressed the button again, and it retracted. I was even more thrilled to learn that it had a leather holster that I could use to carry it on my hip or adjust it to sling on my back.

Within the hour we were packed, and the stable boy brought out two horses for us.

Eden was weepy-eyed and gave me a quick hug before disappearing inside. Not wanting to burden me with her overwhelming emotions.

Dorian held out his arms, and I stepped forward into a brotherly hug as he whispered, "Liam is a good guy, and my friend. He lives by the code, and he will protect you."

"I know."

When it came time to mount the horse, I faltered. Damsel,

the roan my sister gave me, was a few hands taller than our workhorse. I put my foot in the stirrup, and on my second attempt could swing up into the saddle, thankful for the split riding skirt.

"I've sent men ahead of you to alert your troops of your whereabouts. They should meet you on the Marshwam pass to escort you home."

"Thank you, my friend." Liam reached out and shook hands with Dorian.

"If you need anything, Candor will come to your aid."

"I appreciate that, but this is Rya's problem and we will deal with it."

"Safe travels." Dorian waved, and we headed out the gate.

Navigating out of the city proved difficult. I struggled with the noise and chatter. I was scared that I would have a permanent worry line on my forehead from trying to filter out the background from the important things.

We passed a stall where a young, bedraggled child was hanging around a vendor's table full of food.

So hungry. I need food for my grandma so she will get better.

The vendor, a thin man with a wiry mustache and dark eyes, was aware of the child's intentions. His hand rested on a knife at his hip.

He will not steal from me this time. I will take his hand for it.

The boy made his move.

"Stop!" I pulled on the reins and slid from my horse, reaching into my satchel filled with coins, a gift from Eden. I quickly paid for bread, eggs and cheese and handed them to the boy, plus an extra five gold pieces. "Here, for your family. Never come to this booth again, do you hear me?"

He nodded.

I confronted the shop manager. "Taking a boy's hand for stealing is barbaric and wrong."

Liam had moved from his horse and placed a hand on my arm. I flung it off and raced down two more alleys, forcing Liam to follow with our horses.

"Aura," he called out, but I couldn't stop. My heart was pounding with newfound knowledge. I could pinpoint the voices if I got close enough to them. I rushed into a dark building and saw an old woman covered in blankets, in too much pain to get up and even feed herself. I opened the window and collapsed in front of her. Reaching for her hand, I instinctively drew her aches into my own body. Her eyes opened, and she breathed out a sigh of relief.

"Bless you, child, are you an angel?"

"No, but your grandson needs you. He almost lost a hand for stealing. Can you get up?"

She nodded. "Yes, yes. I can. I haven't felt this good in ages."

I struggled to my feet and my back stiffened, my feet burned with every step I took. I moved to the doorway where Liam watched me silently.

"You took her pain, didn't you," he stated.

I waddled past him, grabbed Damsel's saddle horn and tried to pull myself up. My arms gave out, and I slid back to the ground. Liam caught me, his body pressed against mine. His breath warm in my hair as he admonished me. "You're hardly in any shape to ride now."

"Just give me a boost. I can hold on."

His hands gripped around my waist and he easily lifted me up into the saddle. I groaned as my hips tried to get comfortable. They felt ninety years old. Plus the buzzing of voices grew more intense.

When Liam mounted behind me, it jolted me out of my reverie. He tied his mount's reins so that Pern could follow behind us. His arm wrapped around my waist and pressed me close when I tried to move away.

"What are you doing?"

"One, you're about to fall off your horse, and two, I'm shielding you."

"But I can't—"

"You can't help them all, Aura." He flicked the reins, and we began moving, his will so strong, I didn't hear a single voice. And as we rode past, I looked at the faces of the men, women, and children, I almost felt sad that I couldn't help them.

Even when we cleared the capital city, Liam didn't switch mounts, but rode behind me, letting me rest my weight against his chest. A few times he needed to adjust the reins, and he'd bend down, his cheek brushing against mine.

Each time was just a passing touch, but every single one felt like a kiss against my skin. But he was silent, and I was frustrated that I couldn't hear what he was thinking.

We stayed on the smaller roads and avoided all large cities. And even when we had the chance to stay at an inn, Liam avoided the comforts because of me, choosing instead to camp under the stars.

Dinner consisted of dried meat and rations. Liam laid our bedrolls out on opposite sides of the fire, a safe distance from each other. He was unusually silent. The opposite of me, where I loved chatting, but I didn't know what to talk about.

"Tell me about yourself," I asked. "I know that you're a knight, but what else. Tell me about your parents."

"I have no parents," he said. "As soon as I was old enough,

I enlisted and trained to become a knight and protect the kingdom of Rya. Now, I'm the commander of the king's guard." He stoked the fire and added more kindling. The glow lit his handsome face, revealing his sad and haunted eyes. There was something from his past that hurt, and I wanted to know what it was so I could help.

I pressed for answers and those green eyes flicked up at me. "Don't," he warned.

"You could feel that?" I asked in surprise. "Usually no one can tell when I pry."

"Yes." He broke a stick and tossed it into the fire. He looked uncomfortable. "It, uh . . . tickled."

"Really," I chuckled. "Let me try again." I pushed back even harder, but I wasn't aiming for any answers in particular. I wanted to see his expression turn from sad to laughter as I mentally tickled him, testing his power and limits.

I wasn't prepared for his response, which felt like a mental slap in the face. I gasped in pain, and my hand touched my cheek where it felt warm from the fresh stinging ache.

Liam looked at me in horror. "Aura, I'm so sorry."

"It's fine." I sniffed, trying to hold back the tears of pain. The playful mood I was aiming for shot down. "I shouldn't have done that. It was wrong of me."

"No really, that was uncalled for. I didn't even know I could do that." His voice was filled with remorse.

I curled up on my side and pulled the blanket over my chin, focusing on listening to the crickets and the crackling of the fire.

"I'm sorry," he said again. "But it's better if you don't pry into my past. You won't like what you find, and the thought of you hating me is more than I can bear."

CHAPTER ELEVEN

Our second day on the road was filled with light conversation. It seemed Liam was trying to make up for the previous day's lack of discussion. He asked me to tell him what it was like growing up with Lady Eville. What kind of training did I go through? I explained to him what we were doing the day I found him.

"My cat, Hack, would always give me clues as long as I promised to feed him." I laughed. "I can find anyone, anywhere."

"No doubt." He grinned and challenged me. "I bet you wouldn't be able to find me."

"I bet I could find you within minutes," I said confidently, tucking a strand of my pale hair behind my ear. "But you would never find me. Not if I didn't want to be found."

His horse walked close, and our legs bumped together. His eyes met mine, and he became very somber. "It wouldn't matter how long it took. I will always find you." It wasn't a statement, but a promise.

I broke eye contact and looked toward the skyline and frowned. Liam followed my gaze and saw the dark clouds forming.

"It's another storm. Is there any shelter nearby?" he asked.

I closed my eyes and listened. "I can't tell, but I hear

people. A way station that way, I think." I pointed toward the mountains.

"Aura, I don't want to subject you to that."

I shuddered. "I really don't want to be caught in the rain again."

"Okay, but we must hurry."

We spurred the horses into a gallop. A few times, I had to redirect our course until we came to the way station. As soon as we dismounted at the stable, it began to downpour. I had heard of these part inns, part transport depots where transports would drop off passengers and pick up new ones as they headed to different kingdoms. There was a restaurant, bathing rooms, driver rooms, and rooms for rent. Thankfully, this was one of the smaller way stations and Liam could get us food and two rooms.

We ate dinner in silence as I worried more about trying to keep the random thoughts from the other people out of my head. It was a simple fare of soup and bread, but I struggled to enjoy it.

Across the room, I saw a magical notice board of maps that glowed, changed, and shifted, revealing new open roads, and blocked passages, followed by the bounty board. I froze when I saw a Wanted for Murder poster with the familiar face of my sister, Meri. I cupped my hand over my mouth and held back the feelings of guilt that followed. The next notice was a warning as more posters appeared of missing girls. All young women between the ages of sixteen and twenty that had disappeared from the area. I couldn't tear my eyes away from the portrait of a missing young girl with dark curls, freckles, and a haunted expression. None of them had been found, and there was a reward for their safe return.

Others had noticed the same board, and they speculated

what happened to the young women.

I hope that doesn't happen to Rebekah. I should make sure she is never alone until they catch the culprit.

Probably ran away with a boy.

Bet she got herself pregnant and will show up in ten months.

Liam saw my creased brow and stretched out his leg under the table and gently rested it against mine. Immediately, I could breathe easier as the tension faded. After a bit, the conversation started up.

Just a slight pressure of his touch easily canceled out my magic, and it scared me how much I was depending on him.

Because of Liam, I had gone to the palace in Candor. I saw my sister, a queen, made it through one of the busiest cities in the kingdom, went dress shopping, and sat for a meal in public. My spoon stopped midair in my hand when I realized that this would soon be over once we reached Rya and conquered the blight.

"What's wrong? You suddenly became quiet."

"I just realized . . . thank you," I said, putting the spoon down.

"For what?"

"For showing me what it's like to be normal."

Liam looked around the room full of strangers and said, "This is nothing."

"No, it's *everything* to me. I didn't know I was trapped until you came along and forced me to face my fears."

"I kidnapped you," Liam pointed out. He dipped his bread into his soup. "Don't gloss over that fact. Though my intentions were noble, I wasn't thinking and acted selfishly. I shouldn't have done that."

"I know. But because of you, I left home and I've seen so

much of the world already."

"Aura, we've barely scratched the surface. You've seen dirty roads, caves, and one kingdom. This isn't the world, just a neck of the woods. Just wait until you see Rya." Now it was his turn to become solemn. "That is, if we save it from the blight."

"We will," I said firmly. "And I just wanted to say I appreciate all you've done for me. Sticking by me." I nudged my leg against his. Liam smiled and nudged back. "Helping me just take it day by day. I know it must be a pain, but it means so much to me. Thank you."

"That's what friends are for," he said.

"Friends, yeah." My mouth went dry as his eyes became filled with shadow and hurt again. He was definitely hiding something.

He slurped the rest of his soup and looked up the stairs toward our rooms. "You ready?"

I stilled, and my heart raced. "As ready as I'll ever be." My hands balled into fists and my feet were leaded weights as we walked up the stairs to the second floor and turned the corner. Our rooms were next to each other.

Liam opened his door and went in. "If you need me, knock. I'm right here."

"You can't sleep in a chair next to my bed every night. I can survive one night of restless sleep," I lied, keeping my face neutral.

He didn't seem to be buying it. "You promise, if you need me."

"I won't," I said, slipping into my room and shutting the door. I pressed my back against the wood and massaged my temples. This wouldn't work. I could hear the angry thoughts of the chef in the kitchen. The grumbling of the underpaid servant. A man puking his guts out in the bathing room and a couple across the hall making love. My mind was flashing with thoughts of lust, hate, sickness, and I could feel myself dry heave. I waited, giving Liam plenty of time to settle in for the night before I made my move.

I pressed my ear to the door and listened. Slowly, I opened it and slipped out into the hall, carefully turning the latch with nary a whisper. I turned around and was confronted by Liam. He was waiting for me. Hidden in shadow, his arms crossed over his chest, his right foot bent and supported by the wall.

"I knew you were going to be a problem." He sighed and pushed away from the wall. "Where were you going?"

"I was going to sleep in the stables. I think it will be much easier for me to rest there."

"But not for me." He took my elbow and pulled me into his room. I spun and lost my balance, landing on the bed. The door slammed after us with an ominous thud. I heard him turn the key in the lock. "How do you think it makes me feel knowing you would rather sleep in the stables than be anywhere near me?"

"Because we can't keep doing this," I said. "I can't ask you to be my guard dog and sleep on the floor or in a chair every night. It's not right."

I was struggling to breathe, as I was feeling extremely hot. I pulled at the collar of my dress as the aura from the couple next door permeated my mind. I flushed and felt hot all over. I needed to leave. I got up and headed for the door.

Liam intercepted me and gave me a wry grin. "I don't plan on sleeping on the floor or the chair tonight."

"I'm sorry you're angry. I was just putting your needs first."

His voice turned husky. "So self-sacrificing again. That's funny, that you mention needs." He pushed me back on the bed and I hit the pillow and bounced. "What I *need* is a good long rest on an actual bed, and if that means I have to tie you to the bed frame so you actually sleep and not run off to the stables, I'll do it." His eyes glittered with mischief, and I blushed.

He took off his cloak and folded it up on the chair and stretched out on the bed next to me. I sat with my back against the wall, feet curled up. Liam patted the mattress next to him. "You should know by now that I won't harm you."

I relaxed and laid down next to him, facing the wall. The room was tiny. The bed wedged into a corner. To escape, it would mean I had to crawl over him. I laid as still as I could as Liam rolled to his side, and his arm draped over my hip. I stiffened, and then relaxed when he didn't move again.

I shifted in my sleep and pulled away. My dreams became restless, filled with horrid thoughts of being lost in a fog and the terrible monsters within. I shuddered and Liam pulled me closer into the crook of his body. Fully spooning me, his face nuzzled into my neck as he whispered, "Shh, my sleeping beauty, your knight is here."

∽

When morning came, I opened my eyes and saw Liam's chest, his chin rested on the top of my head. One arm laid over my waist possessively, and I looked down at his leg threaded through mine.

My heart raced and my breathing picked up. This was too close. I tried to move away, but Liam murmured and pulled me even closer. I could feel the gentle movement of his thumb brushing across my back.

"You're awake," I accused.

"So are you," he breathed, and pulled back to look down at

me. His eyes flickered to my mouth briefly, and I swallowed. Liam reached out and cupped my cheek, his thumb brushing across my lips. He leaned forward, his lips parted.

My breath caught in my chest and I let out a little gasp. It broke the spell.

"Um, you're drooling," Liam said, brushing the corner of my mouth and pulling away. My head hit the mattress as his right arm slid out from under my neck.

I was jarred awake by the rejection, and I caught a flicker of his intent. Liam had wanted to kiss me. I saw it clearly in his mind, but then his will hit me.

She is a distraction. You're stronger than this. Remember your promise. Your mission. Liam moved across the room and grabbed his cloak.

I groaned in embarrassment. I couldn't keep doing this. It would destroy me being so near Liam. I could easily fall in love with him, and then it would end in heartbreak. I couldn't have him. I couldn't ask anyone to tether themselves to me permanently like that. It was no way to live, to constantly be touching me to keep me sane.

Grumpily, I crawled out of bed and saw that I was still fully dressed. I made my way back to my room and Liam called after me. "Meet you downstairs shortly."

I nodded and quickly changed and gathered my things before heading down. Liam was already waiting for me at a table by a window.

The server, a young girl about my age, brought his drink to him. Her smile faltered when she saw me.

"Oh, I didn't know you were with someone." *Oh, we hardly ever get any single good-looking guys. I should have known.*

"Olivena, meet Aura, my sister." Liam gave me a sly smile. *She looks adorable.*

My shoulders hunched as I picked up Liam's thoughts that must've been directed to our server.

Oh, sister, then. Maybe I could convince him to meet me in the back stable. "Oh, how do you do?" Olivena bobbed her head. "What can I get you to drink?"

"Um, whatever," I said nonchalantly.

"Whatever is coming right up." *Stars above, the sister is dim.* Olivena gave Liam a sly wink.

Liam leaned back and sighed. *I can't wait. Maybe I should skip breakfast and head right to the stables.*

My head was pounding as I had to witness their flirting and obvious rendezvous they had planned. Liam noticed my balled fists.

"Sorry, I forgot." He immediately reached his leg across and leaned it against mine and the thoughts muffled, but it was too late.

I stood up, my chair screeching across the wood floor. "I need some air."

"I'll go with you." He moved as if to follow.

"No, I want to be alone."

Liam sat back down. "But what about—" He pointed to my head.

I spoke through gritted teeth. "I'll be fine the farther I get from you two lovebirds."

Liam frowned. "What do you mean, lovebirds?"

"Olive, er, Olivena, or whatever her name is, likes you. She is even willing to take a tumble in the stables with you."

Liam's serious face broke into an outburst of laughs. "You're jealous."

"No. I just don't want to hear you two moon for each other in my head anymore." I stormed out of the inn and marched across the road to an empty field and kept walking. If they were going to meet in the stables, then I wanted to be as far away as possible. Yes, maybe I was jealous. But I didn't want to be privy to their intimate conversations.

I sat on a hill that faced north. I could see the mountains, and through the mountains—a day's ride on the other side—was the Marshwam pass. That is where we were going to meet the rest of his troops. I had to figure out what in the world I was going to do. I needed a plan. A way to stay sane surrounded by the troops and what would happen if there were actual fighting, and people dying. I knew I might not come out of this whole. My mind could be permanently damaged or broken into a hundred pieces.

I pulled at the grass angrily and stacked it in a pile. It was better to live saving others than to die never having truly lived. I was doomed to live a shortened life, anyway. So why couldn't I do the most goodwill while I was here?

A human shadow passed over me.

"Go away, Liam. I said I wanted to be alone." I stiffened as the dark aura hit me. It wasn't Liam.

"Well, look at this, Bart? Have you ever seen hair as white as this, or that skin?"

"No, I haven't, Smitty." *She will surely fetch us a nice price.*

I turned to look over my shoulder at the two men who hovered over me. A tall, gangly man with a patch of hair under his lip, and the other round with balding hair and ropes in his hands.

My body screamed at me to run, but my mind froze, and I became paralyzed like a terrified doe.

"It's a pity about the bruise."

Bruise, what bruise? I thought as his fist connected with my face.

CHAPTER TWELVE

Dirt rained down on me as I bounced around in the darkness. I opened my eyes and winced. One of them was swollen shut, and I could taste blood in my mouth.

The blighter had hit me. I tried to move, but was gagged, bound, and pressed inside of what I could only assume was a pine box. Was it a coffin? More dirt rained down from above, and I feared I was being buried alive until I remembered one of the men mentioned something about a price. They must need me alive. I tried to gauge my surroundings. As my one good eye adjusted, I could see daylight filtering through the box as hay and dirt rained down on me from above. Then my body sensed the rocking motion and the dip as we hit potholes.

I was in the back of a wagon, and judging by the area of the small space, I assumed I was in a hidden compartment used for transporting black market items—or in my case, women. This must be what happened to the other girls. I tried to cast aside my fear and panic as the men in the front spoke quietly among themselves.

"Maybe we should keep this one for us instead of turning her over to Madam," Bart said.

"Nah, you saw the hair and eyes on this one. Madam is specifically looking for those special ones. Besides, we can always have our turn with her after they have broken her in," Smitty argued.

"I like it when they fight. They're not fun when their spirits are gone."

"Shush it. I don't want any more talk like that," Smitty commanded.

I pounded my fist against the flat board, and they laughed.

"Someone's awake," Bart said.

Smitty pounded his fist against the side. "Stop that racket, or we'll pull over and beat you to a pulp."

I stopped pounding and laid there debating what to do. My only plan was a stupid one. One that would probably end up with me dead and burned to a crisp, but it seemed the better alternative than ending up in a brothel. Reaching my left hand as far away from my body as I could, I worked my fingers through the crack of the floorboard and whispered.

Fiergo.

A small spark started and quickly caught the hay on fire. I pulled the neckline of my dress up to cover my mouth from the smoke and waited for them to notice.

"Bart, the wagon's on fire!"

The horses screamed, the wagon stopped, and I heard them scrambling to try to douse the flames. I kicked at the floorboards but could only move my legs a few inches as I searched for a weak point. My lungs burned as I breathed in more smoke and ash rained down on me, burning my skin.

Smitty crawled on top of the wagon and I heard the jangle of keys as he unlocked the hidden compartment. The door swung open, and he reached down to pull me out. I stumbled and fell and had to be dragged out of the wagon. My entire plan relied on reading them correctly. They wouldn't let me die.

As I lay in the grass, choking and coughing. I watched as one tried to unload the burning hay, while the other had unhitched the horses and was trying to keep them from bolting.

I turned and raced for the woods. Hoping that I could get a far enough head start. My feet and lungs betrayed me. My lungs burned, and with every step it felt they were constricting tighter. I fell to my knees and passed out.

Smoke! I was choking on smoke. Gasping, I sat up. Covering my mouth and nose with my arm, to ease my breathing. My eyes were crusted, and my throat raw from my near-death escape. But I was alive.

Rubbing at my eyes, I tried to figure out what the horrible cloying smell was that was cloaking the room. I couldn't place it, but instinctively knew it wasn't good for me.

They replaced my red dress with a soft pink silk skirt with long slits. My skinny legs peaked through the fabric, the dark bruises on my knees stark compared to my pale skin. The short top scooped low, leaving my neck and shoulders bare while barely covering my stomach. Bandages covered the burns on my arms and my wrists, while my ankles were bound with silk.

The room spun, and I saw a woman sitting in the corner next to a lamp. The golden incense lamp had stars inside, and the scent was drugging me.

"Shh, my sleeping beauty. I've waited a long time for one like you to come along again."

"No." I fought against the drugs. "Don't call me that."

"Hush, I know how fond you are of that name. I plucked it from your memories. What's his name? The tall golden-haired one, Liam. He called you that."

The woman came closer, her hair the same pale color as mine. But her eyes were soft pink, like a rat. She looked to be in her forties. "You may call me Madam Esme, and I'm like you—an empath."

My head bobbed on my shoulders as I tried to follow her movement around the room. She wore a silk dress with a long blue floor-length shawl.

"How are you still . . ."

"How have I survived this long without going crazy?" She laughed and puffed on a pipe that connected to a bubbling clear vase. She gave a puff and pink smoke tendrils filled the air. "It's easy. I learned to not care."

"How?"

She gestured to her pipe. "I no longer feel anything, and soon you will too."

"Y-you're mad," I stuttered.

"Yes, I probably am. After all, our kind turn out that way. Except me. I've outlived them all." She took another long puff. "I like you, Aurora."

"Aura," I corrected.

"Not anymore. In my establishment, we will call you Aurora."

My head bobbed toward the silk-covered windows. Just outside the door, I could see a man standing guard.

"W-what?" The incense was making it hard for me to form words, but it dulled my senses and I couldn't hear her thoughts. In fact, I couldn't hear anyone's. I was numb to it all, and for the first time since Liam, I was at peace.

"It's my brothel, and you will be my newest addition." She came and ran her painted fingers along my cheek. "Such a pity that I can't debut you tonight. I'll have to wait until your eye and the bruises on your body heal. I can't have my star attraction sullied. And it was so nice of you to save yourself for me. I can't tell how surprised I was to find out you're a virgin."

"You're the devil," I spat out and tried to fight against my bonds. "How dare you . . ."

"Relax, Aurora." Esme came forward and pulled at the blue and purple drawstring pouch. Her hand reached inside. "You will eventually come to accept this new life. You will see. You'll even thank me for it. Because empaths, even with our powers nullified, can't help but please others."

"I will never be a whore," I gritted out, fighting against the fog. I tried to form a spell in my mind. *"Incendi-"*

Esme took out the powder and blew it in my face. I inhaled, and it immediately made me numb.

"Your magic is no more."

The spell died on my tongue.

Esme sat on the edge of the bed and crossed her legs. "That, my dear, is a taste of devil's breath. I heard about what you did to Bart and Smitty's wagon. Not only are you an empath, but also trained in magic. And well, I can't have you burning down my establishment. I will just have to keep you under heavy sedation at all times." She patted my cheek. "Now be a good girl for Esme and go to sleep."

I collapsed on the silk pillows, and my eyes closed against my will.

∼

I woke up to someone stroking my leg. I jerked away and recognized the young woman with dark hair and freckles from the missing poster. Her eyes were glassy as she dipped a sponge into a bowl of water and reached out to run it over my arms.

"Hello?"

She didn't answer.

I looked into her dilated eyes, and what I found terrified me, or rather it was the lack thereof. Her mind gone, locked away deep inside her. Was that my fate? Eventually my mind would succumb to the drugs?

"Can you help me?"

She wrung the sponge out and dabbed it gently on my face around my eye. The silk curtain moved to the side, and Madam Esme stepped inside and moved over to the lamp. She replaced the incense, and the drugged fog filled my small room again.

"Good news, Aurora. After the initial query to my secret buyers, your beauty may have caught the attention of some very rich and powerful men. Offers have already begun pouring in. Your injuries healed pretty well, and with a bit of makeup, we can cover the bruises and burns." She held a pink paper in her hands and waved it under my nose, and I caught a whiff of rose water. She fanned herself with the paper and grinned.

"I will have to make the most of this debut. Maybe have something special planned. I know. I will inform everyone it will be an auction."

"N-no," I muttered. My tongue was thick, and I struggled to form words.

Esme frowned. "Now, don't be difficult. I want you to be the perfect little angel for me."

"I will never stop fighting," I seethed and pulled at my bindings.

"Oh dear. I was afraid of this." She reached into her pouch and blew the stronger dose of the hated devil's breath in my face.

I was prepared and held my breath, pretending to come under the effects. I let my head droop and shoulders slouch.

"You think you're so smart, holding your breath, but I've been doing this a long time. What do you think Tamara is bathing you with? It's the same drug. It's already in your bloodstream. And in the incense, and your food. But get some rest. Your debut will be in a few days' time, and you will make me very rich."

She was right. I could feel my eyelids drooping as I fell into a drugged slumber.

Night came. Then another day. Then night again.

I wasn't sure how long I'd been drugged or kept as a prisoner of Madam Esme's. Time did not matter. When food came, it wasn't at inconsistent times, or I was too drugged to remember eating. It was only by the yellow-green hue of my bruises that I was able to estimate that I had been a prisoner for close to a week.

Seven days and no one had come for me. Liam hadn't found me like he promised. But then again, maybe I had dreamed of him. Maybe everything was a dream. The longer I was there, the more real this life became, and my other life was just a fantasy.

A candle on my bedside table had flickered out and the tip of the wick faded from red to black. Slowly, I raised my head and focused on the wick.

"*Fiergo.*"

Nothing. The trails of smoke disappeared.

"*Fiergo,*" I said more firmly. The wick didn't even glow or flicker. I plopped my head back onto my pillow, feeling helpless. My magic was truly gone.

"It's the drugs." Tamara came in with a basket full of cosmetics. She sat by my bedside and set out powders on the table. "The devil's breath makes you compliant to the power of suggestion. They compel you to obey."

"You speak?"

She nodded. "Today is a good day. I can remember more of myself, of who I am."

"And the other days?" I asked.

"Not so much." She sighed and pulled out an expensive jar of perfume. Her hand trembled slightly, and it clattered against the wood. She clasped her hands together to keep the shakes from a minimum.

"You're having a withdrawal," I said. I knew the signs, having seen my mother treat addicts before.

"Yes," she breathed out. "After a few days, I say I'm fine. I can go without, but by nightfall, I'm begging for more." She dropped her head in shame. "It's too much. This place is a nightmare. The drugs are the only escape we have. When we no longer feel, we forget."

"Then let's escape. Untie my hands, and we will escape right now."

Her head rose and those soulful brown eyes filled with hope, but then I saw it die. She pulled out a brush and placed it next to the perfume bottle.

"We can't. They filled the place with guards and powerful men since tonight is your debut."

"Untie me, please," I begged, but she shook her head.

"There's no escape, and if you try to run away, you disappear."

"Disappear? Maybe it's because the girls escaped."

"Not disappear as in escape, more like killed and dropped in a hole."

"Please, Tamara. Help me," I whispered, hearing a commotion coming down the hall toward our room.

"I can't. I'll get in trouble." Her eyes flickered to the door just as it opened, and Madam Esme stepped through.

"I thought you would be finished by now, Tamara?"

Tamara picked up a porcelain dish of face powder and applied it to my face.

"Not too much. I want her to look innocent," Esme ordered.

She turned to me. "Tonight is the night. You have gathered quite the honored crowd. Some of my best clients with the biggest purses will be here. They're all so excited to meet you."

I screamed internally as I underwent hours of treatment under the watchful eye of Madam Esme and Tamara, or her guards. I bathed with bath salts and perfume, hair brushed and curled. My nails were painted, and my lips decorated with a soft rouge. Tamara brought a mirror to me and I saw my reflection and I didn't recognize the woman before me. My white blonde hair shimmered like moonlight, my pale skin looked like alabaster. A soft lavender veil draped across my mouth and they accented my eyes with charcoal to make them look bigger. The drugs dilated my pupils, and I looked like a scared doe.

Madam Esme returned, wearing a velvet red dress with gold bangles on her wrists. Her hair curled and pinned on top of her head. Her nails were a deep blood red. She sauntered over to me and lifted my chin and gazed into my eyes.

"Because I know that you're the fighting kind. I've prepared a special dose for you." She waved in the guard, and a man came with a long needle attached to a glass jar. He pricked it into my skin, and I watched helplessly as they pumped the drug into my system.

"Listen to my command, Aurora, your powers are gone. You're nothing more than a slave to man's desire. Aura is no more."

I would have cried, if I could, but even my body didn't obey.

"Repeat after me," she commanded. "My powers are gone."

I couldn't disobey. "My powers are gone." My mouth moved on its own.

"I obey man's desire."

"I obey man's desire." I wanted to throw up. Rail against the woman.

This time a single tear escaped.

"Drat, you ruined your makeup. Tamara!" Esme screamed and the poor girl came scrambling in to fix my eye makeup.

"No more crying, do you hear me?" she ordered.

"Yes," I answered.

"Then it's time."

It was the first time I left my room, and I was scared. The silken room was the only constant along with Tamara in this drugged-induced prison, and I knew what to expect within the fuchsia-colored walls. I didn't know what dangers lay beyond.

I remember stairs. Stumbling on carpets, and someone having to hold me upright as I navigated the twists and turns that never seemed to end. Lanterns flickered at each passage and I felt a draft as we entered a room, and the ceiling rose. I smelled incense, but then something else. Earth. As though we were underground.

The room brightened, and they led me to the middle of a group of men where they forced me to kneel on a silken pillow. I was glad I was kneeling because I didn't think I could stand anymore.

The lanterns behind the men cast them into hazy silhouettes. My glazed vision couldn't focus, and it looked packed. For once, I wasn't afraid to be around this many men because I couldn't hear what they were thinking. Yes, it was probably horrid thoughts, but I didn't know. I sat there, my hands in my lap, and I couldn't stop staring at the jewel embedded into my painted thumbnail.

Who would do that? It was impractical.

"What's wrong with her?" someone asked.

"It's the drugs. All the girls are on it, and it keeps them compliant," an older man answered.

"I don't know, it seems to take all the fun out of it."

"On the contrary, they will do anything you ask of them. Their free will's gone. If you want them to fight, they will fight. If you want them to act like a cat, they will act like a cat."

"A cat? Is that the best that you can come up with?"

"It's too dark, can we see her?" a firm voice called out.

"Why, certainly." Esme stepped forward and lifted my chin up. I couldn't focus on the speaker. My eyes closed and my head fell forward.

"Let's start the bidding at thirty gold pieces."

"Forty."

"Fifty."

Numbers . . . numbers. It could have been colors for all I cared. Nothing mattered except the nothingness I felt.

"Five hundred gold pieces," a voice called out.

The room fell silent, and I turned to face the shadowy voice. I didn't recognize him, but he came forward and pulled a bag of money from under his cloak. His hair was dark and unruly, his eyes cunning.

"For that price, you could have multiple girls," Esme replied.

"I only want her." He came and held out the bag to Esme.

She was hesitant to take the gold. "You know, it's just for one night. She's way too valuable to me to just give her up."

"One night with her is all I need to fulfill enough fantasies for a lifetime," the stranger added.

"Right you are." Esme snatched the bag from the rich bidder and pointed toward a hallway.

Guards grabbed me under the arms and lifted me up to follow Esme to a back room. The stranger followed behind and they unceremoniously dumped me onto an enormous bed covered with pillows and blankets. They pushed the stranger inside after me. The door slammed behind him, and a deadbolt slid into the lock.

He cursed under his breath. "I wasn't expecting that. Now we're really stuck here."

I whimpered as he came and sat on the bed next to me. He reached out to help me sit up, placing a stack of pillows behind my neck. His eyes sparkled and looked like giant, jet-black jewels. No, it wasn't his eyes. It was the drugs that made his eyes sparkle.

"You really are beautiful. Stunning, really. I really thought you would be more aware. This really hampers my plans. But wait, you're supposed to do anything I tell you to."

It was coming. My heart thudded loudly in my chest. The moment I had been dreading.

The stranger leaned forward, his lips inches from mine, his breath warm on my skin. He ran a finger down the side of my face. "I can't help but wonder what it would be like to kiss you."

I leaned forward and pressed my lips to his, and he pulled back. "No, sorry, that wasn't a command. Your beauty momentarily distracted me. That was just my wishful thinking. I'm sorry I worded that wrong. I'm an idiot."

I shouldn't have been able to cry. They commanded me not to, but I did. A single tear slid down my cheek.

"Oh, Aura, don't cry." He leaned close and wiped the tear away.

Aura. This man called me Aura when Esme had me billed as Aurora. An icy chill ran through my body. Who was this man? How did he know me?

"I'm really sorry about stealing that kiss from you. It wasn't my intent. I'm not here to harm you."

I blinked in confusion.

He flashed me a debonair smile. "I'm sorry, I didn't introduce myself and explain earlier. I'm Devin Hapsturn, and I'm here to kidnap you."

I inhaled and leaned back.

"No, wait. I mean, kidnap you from the kidnappers. This is a rescue attempt, although we probably need rescuing ourselves now."

My hands trembled and Devin clasped them between his and rubbed them as if to bring feeling back to the tips of my fingers.

He rubbed them, and they tingled. "Can you feel that?"

I nodded.

"I'm friends with Liam. Don't worry. We'll get you out of here."

My heart thudded at hearing Liam's name. I wanted to ask a million questions. Was he here? Where was he? But I could not get my thoughts to form into words.

"Thank you," I said.

"You're welcome, but don't thank me until I figure out how to get out of a locked room."

Heavy footfalls came near, and they slowed just outside our door. We waited with bated breath. They continued on down the hall, and I released a sigh.

Devin leaned nearer. "That was close. They're expecting

us to spend the night together, so I'm going to douse the lights to keep the guards from spying on us while I think of something."

He got up and moved around the room, snuffing out each candle and dousing the lanterns until nothing remained lit except for a light in the hall that shone under the door. Devin came back and sat on the bed next to me.

"Is this okay, am I too close? I just want to be near enough if they come to check on us, we can *pretend*."

I nodded as more tears fell from my eyes. I couldn't believe it. It seemed too good to be true. Was I truly going to be rescued?

We laid in the dark, shoulder to shoulder, and I wasn't afraid because Devin was near me. He reached out and placed his hand over mine comfortingly. A few candle marks later we heard footsteps rushing down the hall. Devin rolled on top of me, using his forearms to keep himself elevated inches above me. He leaned down and his breath felt like little kisses across my neck.

"It's okay. I suspected they might do this. If you can, wrap your arms around my neck. All we have to do is fool them if they slide the spy hatch open and look in. Then maybe they will leave us alone."

I heard the footsteps stop in front of our door. Terrified that Esme or her men would suspect something was amiss, I did more than wrap my hands around Devin. I pulled him down on top of me and painfully smashed my lips against his.

I caught Devin off guard, and at first, he pulled away, but then he remembered who we were trying to fool. He kept still. His lips pressed against mine and we stayed frozen like that. Immobile. Then his lips parted, and he kissed me for real. A soft nibble on my bottom lip, and I gasped. My fingers digging into the back of his hair. He took it for consent and kissed me deeper. But then he pulled back and looked at me.

"I'm so sorry. I want to, but I shouldn't."

And all I remembered was his verbal desire for me to kiss him. I reached up and pulled his mouth down on mine and we kissed again, the heat building between us because of my drugged state.

The deadbolt slid open, and someone entered.

"Devin, what in the world is going on here?" a familiar male voice yelled. A lantern swung our way, illuminating Devin and I, our bodies entwined together.

Standing over us, his face a stony mask, was Liam.

Devin rolled away and stood at attention. "Sorry, Liam, I was just doing my part to protect her virtue."

"Protect it," Liam snarled. "It seems like you were destroying it."

I had never seen Liam so angry, so unsettled. He was a different person. Nothing like my gentle shield. Here was a man undone.

"Aura," he called my name, the lantern swung toward my dilated eyes.

I cried out as the light was painful. He lowered the lantern to the floor and moved to sit on the bed. I watched as he took in my hair, my skimpy clothes, and he glanced away in shame. It was the biggest rejection by far.

His astute eyes picked out the bruise on my cheek that the makeup couldn't hide. He ran a finger along my yellowed eye. He scanned the rest of my body and saw the minor burns and bruises.

"This is all my fault." His voice filled with regret. "I couldn't find you. I could not protect you."

"You found me," I whispered.

"Just too late," he groaned.

I wanted him to wrap those arms around me the way he used to, to shield me, but after what he saw with Devin, I knew he wouldn't touch me again.

He leaned forward and buried his face in his hands, and even though I shouldn't have, I cried.

CHAPTER THIRTEEN

When I stepped out into the fresh air, I winced as the sunlight burned my eyes. I wasn't the only one affected by the change. A cry of pain from my right as Tamara and a young woman with olive skin covered their eyes and released sobs of joy.

Devin handed me his cloak and buttoned it around my neck, covering my silk outfit

"Thank you," I said.

Devin held my elbow and guided me to a wagon. Lowering the backboard, he lifted me up and set me down with care.

"Let me go!" Smitty screamed as he was dragged out of the tunnels by a guard, his wrists bound in chains.

"I charge you and your accomplice with kidnapping and trafficking of women," Liam declared.

"We only done what we were paid to," Bart whined. On his knees, hands bound, he didn't seem that threatening.

"You will be imprisoned and await your sentencing at Highbridge Tower," Liam snapped his fingers and they chained Smitty and Bart to a wagon, put under guard along with all the other men captured in the illegal brothel.

Liam paced in front of the hideout as he waited for Madam Esme to appear.

"Commander, she's gone!" A soldier came running out of the cave.

"Hayes, what do you mean she's gone?"

"I found Berk and Frederick, unconscious, the Madam's chains discarded on the ground. Should we go after her?"

Liam spun and looked at me sitting on the sideboard of the wagon and then back to the forest. He shook his head in frustration. "No, we don't have time. We must track her on a different day. We need to hurry toward Somnielle before it's too late."

"Yes, Commander."

I felt Liam's frustration. I, too, wanted to bring the woman to justice, for I knew her kind. She was a slippery weasel, and with her drugs, she could easily disappear and pop up again and start over.

The raid on the illegal brothel brought to light a dark and hidden secret. An ongoing problem that many had turned a blind eye to, and it needed to be stopped. And I knew if I ever crossed paths again with that wretched woman, it would be *she* that would be forced to do my bidding.

"I heard this girl belongs to you?" Devin walked to the wagon with my horse.

"Damsel!" Grinning, I reached out and gently stroked her soft brown mane. I was glad that she was here. "How"—I swallowed, my mouth still dry—"did you find me?" I looked at his lack of uniform and soldier haircut, and knew he wasn't one of Rya's royal guards.

"I'm a ranger and have close connections with Liam. He trained me before I left the guard and went out on my own." He saw my look and shrugged. "I'm not great at settling down or obeying orders. But I'm fine as a hired sword. I was already tracking the chain of missing girls when Liam sent word to me. He thought the same group took you."

"How come no one found them before now?"

"All the girls were kidnapped across the border from neighboring kingdoms, then transported to Madam Esme's hidden brothel in Rya," Devin answered. "She caters to high-profile clients with money and secrets. I had just zeroed in on her hideout when I intercepted a call sheet for one with hair like moonlight and skin like milk. I mean it could have been an auction for a horse for all I know. I got word back to Liam, and he said it had to be you, and that he would bring the troops and rescue you by morning."

I glanced over to Liam. He marched around the field, giving orders, sending troops to escort the men captured during the raid to High Tower, the closest prison.

"Except that you were being sold that night. Morning would have been too late. So I tracked a noble I suspected of using her services. I relieved him of his money purse and invitation and entered the auction on my own." He grinned. "I'm glad you weren't a horse."

I smiled. "That was incredibly—"

Devin interrupted. "Brave, I know."

"Stupid," Liam said, having appeared out of nowhere. His face void of all emotion. "We're loading up. Are you coming, Devin, or are you on to your next assignment?"

"Ah, you know me. I go wherever adventure takes me. I think I'll tag along for a bit." He shot me a wink.

Liam glowered and stormed off. Three of Rya's men headed into the cave, tossing burning torches down each of the tunnels.

Devin reached up to scratch Damsel's forehead. "Looks

like we're ready to leave. Do you want to ride her, or sit in the wagon?"

I glanced at the wagon full of women and turned back assuredly to my quiet horse. "I would like to ride Damsel."

"You sure? You're still recovering from quite an ordeal."

"I'm sure. I'll tie myself to her if I have to."

Devin laughed and helped me onto Damsel, but I could barely hold on to the reins. They kept slipping through my clumsy and numb fingers.

"It's okay." Devin tied Damsel's reins to his pommel and mounted his own horse. Choosing to lead me instead of forcing me to give up the freedom of riding as we headed deeper into the mountains.

We headed out, leaving the burning brothel behind us. A dark trail of smoke rose into the sky, signaling the end of our nightmare. But I knew I would never truly be free from the horrors of what happened here. They would haunt me forever.

Now that their commander had returned to the troops, they were regrouping to take another stab at fighting their way through the blight. He had returned with a powerful sorceress. Except I knew that was no longer the case. I didn't know what I was anymore, and I didn't know how to tell Liam.

As we rode, Liam kept leaving his post at the front of the troops and dropping to the back to ride near me. He watched me closely. I assumed to see if I struggled amongst the large group of men. But I felt nothing. I stared back at him—expressionless.

He frowned. Liam reached out to brush his hand along my arm, but he pulled back as Devin steered us out of his reach, pulling me along.

Liam scowled, but Devin didn't flinch. After the way Liam

had reacted to finding me, Devin had taken it as his job to be my guardian.

Later that evening we stopped to make camp, even though Liam was eager to keep moving. He couldn't keep the pace he was going with a wagon full of women who slowed his quest. The men laid out their bedrolls under the stars and spent the added time to put up three large tents for the women rescued from the brothel.

I headed toward the one I saw Tamara enter, but Devin was waiting just outside the first tent. "I'm sorry, but the commander has asked me to set up your tent in a different location."

I looked at him blankly and shook my head and tried to enter the tent.

Devin grabbed my elbow. "I'm sorry, Aura. It wasn't a request. It was an order."

"But you're not a soldier."

"No, but I still obey Liam."

"Why?" I asked.

"Because he's saved me time and time again." He gave me a grin. "Usually, it was from my own stupidity."

I let Devin guide me over to where he tethered his horse. He helped me up, and we rode double a mile away from camp until we came to a small clearing nestled next to a stream. Then I saw the lone tent sitting under a maple tree. I was proud that I dismounted and could keep my feet under me. It hurt that it was Devin and not Liam that was now seeing to my needs. It was as if the commander no longer wanted anything to do with me.

Devin undid an extra pack from his horse and left it leaning against the trunk.

"I will be back in the morning to help pack up your tent and things."

I looked at the tent that was big enough for one person and my shoulders dropped. Normally, I would find this spot a perfect retreat. A moment of serenity. But now that I couldn't hear anything or anyone, it felt like unnecessary punishment.

I entered the tent, letting the flap close behind me.

The clip of hooves echoed as Devin rode away, and I collapsed on the bedroll. I should open up the provisions and maybe cook something over the fire, but I was exhausted and unmotivated. I pulled the blanket over my shoulder up to my chin and closed my eyes and fell asleep.

The crackling of a log startled me awake. Outside my tent, I saw the glow of a fire and a shadow of someone moving around. I lifted the flap. Liam was kneeling over and going through my pack.

"I sent you food so you would eat. And here you are, not even with a lick of sense to start a fire. Do you know how cold it gets at night in the north?"

I shrugged weakly.

I wanted to run to him and wrap my arms around him and let him comfort me. But that was a silly notion. He only did that when he was trying to shield my magic. Now I had none. I wrapped the blanket around my shoulders and watched Liam, memorizing every inch of his frame. The color of his golden hair, the green of his eyes and his angular jaw.

He held up a piece of hardtack. I shook my head, the thought of food making me queasy.

"Here," he said firmly. "You've lost weight. You're nothing but skin and bones."

"I can't." It was true. After spending a week eating drugged food, I'd lost my appetite.

"Eat," he commanded, and I felt my hand reach for it and put it in my mouth. I didn't want to eat. My stomach was roiling, but my body was reacting to the command.

I chewed on the biscuit, and the taste made me gag. I crawled on my knees away from him and coughed.

"I'm sorry," Liam said, kneeling next to me and handing me a handkerchief. "I should have known it was too soon. Devin mentioned they used drugs to control you."

I nodded and wiped my mouth before moving closer to the fire. I couldn't stop shivering.

Liam kept his distance and stayed on the opposite side of the blaze.

He watched the fire dance. The reflection made his eyes glow. "He also said that the drug made you susceptible to commands, is this true?"

I nodded again, tears forming in my eyes.

"I have to know." Liam took a deep, agonizing breath and met my gaze. "What I saw when I walked in—did Devin command you—did he force you against your will? If he did, I will kill him, and no childhood pact would save him."

I vehemently shook my head and struggled to form my words with conviction. I didn't want Devin punished for something he didn't do. "No."

"I see." Liam's head dropped, and he rubbed his palm over his face. He was struggling with what he learned, but could he not also see that I was struggling just as much?

Oh stars, I wanted a signal, a flash of an aura, something to tell me what he thought of me. Not knowing was almost worse than knowing.

He pulled back and pleaded with me. "Tell me what happened when you left the inn. You do not understand the agony, guilt, and fear that coursed through me when you disappeared. Only to find out you were kidnapped and sold to a . . . I can't even say it. I keep running it through my mind, blaming myself for not running after you."

I never even thought of what the experience did to Liam. How traumatic it must have been, not only for me, but to him. The guilt he felt as well. I didn't want to tell him everything, but I explained how they took me from the hillside, the hidden wagon, and my foolish attempt at escape. With each additional detail, I could see the anguish and guilt eating him up. I decided it was best to stop and spare him the details.

"You're different," he said.

My breath hitched. Was this sadness I heard in his voice, or accusation?

"Of course, I'm different. One does not walk through the fire and leave unscathed. We all have scars that haunt us for life. Some are physical, others emotional. I'd be a fool to assume that I'm any different."

"I failed you."

"It's no one's fault. It's over. It's in the past," I said firmly, trying to make myself believe my own words. "And we're both changed because of this experience, and we'll have to learn to adjust to our new circumstances."

He looked at me, and I heard him swear under his breath. Feeling like I was just disappointing him more, I retreated into my tent and stared at the bedroll.

"Aura. Look, I'm sorry, I failed you. But I promise to protect you from now on." His voice was full of determination.

I pulled a blanket around my shoulders, lifted my chin, and stepped out of the tent to confront him. To tell him the truth he didn't want to hear.

"There's no need. There's nothing left to protect."

"What do you mean?"

"I can't use my magic anymore. The world has become silent. I can't hear anyone's thoughts."

"They can't be gone." He grasped my upper arms and shook me so I would look at him. "Just listen, Aura. Listen to me." His forehead scrunched up, and I could tell he was trying to think or send me images.

Burning built up in the corner of my eyes, and I dropped my head to hide my shame. "Stop. It's no use."

"Will it come back?" he asked.

"I don't know. Maybe it will, maybe it won't."

"What if we go to a healer? Do you think they could fix you?"

"Fix me?" I blurted, feeling my anger rise. "There's nothing wrong with me, and maybe"—I took a deep breath—"maybe I don't want to get them back."

"What?" My confession surprised him. "You can't be serious?"

"I am. Maybe I don't want to be saddled with powers that don't let me near people and are destined to make me go crazy. Did you think of that?"

He dropped his hands from my shoulders and turned away. The frustration was apparent as he stared north. I could see his mind working as he debated his options. I was no longer useful to him, and I was nothing more than a liability.

"Maybe this is for the better," I said. "Now I'm just like every other woman."

"I don't agree," he said stiffly, turning back to me. "You'll never be like other women."

Confused and hurt by his words, I shook my head and whispered. "Just go."

His eyes full of sorrow, he mounted his horse and rode away.

"Hey, wake up, buttercup," a cheerful voice announced outside my tent.

I could smell it was early morning and moisture covered my blankets. My fire had gone out, and I was freezing. I peeked my head out to see Devin standing over my fire with a concerned look.

"You had plenty of firewood. How come you let it go out? Do you know how cold it gets in the north?" he asked.

I shivered and groaned as he repeated Liam's warning. It occurred to me that I didn't have a lick of survival skills. I'd always used my magic to start the kindling. I didn't even know another way of starting the fire.

I felt better after a full night's sleep and my head was less foggy. I popped backed into my tent and saw that my pack was tucked in the corner. I changed into the men's pants and long overshirt, grateful that I didn't have to deal with buttons on a dress. The old Aura wouldn't be caught dead in pants, preferring dresses and curls and braids. But that Aura was dead. This one needed to find an alternate way to survive. I pulled on my boots, then it took me forever to roll up my bedroll and blankets. My fine motor skills weren't working yet, and I was almost in tears trying to tie a knot around my bedroll. I made a makeshift knot and stepped out, tossed it on the ground, just as Devin released the tent line and it came collapsing down, just missing me.

"Ah, I almost caught a girl." He shot me a grin and I couldn't help but smile wanly. He really knew how to lighten the mood.

"Well, what would you have done if you caught one?" I asked, pleased I didn't stutter.

"Why, marry her, of course. She'd cook for me, clean up after my messes, and I could kiss her anytime I wanted . . ." Devin's joke trailed away when we made eye contact and we both remembered the kiss. His eyes glanced to my lips and then he looked away. "Well, there's always next time."

"Next time," I breathed to myself and felt a blush warm my cheeks.

Devin moved to finish breaking down my tent. I sat on a log, wanting to help, but still not feeling in control of my limbs. My mind was a hazy mess, and I frequently found myself lost in a daydream.

"Aura." Devin snapped his fingers in front of my face, and I struggled to focus on him. "Hey, where were you? I called your name three times."

"I'm here. I'm fine. I think." I stood up, and the world spun, and I immediately fell forward.

"Whoa." Devin stepped in and caught me. "I got you." He held me in his arms and didn't release me. I could feel his silent perusal of me. "You're even prettier without all the makeup."

I looked away, and he grasped my chin, and I gazed into his serious eyes. "Don't be ashamed about what happened between us. I'm not. It was *just* a kiss."

Just a kiss, but to Liam it probably seemed more like a betrayal. I should explain what happened. Try to make things right between us. But I kept seeing Liam's disappointed face, and I remembered that maybe it was better this way.

Devin gently released me and then worked on getting me on his horse. He hopped up behind me, and we were on our way to catch up with the rest of the company. They were already on the road, heading further into the woods. I couldn't see Liam anywhere, and Devin could tell where my focus was.

"He's not here."

"What do you mean he's not here?" I asked. "Where'd he go?"

"He left in the middle of the night. Went on ahead to Duke Tallywood's home to see if he can take the women we rescued and help them go back to their families."

"Oh. Who is Duke Tallywood?" I didn't realize how sad I'd be that Liam had left without saying anything to me.

Devin's face brightened. "Everyone knows Duke Tallywood. He is a rich, old man who has a fondness for taking in orphans. You won't find a kinder man than him. Don't worry. We'll get there by nightfall. It's on our way, and I'm here to entertain you with the stories of my many daring exploits." I smiled. "Not to mention all the dazzling ladies I've wooed, including one who had six toes on her right foot."

I laughed hard. It felt good to laugh, considering a week ago I didn't know if I ever would laugh again. Devin kept me occupied laughing most of the morning. Around noon, we stopped to stretch our legs, and I checked on Tamara. She was sitting in the grass away from the other women, watching a butterfly hovering over a wildflower. I counted twelve women. Twelve girls that would never be beaten, sold, or trafficked again.

"Tamara."

She looked up at me and smiled. "I thought I was dreaming. That it was just a horrible dream, and I kept telling myself that it's all right. One day I'll wake up from it." She reached for the butterfly, but it flew away. "But it wasn't a dream, was it?"

I kneeled next to her and gently placed my hand on her shoulder. "No, it was real."

"I can't tell what's real and what's a dream anymore. Is this . . . right now . . . real, or a dream?"

"Real," I said, my heart breaking for her.

She picked a flower, brought it to her nose and inhaled. "I hoped so." She turned and gave me a hopeful smile. "One soldier told me we are going to a duke's house this evening, and they'll be helping us return home." Her smile faded.

"What's the matter?"

"I just don't know if I want to return home, yet. I don't know if I can face my family. How do I explain what happened? They'll look at me differently. Think I'm less. They'll know." Her thin hands covered her face in shame. "I can't face them."

I grasped her hands and I repeated the words of wisdom my sisters had spoke to me when I was attacked by Tobias and Clive. The day that Armon was killed. The guilt I felt—the shame. It was the same. "Tamara, you were the victim. You did nothing wrong. What happened to you was against your will, and it's in the past. That incident does not define you. It doesn't make you a bad person. Do you understand me? You're strong, beautiful, and full of wisdom. You have a bright future ahead of you. It's just going to take a few things."

"What's that?" she asked hesitantly.

"Time. It will take time to heal here." I touched her heart. "And here." I pointed to her temple. "And you'll need courage to face the future, for the road to recovery isn't easy, but with the right people by your side—whether family or friends—I see no reason you can't have a normal life. You're a survivor, and all the stronger for it. If you need anything, I'm here." I realized as I said the words, they were not only for her benefit—I needed to hear them as well.

Tamara's eyes filled with tears. She reached for me and sobbed loudly. I hugged her as she began the first step in her healing process. I ran my hands over her hair comfortingly.

We sat like that until her sobs ebbed away, and the pain lessened. It wasn't gone fully. There would still be feelings of guilt. Even though she was the victim, she carried a heavy load, and there would be self-esteem struggles she would have to overcome. They all would. No one could bounce back quickly from any kind of abuse. It's a long healing process, and they would need understanding and patience from family and a powerful support group.

Tamara sniffed, wiped her nose. "Maybe the lord would hire us on as servants . . . until I'm ready to go home."

"Maybe."

"I hope so. It would be nice to make new memories. Ones that didn't include *that* place."

I closed my eyes and was grateful that I couldn't feel all of her previous painful memories. I didn't experience the horrors she lived through, nor could I fully comprehend them. I had only been there a week, and others were there for much longer. I desperately wanted to reach out and take that pain from her. Make it vanish. With my powers gone, I couldn't do that. But I could help her on her new journey, one of healing. So I did what Eden would do for me when the mental and emotional turmoil of crowds overwhelmed me. I was present with her, and patient.

I listened to Tamara talk of her dreams. She wanted to open a pastry shop one day, get married, and have little children running around.

"But do you think any man will want me after . . . what happened?"

I ran my hand over hers and gave it a reassuring squeeze. "The right man won't care." I instantly thought of Liam. I needed to explain what really happened, but maybe he should ask instead of assuming.

Tamara blushed and smiled. "What do you dream of?" she asked me.

"I don't know," I said. "I have unusual circumstances, so I never allowed myself to have dreams of the future. Instead, I live in the moment."

"How sad. Without dreams, there's no hope, and a life without hope is dark, indeed."

Tamara had such insight and wisdom for someone so young.

"Well, then I hope to live a long and glorious life."

"Ahem." We turned, and Devin was waving for us to get going.

I gave Tamara's shoulder a squeeze and headed back toward the troops. Tamara crawled up into the supply wagon with the other ladies, and I headed over to my horse.

"You feel up to riding solo?"

"I have to," I said. "I can't continue to rely on others." It took two tries, but I mounted by myself, and we were back on the road. Devin wanted to continue on with his tales, but I was in a somber mood and interrupted his story. "Devin, what can you tell me about the blight?"

He shrugged. "It appeared a few weeks ago. A great fog rolled inland from the sea, and anyone who enters the fog hears voices. Most of them wander around and die of starvation and thirst.

"If you survive the fog, then there are the miles of enchanted thorns. Twisting and devilish snares that are slowly moving across the land like snakes, heading deeper into the heart of our kingdom. But the thorns are sharp as daggers, and their scratch is poisonous.

"We've tried to attack it with fire and steel, but they do nothing. Rya's forces have been working on trying to get through the fog to find the heart of the blight, but most that go into the fog don't come out."

It was too horrible to imagine. That meant if we didn't stop it here in Rya, then nowhere was safe. Not even the town of Nihill. The news weighed heavy on my heart.

CHAPTER FOURTEEN

We arrived at Tallywood estate, a sprawling manor that overlooked a massive garden and over sixty acres of land. It was just as picturesque as a fairytale, with its lake filled with swans, a grove of weeping willows, and numerous cherry blossom trees. I wasn't the only one who noticed, for the women in the wagon with Tamara chattered excitedly among themselves.

The contingent of troops in our party numbered twenty members total. That was after they sent six to escort the prisoners to Highbridge Tower. The men brought their supplies around toward the stables and set up camp in the back.

At the front steps stood an elderly man with spectacles, dressed in velvet pajamas and slippers, despite it being early evening.

"Good morning." He flapped his hand jovially.

"Don't you mean good evening, sir?" Devin corrected.

He blinked at the setting sun. "Ah, yes, Devin, I see it is evening. Well, I guess I should cancel my eggs and bacon, and can focus on dessert." He slapped his gums together and tottered back inside.

The delightful old man made me giggle. He seemed harmless, and already the women seemed smitten with the one who would be their guardian.

Hayes drove the wagon up in front as Liam came out of the manor. His blonde hair was slicked back, his uniform and armor replaced by black pants, a pressed shirt, and a blue button-up uniform jacket with gold cufflinks.

He looked highborn, as if he were a noble. Which, as a knight, he probably was. Our eyes met across the drive, and my heart fluttered at seeing him.

He adjusted the cravat at his throat and cleared his throat. "Duke Tally, do you have anything to say to your guests?"

Duke Tally pulled off his spectacles and polished them on his robe. "Oh, that's right. I have guests." He plopped the glasses upside down on his nose and spread his arms wide. "Welcome to Tallywood Manor, I'm the Duke of Tallywood, but you can call me Tally."

"No, he's Duke Tally to you," Liam corrected, rubbing his forehead. "He's graciously offered his home to the ladies as we work on turning them to their family." He turned those stern green eyes toward the wagon. "And for those that have nowhere else to go, you have the option of staying on as an employee. It's hard work, but it is honest work, and you'll be paid and housed in the servant's quarters. You can stay as long as you like. You are not slaves, but free people."

"Thank you, Duke Tally!" Calah called out.

"Yes, bless you, Duke Tally," Tamara intoned.

As each of the women sang their thanks, Duke Tally's cheeks turned a deeper red of embarrassment.

"Ah, speak nothing of it. As long as you work hard and continue to sneak me candy whenever my daughter, the warden, denies me my vices, we shall get along splendidly." He patted his round belly.

More laughter followed as Duke Tally tottered inside to his study.

"Dinner has already been prepared, and it is awaiting you inside." Liam gestured to the doors, and Devin and Hayes helped the women out of the wagon. I slid off Damsel and was patting her nose when I saw a beautiful woman with brunette locks step out of the house.

Her dress was a soft cornflower yellow, her eyes a bright green, and she had the softest rouge to her cheeks. "There you are, Liam." She clutched his elbow possessively and then turned to survey the yard and wagon. Her perfect lips turned into a frown. "Are these the questionable women father agreed to employ?"

I gasped at the insult, and my fingers dug into Damsel's reins.

"Delphine, I already explained the extenuating circumstances in detail," Liam said.

"Really, Liam. I know that you have a noble heart, but don't you think this is going a bit too far? It's not appropriate to have these women under the same house as me. Aren't *you* worried about *my* reputation?"

"Delphine," he turned and clasped her hands between his, "your reputation is above reproach, and I think it will only spread further if the people understand how magnanimous your charity is." He patted her knuckles, and she preened.

"Yes, once again you are right." She smiled and then turned to the women in the yard. "Very well, come in. I will show you to your quarters." She snapped her fingers and spun without waiting to see if anyone would follow.

The earlier anticipation faltered, but only a little. The women eagerly accompanied Delphine. I balked, refusing to enter the house of that woman. There was something about her I didn't like, and I didn't need my gift to know that she was spoiled.

Liam waited until the last woman entered, and he turned and looked at me.

It was a silent standoff. He would either follow Delphine into the house or walk to me. He took a single step toward me, then halted.

"Liam!" Delphine called from inside the manor. He turned and followed her call.

I took my horse and headed around the side of the house. The stables were far larger and capable of housing more horses that were currently kept on the property. Many of the men had claimed the empty stalls for themselves to sleep in, choosing to release their own horses into the fields.

I found an empty stall and removed Damsel's tack and brushed her down.

"You're a beautiful lady," I said, speaking to my horse. "And I wish I could hear your thoughts." I ran my hands up her nose and scratched her in all the spots the bridle would rub.

She bobbed her head and pushed her nose into my chest and snuffed loudly. I closed my eyes and leaned into her nose, trying to open myself up to her. If there was any sign of me getting my powers back, it would be through her. The first time I heard thoughts, I was five. It was one of our chickens as it chased a grasshopper in the yard. I fondly remembered the chicken's thoughts.

Eat hopper. Stop jumping. Eat hopper. Eat hopper.

My sisters didn't understand my ramblings, and they teased me mercilessly.

I sighed and looked into my horse's deep brown eyes. "You got nothing for me? Well, at least I tried."

As night fell, it became darker, and the cold set in. The manor house lit up with lights and music, and most of the soldiers had found their way inside. From my spot in the stables, I could look through the side alcove into the ballroom and see that there was an impromptu dance going on. Tamara played the piano, Hayes was on the violin, and a few of the other soldiers were swinging the girls around the room in a dance.

I moved forward a few steps to watch through the glass. I had said I was just like the others, but here I was. Once again, I found myself on the outside looking in. Afraid to be normal. Afraid to make connections with people, avoiding large groups.

The chandeliers cast a sparkling glow across the grass, and I grabbed my skirt and lifted my right arm, pretending to dance with an invisible partner. Frequently, I would look over my shoulder to correct my stance, and more often than not, I turned the wrong way, and I even stepped on my own foot.

"Ouch!" I cried, laughing at myself.

The music stopped, and I waited for the next song, my hands clasped in front of me. It was a slow waltz, one meant for lovers and partners. In the hall, Patrick moved toward Tamara, and within minutes, each of the ladies had a dancing partner.

"May I have this dance?" a voice came from the darkness.

I spun around in surprise and saw a man with dark blond hair, whom I didn't recognize. He wore a cloak and long sleeves that covered his arms. His face was angular and oddly familiar, but I wasn't sure how I knew him.

"Who are you?" I asked.

"An old friend of the family," he answered.

"Oh, then shouldn't you be inside?"

"Like you, crowds make me uncomfortable." He bowed gracefully and extended his hand to me. I curtseyed and grasped his fingertips. He pulled me close, one hand on my waist, and with practiced ease, he led me through the steps for the waltz.

"I see you've danced before," I said.

"They forced me to take lessons as a child. Although boring, they do come in handy. You're a quick learner."

"I'm barely keeping up with you," I said, out of breath.

He smiled and leaned close to me. "You're so fascinating, Aura."

"How do you know my name?"

"I said I'm a friend of the family. I just didn't say whose family."

"I've never met you before in my life."

"But I've seen you. I watched you from afar as you gallantly tried to save Meri and failed."

I stopped dancing and tried to pull away, but his grasp on my waist and wrist tightened painfully. "Who are you?"

"Now really, I expected more from a daughter of Eville." He laughed. "I hardly sense any magic in you. Why would *he* go to all the trouble to find a daughter of Eville to fight the blight and bring you?"

"Let me go," I snapped.

As I fought, his sleeve slipped, and I noticed dark tattoos lining his arm. I knew those tattoos and what they symbolized. Dark magic.

"I know you," I hissed. "You're Aspen, Allemar's apprentice."

"You're smart. Too bad you're so weak. I could squash you like a bug." He chanted, the tattoos on his arms glowed with power and his fingers burned into my wrist.

I yelped in pain as I tried to pull away, but he overpowered me. "Killing you will be the sweetest revenge on my sister, Rosalie."

I screamed and kicked Aspen. I was aiming for his legs, but he turned, and I kicked his knee. He lost his grip, and I turned to run.

Aspen tackled me, bringing me to the ground. I tried to crawl away, but he flipped me over and hit me in the face.

Blinding stars exploded in my brain, and I felt a warm trickle down my lip as I tasted blood.

"I'm going to kill you, and you're so pathetic I don't even need magic to do it." His hands reached for my throat as he chanted again, his arms glowing. "Go ahead, scream. Cry out for help. No one will save you. I want to hear those pretty lips beg for mercy."

"I'll never beg," I hissed.

"Then die." His hands pressed against my throat and I pulled at his wrists as I fought for each breath. All I could think about was Liam. How I had let him down in so many ways. He was right. I needed to learn to defend myself.

Liam, I'm so sorry. I failed you.

Aspen's grip lessened, and he looked at me with confusion. "What was that?"

I gasped and coughed.

"What did you just do? I felt it. You did something. Where did it come from? How there was nothing there a minute ago and now it appeared."

I couldn't answer, and he quickly changed his mind. "Never mind. It won't matter once you're dead." He grabbed my neck again, and I was losing consciousness. My vision was narrowing as darkness took over. "Allemar looks down on me. Said that I'm not strong enough to beat one of Lorelai's daughters. I will prove him wrong. You're nothing but a weak girl."

I choked. Anger boiling up within me. I'm not weak. I'm strong, and I refused to die without a fight. I released my hold on his wrist and felt along my hip for the staff. Digging with my fingers on the strap, I released it from the leather harness and put it between our bodies. I pressed the button, and the staff extended, knocking Aspen backwards. He groaned in pain and his hands went to his midsection.

I swung my weapon like a club, hitting him in the temple. He lilted to the side, but it wasn't a powerful hit because he recovered quickly.

"Why, you little . . . ." Aspen lunged for me, and I braced myself for the attack that never landed.

A fist connected with Aspen's face. His head snapped back. He dodged the second attack and ducked. The two men circled each other warily. I lay on the ground, my focus coming in and out in waves.

Aspen's hand glowed as he released a fireball, and the other person jumped to the side. When the smoke cleared, Aspen had disappeared.

The figure ran to me, and Devin materialized as he leaned over me. "Aura, are you okay? Answer me."

"I'm sorry," I croaked out.

He shook his head. Devin helped me sit up, and he accidentally touched my burned wrist. I cried out and looked at the four-and-one blister pattern.

"You have nothing to be sorry about. He attacked you."

"I couldn't stop h-him. I was so upset I let him overpower me and get away," I hiccupped.

"Shh, I don't care about him. I care about you." Devin pulled me into a hug. One that I didn't even know I needed. Huge, gut-wrenching, guilty sobs racked my body as I wished it were Liam holding me, comforting me.

I wanted it to be Liam.

"Aura!" Liam cried out. His shirt had come undone, and

his hair was in disarray, as if he had run from far away. "What happened?"

"A mage attacked her. He went that way," Devin answered, pointing toward the edge of the property.

Liam saw my burned wrist and his fists clenched, his face turning dark.

"I'm taking her to get her wrist bandaged," Devin said, lifting me up into the air. He carried me into the manor house, my skin blistered and red, giving off an odd stench of burning flesh.

"N-no," I murmured into his shoulder. "No, I'm fine. I can do it myself."

"There's nowhere else to go. I have to get you to a healer." Devin walked past the ballroom and headed down the hall.

A house-elf wandered by. "Fidget, fetch bandages, now," Devin yelled.

The house-elf nodded and scampered into a hidden panel in the wall. Devin moved like he knew his way around the house, and he took me to a study. After he set me down in the chaise lounge, I leaned forward to see if Liam had followed us inside. He hadn't.

I sighed and relaxed on the chair, letting Devin and the house-elf tend to my burn. I was pleased that the elf returned with a large fresh aloe vera leaf and other treatments in her hand.

Devin picked up the aloe leaf and made a face as he smelled it. "Phew."

"Don't worry, I know it stinks, but the smell will go away." He didn't know what to do with it, but I explained, and he worked the knife. "Cut the spines off, slice it in half, score it, and then we can rub it into my wrist." I turned to the house-elf and asked her to show me what else she brought. With my good arm, I pointed to the items I knew would help with the blistering.

"Ah." Devin held up the prepared aloe and carefully applied it to my wrist.

I only whimpered a little at the pressure, but the burning sensation was cooled. It wasn't the first time I'd received an unbearable burn. When I was little, I had grabbed a cauldron handle thinking it was cool and had to endure a similar treatment. Thankfully, Devin bandaged my wrist and gave me a smile.

"How's that?"

"Not bad," I answered, surveying his work.

"Thank you." He grinned.

"Devin, have you seen Liam?" Delphine spoke as she walked into the study. When she saw me on the chaise and Devin leaning over me, she halted. Her eyebrows rose, her mouth pinched together. "What are you doing?"

"Tending to an injury. We had an intruder on the property that attacked Aura. Liam went after him."

"He what?" Delphine and I said in unison. I had no idea.

"What are you doing here? You need to go after him," Delphine screeched, and I was inclined to agree.

Devin looked up at me and gave me a wink. "He's a big boy. He can handle himself."

"Against a dark sorcerer? Please, Devin," I pleaded.

Devin heard the worry in my voice. "Okay, I'll go. You stay here and don't worry."

"I'll be right back."

He followed Delphine out into the hall, and I sat in the study alone, taking in the warm, cozy interior while I waited.

It was hours later when Devin and Liam returned on horseback without a prisoner in tow. I heard the servants rushing to help them, and Liam's voice just outside the door to the study.

"She's asleep," the house-elf whispered.

The handle moved, the door opened, then it shut and closed with a click. Liam's footsteps faded away.

CHAPTER FIFTEEN

A loud thud roused me from my unnaturally deep sleep, and I rubbed my palms over my eyes. It was strange to sleep without having other people's thoughts merging into my dreams. It was oddly peaceful and unnerving. I had a kink in my neck from sleeping on the chaise. I stretched, reached toward the ceiling. Rolling my shoulders, I wandered over to the window that overlooked the courtyard and stables. My hand, despite the severity of the burn, only ached. I would need fresh bandages, more aloe, and pain reliever poultice, but for now the pain was tolerable.

The white lace curtain obscured my view, and I pulled it aside to see most of the troops had their horses saddled and were ready to leave. They were loading more barrels and food onto their supply wagon, and it was that noise that woke me. Devin had already mounted, his face forlorn as he cast a solemn look toward my window.

The door creaked open, and the soft steps on the carpet alerted me to a visitor. Even without my magic, I knew who it was. I could sense Liam.

"Are you okay?" I turned and studied him from head to toe, searching for signs that he had encountered trouble.

"I'm fine. I'm sorry, I couldn't find him," Liam said.

"I'm just glad you're not hurt." I looked out the window. "I overslept," I said.

"I told the servants not to disturb you."

"Why?" I asked, heartbroken, still not turning around.

Liam came closer, stopping inches behind me. So close I could breathe in his scent. "I wanted you to rest so you can recover."

I turned around, ready to spill my heart out to him about the kiss with Devin and how it meant nothing, but his stony look stopped me. He clenched his jaw, his brows furrowed, and I saw the dark circles under his eyes. I hesitated, unsure of the reception I would receive. This didn't seem like the same Liam.

Liam gently grasped my shoulders. "I'm sorry that I failed to protect you a second time. It won't happen again." His voice was full of regret. His hands dropped from my shoulders and he stepped away.

I stared up at him with wide eyes. "What do you mean?" I cast a glance out the window, through the lace, and came to the heartbreaking conclusion. "You're . . . leaving me behind."

"Yes, it's for your own good. I was wrong to ask you to come."

"You don't get to decide what's for my own good," I breathed, holding my temper in check.

"I'm the commander, and I say what goes."

"I won't stay here. I still want to help. I will make my own way to the front lines to fight anyway I know how."

"Aura," Liam warned. "I've lost enough men trying to tackle the blight, and now you're even more of a liability."

"I'm not a liability."

"You are. Last night proves it. I can't bring an unarmed woman to fight the blight. It will be too dangerous."

"I wasn't defenseless. I fought him off using the staff—without magic—but I can get better." I finally found a spring of hope in my dire situation. "Maybe Devin could teach me to fight with it?"

Liam's hands balled into fists. "Is that what you want? Devin?"

"Yes, I just said—"

Liam's shoulders dropped the slightest. "As you wish." He turned and marched out of the room.

"Where are you going?" I asked, quickening my pace to keep up with him.

"If you want to come, we're leaving right now. If you can't handle my pace, then maybe you should reconsider the offer to stay here," he said.

"But I haven't even had breakfast." I slowed when I smelled the fresh ham in the dining room, and I debated if I had time.

"There's an entire kingdom at stake. Food can wait." He marched by and headed out the front doors.

I stood in my half-wrinkled clothes, my bandaged hand throbbing with pain—needing more ointment—and looking at the buffet table full of food.

My stomach let out an unladylike announcement.

"Oh, stars." I raced into the room, and with my bare hands grabbed handfuls of ham, bacon, and toast, and then raced out the door and down the steps. Carefully, I sandwiched the meat between the bread as I stopped in front of Damsel.

"You decided to join us." Devin grinned jovially. "I saddled her for you, just in case."

"I couldn't let you have all the fun without me." I shoved the sandwich in my mouth, pulled myself up into the saddle, only slightly wincing from having to use my injured hand. Then we were off.

The trek was brisk, the hours long, and I suffered in silence. By late evening, we came to a lake, and Liam called a halt so we could rest. Everyone easily dismounted, but I leaned forward and grimaced when I bumped my injured wrist on the pommel. Devin noticed, and he held out his hands for help, and I shook my head.

"I got it." I leaned forward and slid from the saddle to the ground.

"Independent. I like it," he said.

It had nothing to do with being independent. I rarely liked to be touched, and the habit of avoiding people was still strong, unless it came to Liam.

Hayes came over and unloaded the wagon. "It looks like we're going to get a few hours of rest."

"Sounds good. Let me help you." Devin jumped up onto the wagon and helped Hayes unload.

I kept busy and helped Joshun chop the fresh vegetables we got from Duke Tallywood for the evening's supper. After a candle mark, I noticed my hands were shaking, and I was fidgety, struggling to concentrate.

Devin came to check on me and noticed. He leaned forward, and whispered, "Are you okay?"

I flinched as his soft question rammed into my eardrum and split my skull painfully. "I think I just need to take a b-break." I shivered.

Devin patted me on the head and nodded in understanding. I blinked and tried to focus as I headed over to my bedroll by the nook of a tree. I took my cloak and wrapped it around my shoulders, then snuggled into the base, pulling my knees up to my chest as I tried to control my shivering. Sweat dotted my brow, and I could feel a pool of it trail down my back, and the sulfur smell of the fog changed to a sweeter smell—one that terrified me and reminded me of the incense.

Staring off into the woods, I saw a silhouette of Madam Esme materialize as she puffed on her pipe before disappearing into a cloud of fog.

"Oh stars, no," I whispered, realizing that I was hallucinating and that my body was having a withdrawal to a substance I equally wanted and despised.

Devil's breath.

Chills rode up and down my body. I knew I was in for a rough night until I could ride out the withdrawal, but how did I do it without putting the camp in danger or upsetting Liam? I had seen my mother treat an addict back home, and it wasn't pretty. He had lost a leg in a farming accident and had taken to different substances to try to overcome his loss. His wife begged my mother for help and to intervene. It surprised me when Mother agreed.

She had the man chew on guanna root to keep the cravings at bay while we kept him in our barn. She did her best to let him ride it out, and whenever he became dangerous during a hallucination, she would use a spell to put him back to sleep. After a few days, he was almost as good as new. But that first night was a nightmare. It was terrifying to see him screaming and hallucinating. Going from sweet and kind, promising us the world if we would let him go, to threatening to hurt us if we didn't bend to his commands.

Would I go through a similar ordeal? I held up my hands and saw the tremor. I was in for a similar ride, and I couldn't bring myself to disturb my friends.

I grabbed my pack and tucked it behind my back as I leaned against the tree. Liam had his back to me and was speaking with Berk and Hayes. Devin had moved to the edge of camp and was watching the perimeter, having relieved the guard on duty. I leaned my head against the rough bark of the tree, looked up through the canopy at the stars beyond, and prayed that I could overcome this. I laid back and covered myself with my cloak.

∼

You're the worthless sister.
No one can ever love you.
Even Liam can't stand to be near you.
The pack dug into my shoulder as the whispered voices haunted my mind. My mouth was dry, my tongue swollen, and I couldn't stop thinking about the drugs.

"Stop it," I whispered loudly to myself. My cloak muffled my voice.

I dug in my pack for a leather belt strap, placed it between my teeth and bit down, muffling my cries. Time came and went. My tears flowed and dried over and over, coating my cheeks and eyes with crystal salt deposits.

The hallucinations were the worst.

I was back in the brothel with Madam Esme one minute, with strange men gathering around me, calling me names. The next, I was in Nihill, trapped in an alley surrounded by Clive, Tobias and Armon. Another one, I was in the ship's hold as it was sinking, and Meri's rage waged an oceanic war on us. The water filled the cabin and covered my mouth. I couldn't breathe. A silver dagger slipped from my fingers and disappeared into the bottom of the boat as I drowned in the depths of the sea—forgotten.

With a gasp, I sat up. My clothes were soaked with sweat,

my fingers were thin, and my body was sore and ragged, like I had hiked up a mountain and then clumsily fell down the other side. My head pounded, and I rose to my feet, and then stumbled, my muscles weak.

My belt had serious teeth marks embedded in the leather, and it lay discarded on the ground next to me. The men were up and ready for the morning, and I felt like mush—with a constant buzz in my ear. I tried to ignore it, shaking my head and swatting at the air, hoping it would dissipate.

"Here." Devin handed me a tin cup full of dark liquid.

I wrinkled my nose at the bitter smell. "What is it?"

"It will take care of aftereffects of the withdrawal." He pointed to my head.

"I thought I was hiding it well," I said shamefully. Heat rose to my cheeks.

"You did. It was a valiant effort and would have fooled most people."

"But not you."

"I had a friend addicted to various substances. I know the signs and what to look for. This helped him until it couldn't anymore." His smile was forced.

"I'm sorry about your friend." I shuffled the cup in my hands, knowing that Devin was hiding his pain.

"It's okay. But this will stop any cravings or withdrawals in its tracks."

Relieved, I took a large swig of the cup's content.

"No, not that much," Devin warned too late.

I choked and coughed. I handed the cup back to him and felt the drink burn through my throat and sinuses. My eyes watered, and I wanted to sneeze. "Take it away! What poison is that?"

"It's a home brew. Guaranteed to put hair on your chest and get you feeling like yourself again."

The second round was a mix of me coughing and laughing. "I could do without the first part."

"I figured." He winked. "Feel better?"

Slowly, I took a deep breath and took stock of my body. I felt better. I was less achy and sore, and the buzzing lessened.

"Yes. Thanks."

"I will be happy to make you a second cup when we stop later."

"Pass. And pass on all future cups. In fact, never offer that to me again."

"No one respects my medicinal skills." Devin turned toward the wagon, and I followed.

Hayes brought over a cup of water, and was about to comment on my haggard appearance, but I held up a finger and shook my head in warning. He quickly retreated. I drank the water down greedily and did my best to get ready for the day.

When we mounted, I strapped myself to Damsel's saddle horn, in case I fell off. I pulled my hood over my head and kept my face low, trying to hide my shaking hands. I was thankful for the pace we set because no one tried to talk to me, and I tried to get through another arduous day. With each passing candle mark, the shivering lessened as the final dregs of the drugs worked their way out my system, no longer numbing my mind.

By the time we stopped again, I was so exhausted that all I had the energy for was to take my bedroll out and treat my hand, then I promptly fell into a deep sleep.

"Devin, can you train me to fight?" I asked the next morning, feeling exhilarated.

Devin tossed a roll of canvas to Hayes and gave a wary look over to Liam, as if seeking approval.

"You don't need his permission to train me to defend myself, do you?" I taunted.

Devin's cheeks flushed in embarrassment. "Uh, no. I don't."

Hayes snorted. "Maybe you should have me teach you. All Devin is good for is picking up the ladies."

"Am not." Devin took a playful swipe at Haye's shoulder.

Hayes reached down and picked an item out of the wagon. "Watch out," he yelled.

I flinched as he tossed a sheathed sword toward me. It hit the ground.

Devin laughed as he picked up the discarded weapon, patting off the dust. "First lesson, work on your reflexes."

"Hey," Hayes said, his expression brightening. "We should teach you how to use the staff you carry."

My hand reached for the tube at my side and I looked down. Seeing the red scabs left from the burn of Aspen's attack only bolstered my desire to learn to defend myself. I wouldn't be left vulnerable like that again. Dorian believed in me. That's why he gave me the staff. I was grateful that it was still in Damsel's pack and I hadn't lost the gift.

"Okay," I said, and headed into the clearing. I was wearing the pants and overshirt that I had gotten from Eden, pleased that it gave my legs plenty of space to maneuver. I unstrung the leather strap and took out the tube, and with the push of a button, it sprung out into a long staff.

"Nice," Devin commented. He ran over to the wagon and

pulled out a spear, testing the weight in his hands. "Okay, do you know how to block a downward strike?"

I held the staff parallel above my head.

Without warning, he struck, swinging downward, hitting the staff and knocking it from my limp fingers. He pulled his spear before it hit my head.

Devin frowned. "Well, that won't do you any good if you can't hold on to it."

"You startled me." I leaned down to pick up the staff, my fingers already sweaty with nervousness. I didn't know how I was going to keep my grip on the thing.

"Again," Hayes instructed from the sideline. "Expect pain, lean your body forward, brace with your back leg, absorb the strike."

Devin held the spear at his side and waited for me as I clumsily followed along. As soon as I raised the staff, the strike came again. I yelped, and felt the reverberation through my fingers, but I didn't drop the staff.

"Again," Hayes called.

Devin struck a second and third time, and I was becoming less scared, then he changed direction. He feigned a downward attack, but swung his arm inward and up, knocking the staff out of my hands.

"Oh, come on," I grumbled, as I went chasing after the staff as it rolled into the woods.

"Expect the unexpected," Hayes said. "Your enemy won't strike the same way every single time. They are constantly testing you, sizing you up, looking for your weaknesses."

I knew that, but it was different putting it into practice. I hated physical harm. It went against my nature, but I didn't want to give up. I picked up the staff and came back, and this time I waited, watching Devin as he attacked. He swung, I blocked, and as soon as I made contact, I felt the lack of power. It wasn't a full blow. He was feinting. I stepped back as he spun under my staff and hit me in the side of the ribs with the edge of the spear.

I gasped and cried out, falling to one knee. My hand still clutched the staff. Sweat beaded across my brow, but I wasn't ready to give in. I could do better. As we practiced, a crowd grew, and I noticed Liam was watching from the side. Devin was grinning ear to ear while Liam's deep frown showed his disapproval.

Did Liam think I was worthless?

All of a sudden, the need to prove myself became great. I no longer wanted to defend. I wanted to attack. I screamed and raised the staff, swinging it around my head, and attacked Devin. His eyes glinted with mirth as he easily blocked each of my attacks and toyed with me. He became a little carried away and quickened his steps, attack and feint faster, keeping me on my toes. I barely blocked his side hit.

I faltered and became distracted by Liam's intense gaze. The staff felt heavy in my hands, and I struggled to raise it. I was tired, and slowing down.

The staff dropped from my fingers and I looked up as Devin's strike came toward my face.

"Aura!" Hayes yelled in warning.

A golden blur appeared in front of me as Liam pushed me out of the way. I heard his grunt of pain as he took the full force of the hit.

"I'm so sorry, Commander!" Devin cried out, dropping the weapon.

Liam's eyes were closed, his lips pinched into a thin line of pain. He looked up at me, and I saw the hint of a smile as he turned and picked up my dropped staff.

"My turn," Liam challenged.

Devin retreated as Liam bore down on him. Devin signaled to Berk, who tossed him two short swords. He crossed the swords in front of his body, accepting the challenge from his leader.

"This is going to be good," Hayes said.

"Liam is at a disadvantage," I commented. "A staff against two swords."

"Don't let the choice of weapons fool you. It's Devin you should be worried for. He almost injured you, and Liam is going to make sure he pays. He's making a statement."

Devin charged, the swords spinning in a deadly dance. Liam towered over Devin, and with deft movements, he easily sidestepped and blocked, twisting the staff, and pinning Devin's left arm. With a twist, he disarmed him and tossed the sword into the ground.

"What statement?" I asked.

"That no one hurts you, or they answer to him." Hayes gestured with his chin to Liam.

"It was an accident. If I were a man, this wouldn't be an issue."

"If you were a man," Hayes warned, "it would be Liam beating *you* senseless for dropping your weapon. But you're not, so count your blessings."

"That's not fair," I exclaimed, and watched as Liam made quick work of Devin. He jabbed him in the chest, swung the staff, knocking his knees out from behind, and then brought the end up to Devin's throat.

"I yield." Devin swallowed, his Adam's apple bobbing against the pressure of the staff. His hands up in the air.

A roar of approval and taunts came from the surrounding troops. Liam didn't back down, and for a moment, I thought he would strike his friend. His eyes were wild, his nostrils were flared with anger, yet he didn't even seem out of breath.

Liam nodded and held out his hand to help Devin up. He pulled the man close and whispered something into his ear. Devin's face paled, and he looked over at me with fear in his eyes. I wanted to know what he was thinking and hearing.

It was my turn to frown with displeasure.

"Why the long face?" Hayes asked. "I would think most women would love the thought of a man fighting for their honor."

My face flushed. "I'm not most women. And I wouldn't call that fighting for my honor. He beat him within seconds."

"Would you rather he dragged it out and completely humiliated him? Which he's done in the past."

"No. I wished he wouldn't have interfered at all. It makes me seem weak."

Hayes snorted. "Believe me, you have enough weapons at your disposal that you are quite dangerous."

"What weapons?"

Hayes rubbed his palm over his face and groaned. "It's sad that you even have to ask. Just shows that you don't know how to use any of them, which makes you even more innocent." He looked up and grinned.

Devin limped over, a bruise forming on his cheek, a wide smile on his face. "That was fun. I almost had him."

"No, you didn't," Hayes called out.

Devin shrugged. "Come on, your lesson isn't even over yet."

"It's not?" I asked.

"Commander's rule. We don't stop training until you can no longer walk, or until you pass out from exhaustion."

"I'm going to regret this." I sighed.

CHAPTER SIXTEEN

Devin and Hayes spent every break over the next two days training me in combat. They were both right about working me over until I could no longer walk, and I passed out from exhaustion each night. I'd stretched and worked muscles I didn't even know I had, and I felt empowered because of their encouragement.

Liam didn't interfere in my training again. In fact, he was always occupied, even when I wanted to show him I was improving in my skill. He became distant. Cold, even.

Then Liam announced we would stop in Briarwood, the last town, before we would reach the blight. That knowledge made me nervous and on edge.

Devin described Briarwood as a sleepy city compared to the bustling city of Thressia. Slow in pace and atmosphere. The shops were older with thatched roofs, and wooden shingles advertised the alchemy shops, local hedge witches, and even an acupuncturist.

We slowed as we navigated the narrow streets, falling in line, one behind the other, like a string threading its way through a needle. We poked and prodded our way toward our destination. Fae and human alike crowded the streets as they prepared to flee the oncoming darkness. I could feel the underlying fear that coated the air.

As we rode down the main road, I saw wagon after wagon being loaded with furniture and crates. Many of the people that had the means were leaving, trying to outrun the blight that was bearing down on their home.

City guards rode their horses up and down the street, trying to intimidate the townspeople into staying instead of running away. My heart lurched as a father loaded up his children into a cart and pulled them by hand toward the city gate.

One guard blocked his way, and the youngest child cried out in fear. Her tears left a white trail down her soot-stained face.

"Move out of the way," the man yelled at the guard.

"The king needs you to stay and defend the city," the guard ordered.

"I have children." The man gestured to the wagon behind him. "Their mother's gone. If something happens to me, they'll starve."

"If Somnielle falls, then it won't matter where you run to, the blight will follow." The guard puffed up his chest and stared down at the wavering father. "If you don't stay, I'll have you arrested."

The father's bottom lip trembled, and he lowered his head in shame. "I'm a coward," he admitted.

The guard sneered in disdain and gave an ugly gesture. He spurred his horse onward, kicking up mud onto the wagon's occupants. The father tried to wipe the offending mud from his youngest daughter's face.

We watched the same scene play out with each street we passed. Only a few of the fae would stay behind, for other kingdoms weren't as accepting of their kind. As afraid as they were to stay, they were even more terrified to leave.

There was hope. I could see it when the people looked

toward Liam in his fur-trimmed red cloak, his head held high, his gold helm gleaming in the sunlight. He was a beacon in their worried hearts. A symbol much more powerful than I realized. When he passed, people paused, looked on with awe, and pointed. Some bowed, old women cried, and a few clutched their hearts.

I looked toward Devin, his own face was solemn, his lips pressed together and his chin high as he followed in a line behind his commander.

I gathered just as much attention from the crowd.

"Look, Mama, a princess." A young girl with braids pointed and waved at me. My heart raced as I smiled and gave a small wave back. A completely different reception than the one I had back home.

"Yes, dear, she probably is."

We stopped outside a small white stucco inn called the Sleepy Gnome. I hadn't even dismounted when the front door burst open. A cute brunette with dimples and doe eyes rushed out and stopped awkwardly on the first step, her hands pinwheeling so she didn't fall into the street.

She wagged her finger at Devin. "You sure took your time. You promised me a date when you passed through again."

"Anna!" Devin flashed her his most debonair smile and straightened his shirt. "That I did, that I did. And I may very well still keep my promise if you can put us up for the night?"

She turned, smoothing back her hair, and glanced at our small troop. "Oh, and Sir Liam as well? We'd be honored. Come in, get settled. If I'd have known you were coming, I'd have baked you my famous sweet potato pie."

"Oh, love. If you'd known I was coming, you would have baked so much food I'd have no choice but to marry you." Devin chucked her under the chin, and she blushed prettily.

As soon as Anna went inside, Devin held up six fingers and pointed to his toes.

"Liar," I mouthed at the inside joke.

"Yeah, but I almost had you fooled." He grinned cheekily.

"Not for a minute." I smiled. I didn't need to read auras to know he was lying. Devin was a born charmer, pretty smile and smooth lies. I knew better than to fall for that dimpled face. He loved the chase. I don't think he'd be one to settle down soon, if ever. He would always be a free spirit, and I admired that about him.

It wasn't an overly large inn, but they could accommodate everyone, as long as some men didn't mind sharing rooms. I heard Berk mumbling that there were four men in his room.

Anna was sweet enough to show me to a small attic with a single cot. The space barely had enough room to stand because of the slanted ceiling.

"I feel bad for sticking you here, but we rarely get so many people at once. I lent out my room, so my sister, Dana, and I are already doubling up. Since you're the only lady, I thought this would work for you." Anna fussed about the room, knocking down cobwebs and trying to straighten the curtain rod that had half fallen down.

"It's perfect, Anna. I enjoy being away from the rest of the group. Thank you for your hospitality."

Anna beamed and then leaned in close to whisper confidentially. "So, what can you tell me about Devin? Are you two courting?"

I shook my head. "No, he is too rambunctious for me."

She fiddled with her apron and gave a knowing smile. "Ah, so you like the quiet ones."

An image of Liam came to my mind, and I blushed. "I do."

"Do you think if I had hair like moonlight and eyes like yours, then maybe I'd get him to settle down?"

It wasn't the first time that my unique hair color or pale eyes had come up in conversation. Living in my house where my sisters' hair color ran from golden to deep red to raven black, my hair color seemed bland in comparison. I never considered it to be anything special.

"Thank you for the compliment, but I don't think you should change yourself to please others. Now, if you do it to please yourself, that's different. Love yourself, and others will take notice and love you—for you."

Anna grasped my hands, and I expected to wince from her touch, but I received nothing. Not even a stray thought or image. I stared at our clasped hands in awe and was reluctant to let them go.

"Can I trouble you for one more thing?" I asked.

"Sure."

I gave her my list of ingredients for the burn on my wrist. It had scabbed over, but I wanted to continue to treat it so it wouldn't leave a scar. She promised to see what they had and gave me a wink. "I'll have my Oma come visit you."

"Thank you, Anna."

When she left, I noticed there wasn't a true lock on the door, but a wooden latch that swiveled and dropped down. The gap in the door was quite large and hardly left any protection.

A candle mark later, an old woman knocked on my door and let herself in. Her back was as crooked as her nose, and her eyes were as wizened as her skin. She muttered in an old language that I hadn't heard and fussed over my wrist. I thought for sure she would get out the ointment, but she ran a finger over my injury and I felt a tingling sensation. The skin healed.

A hedge witch.

"Gut?" she asked.

"Yes, gut," I repeated, semi-recognizing the word.

She grinned, showing her missing teeth, and then emptied her colorful carpet bag onto my bed.

"Ves," she muttered over and over, and tossed out chicken bones, red candles, and a hex bag.

"I'm sorry, I don't understand?"

"Gut, gut." She spun, holding out an old wooden spindle with golden thread. I stared at the spindle and felt drawn to it, my hand automatically reaching for the tip. At the last second, I withdrew my finger and looked at it through narrowed eyes. There was something magical about it, and I knew to be wary of taking enchanted items from strange, old women.

Oma didn't seem to like my refusal of her gift. She held it up, pushing it into my hand, forcing me to take it. As soon as I did, I felt a hum of magic, and dropped it onto the bed.

Oma jutted her chin out at me, her wrinkly finger wagging as she launched into a long tirade.

Anna happened to return when her granny was in the middle of her rant. I looked up to Anna with desperation in my eyes.

"Oma! Was se?" Anna asked.

Oma repeated her conversation and Anna listened intently, her head bobbing every few seconds, followed by a long sigh.

Anna packed Oma's things into her old bag and paused when she saw the brittle white bones. "Ew, I hope she didn't give you chicken bones. She always believes those will bring the bearer luck."

I held up the spindle.

Anna laughed in relief. "Yeah, I don't know where that came from, only that she's had it forever. I'm surprised she gave it to you."

"I can't possibly take it, then." I placed the spindle on the bedside table, and Oma stamped her feet angrily.

Anna looked up in alarm. "No, you need to take the gift, otherwise she will be upset, and it will take hours to settle her down."

My fingers curled around the spindle, and Oma's loud stomping faded away. She gave me a bright, toothy grin, and pinched my cheeks.

Anna laughed. "Oma said it will bring you luck. It's made of firethorn."

Firethorn was rare and only found deep within the fae woods. It was a giant tree with thorns that ran a foot in length, this spindle carved from one of those thorns. To a sorceress, it held immense power . . . or rather, it would in the right person's hands. In mine, it only hummed.

I bit my lower lip and regretted not having my powers. My head dropped, and Oma noticed my change in mood.

Oma spoke to Anna in a hushed voice before the girl turned to me, and declared, "You haven't lost it."

"What?" I asked.

"Whatever it is you apparently lost." Anna shrugged. "She's not one for details, and says she needs a nap."

Oma shuffled out of the room, and Anna helped her grandma down the steep stairs. I let Oma's words resonate with me. A candle mark later, Anna returned with a tray of food, and the girl seemed hesitant to leave.

"Can you tell me something," I asked. "What do you know about the heir of Rya?"

Anna plopped herself down on the edge of my bed and crossed her feet. She placed her chin in her palm and gave me a look. "There isn't one."

"Oh..."

"I mean, there isn't one anymore. It could just be rumors, and considering who it's coming from, I don't really know what to believe."

"Go on." I waited patiently for her to continue.

Anna took a deep breath. "Oma used to work at the palace a long time ago. When Dana and I were little, she told us a story about King Pharrell and his true love."

"You mean Queen Maris?" I said.

Anna shook her head. "Not the queen. He had an affair with a beautiful fae woman. It's said, the newly married king was out riding one day, and he came upon a young fae woman sleeping in the forest. He fell madly in love and would sneak away from the palace and his queen to come visit her every day."

"I can see why they would keep this silent."

Anna nodded. "It was a scandal. The king married Maris out of duty, but he loved the fae woman. He even snuck her into a hidden wing in the castle and kept her presence secret from the queen. The young fae woman begged to return to her forest home, saying she couldn't stand to live within the cold, lifeless walls of the palace."

"That's so sad," I said.

Anna nodded. "The king locked her in the tower, and rumor has it, she became depressed and took her life."

My fingers dug into the quilt of the bedspread. "No," I gasped.

"A few days later, a dark storm blew in, and with it,

Tatiana, Queen of the lesser fae court. She came seeking vengeance.

"Queen Tatiana said the fae woman was her handmaiden and friend, and she didn't commit suicide, but was murdered. The king denied it, claiming loudly for all to hear that he had loved the woman, and still did. Tatiana called him a liar and vowed to curse his kingdom and take from him what he cherished most. His firstborn child. Days later, a child was born in secret to King Pharrell and Queen Maris. Fearing that Tatiana would take their child, the king ordered an attack on the fae court, killing everyone in it and burning it to the ground. Believing that the fae queen was a casualty of the attack, they thought themselves safe from her curse.

"On the day of the child's christening, Tatiana returned, clothed in black and covered in burns. She claimed that because of the king and queen's betrayal, she would not only take the child, but the kingdom from under them. A great battle ensued between Tatiana and a court sorcerer, and when the battle cleared, both the fae queen and the baby were gone."

Goosebumps ran over my arms, traveling up to my neck, and I couldn't help but wonder if it were really true.

"But again, there's no proof any of it ever happened."

"What do you believe?" I asked.

Anna sighed wistfully. "I think it makes a dramatic bedtime story." Her voice lowered, and she leaned in to whisper. "But there are a few people, Oma being one, that believe the blight marks the return of the king's heir, and that this is the curse coming to fruition."

"Yes, it sounds possible," I said, unsure. Reaching for a piece of bread, I took a bite and chewed.

"But those are just rumors from crazy old ladies." Anna

stood and wished me a good night's sleep before excusing herself.

She left, and I closed the door, flipping the flimsy wood bar down. Thinking over the story and its possibilities,.

I had curled up on my cot and was almost asleep when I heard a soft knock on my door.

"Aura."

I recognized Liam's voice.

Ignoring the knock, I pretended to be asleep. But that lock did nothing to keep someone out. Liam slipped a thin knife between the crack and flipped the lock and let himself inside my room. I sat up and glared at him, but I couldn't be mad for long. The attic was made for short people like Oma and me, not for giant knights like Liam. As soon as he ducked under the short doorframe, he had to tilt his head so his ear touched his shoulder. It couldn't possibly be comfortable.

"What do you want?" I asked, trying to mask my amusement.

Liam sat down on the edge of the cot so he could look at me upright. He frowned and reached out to brush a stray strand of hair out of my face. His finger rested on my cheek, and he didn't pull away. I closed my eyes and pressed my cheek into his hand. Missing him, even as he sat on the bed next to me and touched my face. I felt like there was a giant crevice between us.

"There's something you should know." His voice was raw with emotion.

I looked into his eyes, and I saw the regret he could not hide.

My voice hitched, and my heart raced. "What?"

"The king sent me to the Eville household to bring back a powerful sorceress to fight the blight. I was supposed to beg, supplicate, bribe—and if that didn't work, kidnap one of the seven daughters to fight the curse on our behalf. I've come to the conclusion . . . I mean . . . I made a terrible mistake, and—"

"I'm not a mistake," I interrupted. I found the lack of face unnerving, and my chest compressed with emotion. It was hard to breathe. "I'm not a mistake," I repeated a little louder. "I am strong. I'm not helpless. I'm not—"

Liam surged forward and kissed me, his hand cradling my neck, pulling me into the kiss.

It was such a surprise that I reflexively pulled back and broke it off. I covered my mouth with my fingertips. I was at a loss for words, and I was never at a loss for words.

"I'm sorry." Liam cleared his throat and looked over my shoulder at the wall. "You were getting emotional, and I was trying to calm you down."

"A distraction," I said, slowly. "I see."

My heart broke into a million tiny pieces. He didn't want to kiss me. He was just trying to shut me up. It wasn't the perfect kiss. It was the perfect weapon, and he used it to stab me in the heart.

I shifted away from him, running my fingers through my hair and tucking it behind my ear, giving him my back so he wouldn't see my heartbroken face. For once, I was glad that I couldn't hear his thoughts. I don't think I could have handled another rejection. I steeled my nerves, lifted my chin, and with an icy voice, dismissed him.

"It worked, so you can leave now."

"Aura, I—"

I turned and glared at him. "You had *no* right."

I was furious. My anger was boiling over at being rejected, and I used my words like a sharpened blade to injure him. To dig at his pride and put as much distance between us as possible. Because it was obvious now that Liam didn't have feelings for me. In fact, I wasn't sure if he even had genuine feelings. He just used me like a tool.

"You took what I would have freely given. Used my feelings as a weapon. You're worse than the men at the brothel. Even Devin didn't stoop so low."

Liam paled, and I watched as my words shattered his stony exterior. I wanted to see him crack, and he did. His hands balled into white-knuckled fists. The veins in his neck pulsed, and he stood up so fast, he smashed his head into the ceiling, causing the stucco to crack and fall all over the floor. He spun and ducked under the low doorframe, slamming the door so hard that the latch fell off onto the wooden slat floor.

I picked up the lock and held it, knowing that it was the symbol of what was left of our friendship. Broken.

CHAPTER SEVENTEEN

The next morning, I came downstairs and was met with a somber gathering. Anna had her arms wrapped around her younger sister, Dana, who was crying into her older sister's shoulder.

"What's the matter?" I asked.

Anna wiped at the tears on Dana's face and sent her into the kitchen. Her own face paled, and she wrung her hands. "The blight has reached Birchwood. It's completely covered in fog, and a pack of cù sìth have been sighted near the town." She shook her head, her eyes glassy. Her bottom lip quivered. "My aunt lives there, and my cousins. Do you think they're alright?"

I held back my surprise at the news.

"I'm sure they'll be fine," I said. "We will find a way to stop it."

Liam came down the stairs, our eyes met, and he looked away. The muscle in his jaw tensed, and I could see the stress and guilt that was eating away at him.

Anna's face momentarily brightened before she worried. "Oh no, Miss, you shouldn't leave. It'll be dangerous." She reached for my hands, but I quickly lifted them out of her reach.

"Don't worry. We'll figure out a way to help everyone."

Devin came in through the front door, his normally jovial face was grim. "We're ready, Commander."

"Let's go." Liam gestured with his chin, and I knew it was time.

Anna flung her arms around me, and I let myself be comforted by her hug. It reminded me of my sisters, and it was because of Anna's family that I knew I would have to overcome my obstacles and fight the blight.

When I tried to leave the inn, Liam blocked my way.

"Aura, please reconsider staying behind. We don't know what we are facing, and without your magic, I—you—," he struggled to voice his concerns.

My hands balled into angry fists as I pushed past him and headed outside. Devin had already prepared my horse, and because he knew how sore I was, I allowed him to help me on to Damsel.

Out of the corner of my eye, I saw Liam's frustration at his inability to intimidate me into staying. He flicked his reins, and his horse took off at a gallop. The rest of his troops followed swiftly behind. Without another word, I spurred my horse on and took off after the cloud of dust left by the troops. We rode at breakneck speed for hours, and only slowed when the terrain became too dangerous as we climbed up a great hill and looked out at the valley below. Liam stopped, and I pulled up beside him.

I gasped at the horror of what I saw below. In the far distance was the forlorn silhouette of a castle sitting above a little town. But to the west, a dark sky loomed, and the land was covered by a thick fog.

"Is that where we're going?" I asked, seeing Liam's hesitation.

He looked to the palace and back to the ominous fog,

studying the layout of the woods to the west. "Yes, I'm supposed to take you through Somnielle to the palace." He pointed toward the town, then to the castle built high on a hill. Below it, a forest and steep cliffs surrounded the structure.

A faint hum started in my pocket, and I reached into my cloak to pull out the spindle that Oma had given me. The wood was warm in my hand, and I could feel it pulse softly in my fingers, the golden thread flickering softly. I lifted it in the air, letting my arm swing back and forth like a pendulum . . . until I felt a tug on the spindle. A thread pulled off, and it pulsed harder until I felt a shock in my fingers. I almost dropped the spindle, and I looked at where it had sent off the spark.

I studied the ebb and flow of the fog, taking into account the spindle's magic.

"No," I exclaimed.

"No?" he asked.

"We go there." I pointed. "Just beyond the fog, to the northwest. A swirl in the fog, a miniscule vortex. Do you see it?"

Liam squinted and followed my hand. "I've never noticed it before. What is it?"

"It's the source of your blight."

"What do you think we will find?" He looked at me expectantly.

I shook my head. "I don't know."

His shoulders dropped.

He didn't need to say anything to me. I understood where his hopelessness came from. He had wanted to return with a weapon, but he returned with a liability, and because he searched for me to save me from Madam Esme's, we arrived too late to save the city.

"Where did you get that?" Liam asked, pointing to the spindle in my hand. "Looks old and beat up."

"I got it from the old woman at the inn. It will bring me luck."

"Good, we'll need all the luck we can get to survive the fog."

Devin rode up next to us and surveyed the blight. He let out a low whistle. "I heard, but still never expected it to be this bad. What do you think happened to the second contingent of troops the king sent to stop the blight?"

Liam's face hardened. "If they encountered what I did, then they're gone."

"How do we fight against magic we don't understand?" Devin asked.

Liam glanced at me, and then away. "There are many things in this world we don't understand, and plenty we do. We may not understand magic, or spells, but we have faith, courage, and hope—and it is because of that I believe we will find a way."

Devin smirked. "It didn't work before, why should it work now?"

"Because now we're backed into a corner and we have no choice." Liam turned and gave Devin a malicious grin. "And that's when we become the most dangerous."

I wanted to say something profound or encouraging, but Liam turned toward his men, raised his sword high in the air, and yelled out, "Onward to protect Rya!"

The mood shifted from despair to grim determination. I felt the goosebumps rise along my arms, and I could sense the change in the air. Feel the willpower of the troops led by Liam. Even I felt encouraged by his charisma, spurring my horse and falling in line behind Devin as we began our race toward the fog.

As we ran along the river, I saw flashes of silver as undines were racing downstream and along the banks, while herds of deer, elk, and small forest creatures were quickly evacuating. Specks of black covered the sky as flocks of birds were following the same path—away from the blight.

On the roads we met cart after cart pulled by donkey, horse, or even steer as people evacuated their homes and were heading toward the castle. No one wanted to stay to meet the doom slowly creeping toward their doorstep.

Except for us, and we rode straight toward it.

∽

A howling screech ripped through the air, spooking the horses, and scattering our formation. We entered the fog, and immediately the sky darkened. We could feel a mental oppression weighing heavy on our minds.

"What was that?" I asked.

Devin, Hayes, and Berk drew their swords and moved to the inside of the path, putting themselves between the loud sound and me.

"I don't know. I've never heard that sound before," Devin whispered.

"Banshee," Liam said, his back straight, eyes scanning all the shadows for danger. "Don't stop, men. Keep moving. This is not the part of the woods where you want to dawdle," he warned.

"Why not?" I asked.

"What you're hearing are the dark fae."

"But they're home is a good forty miles west of here," Hayes said.

"Their hunting ground has migrated with the blight. It's best if we go unnoticed. Take off the bridles and armor. We must move through the fog as quietly as we can." Liam raised an eyebrow at me. "Still glad you came?"

"It's going to take more than the threat of dark fae to scare me," I said firmly.

"Good to hear."

He turned and rode back to the front. Using hand signals to direct his men, they switched out the decorated harnesses for simpler leather bridles, tucking away all of their standards, bells, and any piece of metal that jangled or made noise. Berk oiled the axles on the wagon, and I watched the forest, searching the darkness for any hidden threat.

A candle mark later we were on our way again, but at a much slower pace. One man scouted the path and held back tree branches and moved sections of logs that would make noise or slow us down. Sunlight couldn't penetrate the fog to reach the forest floor, and within the cloudy haze, the stench of sulfur was overwhelming. Without the sun, navigating the woods became almost impossible, for every time we made headway, the woods twisted and shifted. The fog thickened, and we found ourselves right back where we'd started.

"I've never seen anything like this?" Devin whispered.

"Me neither." I shuddered.

Only our hunger pangs and exhaustion gave us a clue as to how much time had passed, and once again, we were forced to make camp in the near darkness under a canopy of silence. My training with Devin and Hayes became more of a silent dance than actual training. Something we needed to do to pass the time and take our mind off of our surroundings.

We worked without weapons, for the clang of contact would rattle through the forest. Instead, we mimed hand-to-hand, fighting in slow motion, where whispered punches, dodges, and footwork became our routine. But the long hours and never-ending fog wore on us emotionally, physically, and mentally, and we let our guard down.

In the middle of the third night, lost in the fog, one man slipped away, abandoning his post. Liam was quiet. He didn't mention the deserter, nor would he speak on it. The next night, he made the guard rotations shorter and even took the first watch.

I rolled over onto my side and tried to get comfortable on my bedroll. Keeping the spindle out, I would watch it to see if it glowed or gave me any sign of where to go. It stayed dim.

I missed the privacy of my tent, but until we were past the dense fog, we were sleeping in the open without a fire. Cradling my arm under my head, I stared out across the sleeping forms of Jon and Hayes. The soldiers huddled under their red cloaks on the ground looked like long mushrooms.

Shivering, I pulled my saddle blanket closer to my neck and easily spotted Liam sitting against a trunk watching over the camp. He didn't sleep, or at least I didn't think he did. The dark circles under his eyes told me he'd spent most of the night wide awake watching the fog, and I spent as much time watching him.

With a frustrated sigh, I sat up and felt under my bedroll for the rock that was jabbing painfully into my ribcage. Freeing the stone from the earth, I was about to toss it away when I noticed the empty bedroll closest to me that moments ago had been occupied.

I tossed the stone and hit Hayes in the back. He groaned and sat up. "What?"

"Where's Jon?" I whispered, pointing to the empty bedroll.

Hayes yawned. "Probably went to take a leak. Go back to sleep."

Heat warmed my cheeks, and I lay back down, feeling an absolute fool. He was probably right, and I was overreacting. My eyelids became heavy, and I drifted off.

"He's gone." Hayes shook my shoulder.

Rubbing my eyes, I looked up into Hayes' worried expression.

"Jon didn't come back?" I asked.

He shook his head.

"Go wake Liam," I said.

Hayes silently moved through the camp, and I went to Jon's bedroll and placed my hand upon the cloth. It was cold and damp from the fog, signifying it had been empty for a long time.

They roused the rest of camp from their sleep, and Devin went to check with the guards. I paced back and forth, biting my thumbnail in guilt. Devin walked past, his face grim.

"Any word?" I asked, stopping him.

"No."

Liam and Hayes joined us. "He's not the only one. Another one's missing."

"Maybe they got lost in the fog?" Devin asked.

I caught Liam's dire look. "I don't know. One can only hope for the best, but expect the worst," he said.

My chest hurt and the words just burst forth. "I'm sorry, this is all my fault. One minute Jon was there, and then he was gone. I should have known better."

"No, I was the one that told you to go back to sleep," Hayes interjected.

"Now, what? Do we go looking for them?" I asked.

"Aura, it won't be any use. We can't even find our way out of the fog. I won't risk any more men getting lost." Liam's green eyes met mine. "Unless we have a guide. Someone who can hear thoughts."

I swallowed and stepped back. "I can't."

"Can't, or won't?" Liam snapped.

"You know nothing."

"I think your magic is still there. I think you're just afraid to use it."

"Magic. What magic?" Devin asked. He cocked his head and gave me a strange look.

"She's a sorceress . . . and she can hear your thoughts." Liam gave Devin a sly grin.

"What?" Devin's eyes widened. He glanced my way and blushed. "Oh . . . uh, that may have been good to know earlier."

"I can't hear thoughts anymore," I said. "It's gone." I spun and stormed away, but Liam came after me.

He grasped my wrist, and whispered, "How do you know if you won't even try?"

"Let me go."

"You said you wanted to help, so help. Or are the rumors true about how cold and heartless the daughters of Eville are?"

"Fine." I wrenched my arm free. I moved to the edge of camp and stared into the dense fog. An icy wind blew, batting at my hair, causing goosebumps to run along my arms. Crossing them over my chest, I tried to squeeze warmth into my body as I internally debated with myself. My gifts weren't something that I could turn off and turn on, otherwise I would have had better control over it. It was just always a part of me.

Closing my eyes, I focused on reaching out. Searching, seeking, but I got nothing. Groaning, I focused harder on what Oma said. It wasn't lost. That had to mean it would come back if I wanted it to. The problem was . . . the underlying issue and fear that was blocking me. If I didn't want my empathy gifts back, then I could live a normal life, get married, have children. But to take back my gift, it would doom myself to a life of early madness.

I couldn't help but think back to the pain I was in at the palace in Candor. The thousands of thoughts that dragged through my mind . . . when I would have done anything to silence them and have peace. Funny, now I didn't feel at peace. I felt unsettled, on edge, because I was always guessing what others were thinking instead of just reading them.

Liam watched me. Waiting for me to act. Being normal seemed to create an even greater distance between us, for he had no reason to shield me, and seemed to give that duty to Devin. But I didn't want Devin. I wanted Liam.

I was going crazy being away from him. No matter the choice I made, I would go mad. At least knowing I had a choice, I could make the right one. One that would help the knight who traveled all the way to Nihill. He wanted a savior. I wanted to be that for him. Even if I feared my gifts and my future, I needed them to save Liam's men—even if I destroyed myself doing it.

Closing my eyes, I kneeled and buried my fingers in the dirt, feeling the ground, searching for the magic ley lines deep in the earth, but I couldn't feel or hear anything.

I bit my cheek in frustration. Never had it been this difficult to sense the ley lines. Maybe my connection was truly severed? Dragging my finger in the dirt, I traced the symbol for the word accept.

"I accept," I whispered. "I accept my power." I felt a soft rumble of magic, and then felt it slapped away. "What was that?" I said in surprise. "What happened?"

A shuffle of gravel had me turning to look up at Liam, who stood over me. I stood, dusting off my hands.

"Anything?" he asked.

"Nothing," I snapped irritably.

"Try again," Liam demanded.

I preferred the old Liam over this new angrier, bossy version. "I did." I sighed. "I can't hear or feel anything, even when I reached for it. It's like I'm blocked. I . . ." I trailed off and met Liam's determined green eyes. And then it hit me. "It's *you*." I pointed my finger at him.

"Me?"

"You're blocking me." I snorted. "I haven't lost my powers. Yours have grown."

Liam shook his head and scoffed. "No, that can't be."

Grinning in triumph, I poked him in the chest with my finger. "It is. Your shield magic has grown, and you're shielding me."

I caught him by surprise. "Am not." He raised his hands in surrender.

It made sense. "Ever since Devin rescued me, you've done nothing but blame yourself for my capture. You're consumed with guilt, and that emotion has only increased your desire to protect me. Your shield magic has completely blocked me from accessing mine without even touching me."

Liam's shoulders dropped. "I didn't know. I can't control it."

"And yet, you expect me to control mine." I smirked. "Well, you can drop it now," I said softly, and placed my hand on his arm, feeling his muscles tremble beneath my touch.

Liam's brows knit together, and he tried to concentrate. "How?"

"I don't know." I tried to think of a way to teach him

control when he'd never been trained. I bent down and picked up a river stone. I placed it in his palm and clasped his hand around it. "Hold this stone and squeeze it tight. Now slowly, one by one, open your fingers and let the stone slide out of your palm".

Liam followed my instructions, and we both watched the gray rock fall and hit the ground with a thud.

"Good." I scooped up the stone and had him repeat the exercise.

"Do it again. But this time, visualize that it's me. I'm the stone."

His fingers squeezed so hard his knuckles turned white. His lips turned down and his brows furrowed.

"Let me go," I whispered.

His fist trembled, and he gazed at me. "No, I can't. You'll get hurt."

"That's part of life. You can't protect me forever."

Liam didn't like that answer. "I can try."

This was getting us nowhere. He was refusing to drop his shield magic, and I was useless being this close to him.

"It's not your job to protect me," I said.

"I promised I'd watch over you."

A prickly feeling ran up my spine, and I turned and looked among the men, my gut telling me we were in danger. But from what?

Devin had been a silent observer during our entire exchange. He picked up my nervous energy and moved to my side, giving me a curious look.

I scanned the dense fog. The feeling wasn't leaving, instead it was a growing discomfort in my gut that I couldn't ignore. We were in danger, but I couldn't sense it. "Liam, I need you to back off," I said.

His eyes darkened. "You can't tell me what to—"

Panicked, I yelled at him. "I don't want *you*."

He stepped back, his brows furrowed, and I saw the stubborn line in his jaw. He wasn't going to let go, or he didn't know how, and I was desperate.

I'm sorry, Liam, I cried out mentally. I reached out for Devin's hand and took it in mine. Turning toward him, I went on my tiptoes, my hands wrapping around Devin's neck, pulling myself close. Not sure what to do or how to act, I just hoped that he'd meet me halfway. I pressed my lips to his awkwardly.

I felt a mental slap as Liam's anger grew, and his magic pressed into my mind. I caught Devin by surprise. His hands rested on my hips and he kept the kiss chaste, not willing to kiss me in front of his friend.

But chaste wouldn't get Liam to get angry enough to hate me and drop the shield. I pulled Devin closer, and he must have read my desperation. His lips moved against mine, his hands lifted and wrapped around my back, crushing me to him. He deepened the kiss, and I gave a squeak of surprise that sounded like a moan. He lifted me into the air, my feet dangling as he kissed me. I didn't enjoy it. Instead, the mental power that I felt pressing against me changed. It turned cold. I shivered, and Devin slowly released me, letting my body drag against his as my feet found purchase on the ground.

I didn't dare to look at Liam. I was too ashamed to even make eye contact.

"Is this true?" Liam asked.

I reached for Devin's hand, and he entwined our fingers together. "Yes. I *choose* Devin." The lie soured my stomach.

I felt the moment Liam's shield dropped, and the sheer power that had been smothering me was amazing. Immediately, I gasped and stumbled. Devin supported me as Liam's intense feelings came my way.

Red flashed in my mind, and I felt my knees go weak. Liam was livid, and then I felt his immense pain at being rejected. Devin's arms held me close, keeping me upright as I battled with the onslaught of images, thoughts, and feelings that rushed into my mind.

That was unexpected. But pleasant, Devin thought, then looked at me and his eyes widened. "Tell me you didn't hear that?" he said.

I laughed, nodding, and felt tears of joy build in the corners of my eyes. I could hear and feel again.

I rubbed at the tears in my eyes, and I looked up at Liam. My heart broke. His eyes were distant. His face was stony and unreadable. His thoughts hidden from me.

How could I explain that I only hurt him so he would stop shielding me? So that I could protect everyone else? I didn't think I could. If I did, his magic would smother mine, and it would doom us. It would be better to hide my feelings and keep him at a permanent distance.

Liam, head held high, walked away, leaving me clinging to Devin.

This time when I cried, it was tears of sorrow. Devin patted me on the back, trying to comfort me.

"I'm sure you will clue me in on what just happened," he whispered. "Because as nice as that kiss was, I know you don't care for me like that."

"I'm sorry, you're right." I sighed. "I needed to distance myself from Liam so his magic won't cancel out mine. It's the only way for me to help all of you."

Devin sighed. "He's my best friend. This will be torture for him. You get that, right? By doing this, you are purposely hurting him."

"It's the only way to protect him."

"And yet, he was just trying to protect you."

"He can't. He's untrained, and he doesn't know the extent of his power. He could do more damage than good." I turned to look deep into the fog, and I felt magic surrounding us. A hint of a dark aura made my skin prickle in warning. "There's something out there hunting us . . . and this is the only way I can find it."

CHAPTER EIGHTEEN

Hungry. Sss-ooo h-hungry.

My eyes flew open, and I stared up at the dark sky. Blinking to clear my sleepy thoughts, I looked over to my right and saw the sleeping forms of a few men all bundled up in their wool blankets. Nothing was out of place. Therin sat at his guard post against a tree, a crossbow in his lap, his eyes alert as he kept watch.

I laid back down on my side and turned to face the fog when I heard it again.

Hungry. Need to eat again.

I didn't imagine it.

I reached for the leather pouch, pulled out the tube, and held it out in front of me. I wasn't sure what I was going to do since I couldn't see anything, and I wasn't getting any flashing of auras. As quietly as I could, I crept toward Liam, kneeled down, and shook him awake.

No sooner had I touched him when his eyes came open, a glint of steel flashed at my throat and a hand covered my mouth. When he focused and realized it was me, he released his grip on both.

"Something's out there," I whispered, and nodded toward the woods.

"How do you know?" he asked.

"I can hear it."

He turned his head and listened, straining to hear what I heard.

"No." I motioned to my head. "Here."

"Your powers are back?"

I nodded. "I can hear the creature. It's loud and hungry."

Liam nodded and stood up. Reaching for his sword, he came to my side as I faced the fog and tried to open my senses. He motioned to Therin, who stood and held his crossbow at the ready. I didn't want to say anything, but I was secretly relieved that I could hear the monster because it meant that all wasn't lost.

"Where is it?" Liam asked.

"I don't know." It frustrated me that I couldn't give him more information. I squinted into the darkness. "I can't hear it anymore. Maybe it left?" I said.

"What do you think?" Liam asked.

"I think it's still out there. Watching us," I said truthfully.

"I think you're right."

I heard it too late as a scream echoed into the night air.

We both spun and saw one man, who had been sleeping near the edge of the camp, get dragged into the forest. We charged across the camp as the rest of the troops were roused by the ruckus and armed themselves.

"Did you see what it was?" Liam paused to investigate drag marks and the footprints of the creature.

"No, there was nothing there," I panted, but I didn't pause. I raced after the man into the darkness.

"Aura, no!" Liam cried.

I couldn't stop. Something propelled me after the beast. My hands shook, adrenaline pumping as I chased blindly, following the scattering of leaves and crackling of branches as the monster dragged the man into the fog.

Then the crashing noises stopped, and I slowed and searched the tall grass. I stumbled over a body. It was Frederick, unconscious, his leg dripping with blood, three long gashes down the side. I leaned down to check his pulse. He was still alive, but he wouldn't be for long if I didn't stop the blood flow.

Stupid human.

I spun, clicking the button to release my staff. I held it out and flailed the weapon in the air in front of me, making sure I didn't take a step away from the injured Frederick. I may not have had all of my senses, but I knew I had surprised the creature in my sudden pursuit.

Loud crashing came from the bush. I screamed and swung my staff as Liam appeared.

"Whoa!" He ducked and was nearly struck in the neck.

"Aura, you can't run off like that."

"Shh," I hushed, and pointed to the tree's boughs above me.

Liam's chin rose, and he looked up into the darkness above.

"Where is it?" he whispered.

"Invisible."

He looked at me in disbelief. I held out my hand for his sword, and he wouldn't hand it over. I forcibly took it from him and shoved my staff into his chest. He reached for it, and I shook my head. Making a circle in the clearing, I closed my eyes and tuned out the sound of Liam's breathing . . . the crunch of leaves beneath my feet . . . the soft exhales from Frederick.

Instead, I focused on what I couldn't hear.

Please, please. I mentally tried to find the creature.

Eat. Kill. Eat.

I could hear it so clearly because it was a monster, a creature with a bloodlust so strong it screamed in my head, but it wasn't giving me any clues where it was.

"Aura," Liam warned.

I spun and pointed the sword at him, my arms quivering under the weight of holding the heavy weapon. I glared at him, my mouth pinched together angrily, and he became silent.

I felt a sigh of pain and saw an image of a beautiful woman and a young boy, no more than eight in age. Regret, love, and sorrow washed over me, and I fell to my knees. Tears of empathy filling my eyes, my heart aching.

Releasing a shuddering breath, I stood up, my mind filled with determination. I exhaled slowly. Closed my eyes, like I had done in practice with Lorn. I swung the sword wildly and waited for a response from the beast. A flash of amusement.

In what appeared to be a random sword dance, I worked my way in a circle around and came back toward Liam. I raised the sword up in the air, hovering right over Frederick's body.

Pale blue flashed in my mind. *Worry.*

I smiled in triumph and stabbed straight down with all of my might.

"No!" Liam cried out as I stabbed Frederick's arm.

Fire burned in my own arm, and I cried out.

Frederick's eyes opened, and he let out an inhuman cry. He knocked the sword from my grasp, and Frederick shifted and transformed before us, his body dematerializing and becoming translucent.

"There!" I pointed at the blood dripping down the creature's arm. Apparently, its blood wasn't able to become invisible as the rest of the body did, blurring into the background. The creature tried to run, but Liam intercepted it. He swung his shield and knocked it down as it tried to slither up the tree. He picked up the bloodied sword and finished the creature.

The creature screamed.

I screamed in unison.

Feeling its painful death as my own.

I lay in the grass, my face splattered with blood and my body shaking.

"Aura, are you okay? I forgot what being an empath does to you." Liam rushed over to me and helped me get to my feet.

"I'm okay." I shuddered and used the edge of the cloak to wipe the blood from my face.

"What was that?" Liam asked. "I've never seen something like that come out of the forests before."

"It's an onwae," I answered. "They're rare and prefer to stay hidden deep underground, but it was driven here—"

"By the blight," Liam finished. "But what happened to Frederick?"

"He's over there." Wiping my hands off, I pointed to nearby brush.

Liam rushed forward and pulled back the foliage to reveal Frederick's body. "Hurry, we can still—"

"He's dead," I said solemnly.

"How do you know?"

"I-I felt him die," I said. "I didn't sense it until it was too late. It was his dying thoughts of his family that alerted me to the imposter in front of me. The onwae's plan was to pose as Frederick and have us take him back to camp. If we would have, the onwae would have slaughtered all of us in our sleep. They're that vicious and crafty."

"Then it's good that it's dead," Liam confirmed.

"Is it?" I turned and looked at him. "Was his death necessary?"

My question riled Liam. He pointed at Frederick. "Was his? I'm sorry if I don't feel the same way about the death of that monster as you. I'm a soldier, trained from birth to protect those I care about. He was my friend. So yes, I'm glad the creature is dead."

I understood Liam's feelings. I should never have expected him to feel the same way as I did about living things.

We heard others coming, saw the torch light flicker off the trees, and Devin came through the underbrush. I must not have gotten all the blood off my face because he immediately rushed to me exclaiming. "Aura, you're hurt."

I was, but not in the way he meant.

"I'm fine." I gathered my cloak tighter around my neck, wishing to protect my feelings. "It's not my blood."

Devin's shoulders dropped when he saw Liam standing over Frederick's body. He released a long sigh. *I knew his wife and son.*

I used the distraction to slip away and follow the trail back to camp while the men dealt with the bodies. It was me and the horses, and I wasn't scared of what may or may not be in the woods anymore. I had a feeling I could sense trouble if it got anywhere near me. My hands trembled as I packed up my blankets, my mind and emotions raw with empathy for not one death, but two.

CHAPTER NINETEEN

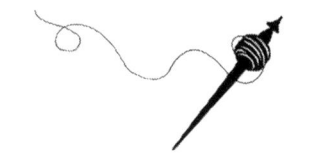

My powers were back, but they came in unreliable spurts. I couldn't selectively hear people anymore, but every candle mark or so I would get stricken by random images and feelings that would cause me to grit my teeth and have mini-blackouts. They were worse than before. Rather than the steady pain I would get from being around people, it was like a vase that would fill up. When it could hold no more, it would dump every thought and emotion on me at once.

What it did was give me longer times of sanity, followed by short bursts of manic episodes where I wasn't sure where I was, as it took my sight with it.

I dismounted my horse, and I was hit with an onslaught.

This is a failed mission.

We're all going to die.

I wonder what will happen to the kingdom.

The commander has no clue what is going on.

I reached out and Devin caught me as I stumbled. His firm hands clamped around my waist, pressing me into his body as he held me up.

"Whoa there," he quipped. "I always knew you'd fall for me, but not literally."

His voice was muffled compared to the voices that were rushing in my head.

I gripped his neck as I buried my face into his chest, breathing hard, fighting to stay conscious as the ground moved beneath my feet.

Devin's muscles stiffened, and I looked over, meeting Liam's turbulent eyes. From this angle, it probably looked like I ran right into his arms and we were embracing like lovers. I pushed away from Devin, but he wouldn't immediately release me.

"Let go," I whispered.

"Are you sure?" His grip lessened, and I stepped back.

"I'm okay now." I could feel Liam's gaze like the sun boring into my back.

Devin flung the pack on his shoulder and turned.

I grimaced and quickly tried to hide my discomfort. Liam gave me a knowing look, and he waited for me to admit defeat. That I needed him to shield me. His eyes narrowed, and one brow rose in question.

I raised my chin in the air.

Liam shook his head. His face fell as I passed him and headed away to the very edge of camp and stopped, wincing in pain as I touched my temple.

Help!

Scared!

Help!

Everything appeared still and calm, but I knew it wasn't the case. I was picking up the thoughts of the forest animals, and I wasn't sure how far away they were.

The crunch of gravel signaled Liam was still with me. He wisely kept quiet.

"I hear them." I gestured to the forest beyond. "The animals. Their fear is growing. I don't know how to stop it," I said helplessly.

Liam came and stood shoulder to shoulder with me. "We'll figure it out."

I smiled softly.

"Tell me," he said. "What are my men thinking?"

I took a deep breath and debated on how much to tell him. "They're afraid, but not for the reasons you think. They're afraid of losing against the blight. That they'll die in vain."

Liam turned to me, and I read the pain in his eyes. "They're not wrong. I've failed before. They entrusted me with five hundred men to stop this blight, and what you see before me is all that I have left. This time it's different. The fog is stronger; harder to pass through. I fear we may not make it further. If we don't find the source, our kingdom will truly be overrun."

"That's why you brought me, or have you forgotten the whole reason you traveled to a backwater town and kidnapped a sleeping girl?" I grinned and patted his arm. "I guess it's a good thing I didn't stay behind in Briarwood either."

"You have a plan to get us out of the fog?"

"I do. You're not going to like it."

CHAPTER TWENTY

I held the scrap of red fabric and grinned.
"This is your plan?" Liam scoffed.
I tied the makeshift blindfold around my eyes and felt Damsel shift beneath me. "Yes."
"Are you crazy?" Devin asked.
"Never ask a woman if she's crazy." I chuckled, putting on an outward show of bravado, but internally—I was quaking.
"What is the point again?" Devin asked. "How are you going to lead us out of here if *you* can't see anything?"
"It's our eyes that are deceiving us. We've been trapped in this mist for days when we should have already made it to our destination."
"How are you going to lead us out, then?"
"I'm not." I leaned forward and patted my horse's neck. "She is."
"We're following a horse?" Hayes rubbed his palm over his face. "This is going to be interesting."
"Stop worrying and don't take your eyes off of me." The abrasive cloth rubbed against my eyelids, and I wanted to rip it off. Instead, I pressed through the feelings and used it to focus outward, then downward, running my fingers through Damsel's mane.
Are you ready to be my eyes?

I lead, Damsel replied.

Thank you.

She started moving forward, and I grasped the pommel, being careful not to pull on her reins and direct her. I had to put my trust into her eyes and her senses.

"Yah," Liam said, spurring his horse after mine. I felt better knowing that he was at my back.

He's nice. Smart, that one, Damsel commented. It was a relief to hear her voice.

Yes, he is.

Gives lots of snacks. You should keep him. Then he'll feed you and you can get fat too. Fat is good.

Maybe. I hid my smile, trying not to show my amusement that my horse was giving me dating advice.

Make lots of foals with that one.

I snorted, covering my mouth with my hand. I definitely didn't need this kind of advice from my horse. No, definitely not.

He was sad when the bad men took you, a deeper voice spoke into my mind.

I blinked as I tried to register who I was hearing.

Hush, Pern, Damsel admonished.

He didn't sleep or eat for days. Pern, Liam's horse, had joined in the mental conversation.

So now you're both going to make me feel guilty, are you?

Of course. You worried the golden one, Pern said.

Golden one? Ah, that must be Liam. He did kind of give off a golden aura.

"Uh, Aura?" I heard Liam's warning. "I think you need to turn."

Do we? I asked her quickly and gripped the reins, preparing to course correct.

Damsel snorted, tossing her head in frustration. *No. I take back what I said. He's not smart. Dumb.*

We'd have been out of here days ago if he let me lead, Pern added. *But he fought me every inch.*

Behind me, others pulled on the reins, and I heard the horses being redirected. Their hooves scraping against the gravel. Voices raised as men fought to turn the horses.

Hold tight, Damsel warned.

Out of curiosity, I raised the corner of my blindfold and gasped. We were walking off a cliff. I gripped the reins and was about to do the same, but I felt no fear from Pern and Damsel, only confidence.

Even though I was terrified, I turned in my saddle and gave Liam and the men a confident smile before pulling the blindfold back over my eyes and gripping the pommel. My heart jumped into my throat as my mind told me we were going to fall to our death.

I waited and counted down the steps, expecting to plummet. Instead, my weight shifted forward, and I had to lean back as Damsel started down a small incline.

There's a trail, I said to Damsel in relief.

Of course, there's a trail. This is the way.

But a few seconds ago, it was a cliff.

No, no cliff. Only path.

I lifted my blindfold and looked back, and all I saw was fog as thick as molasses. I couldn't even see Liam or the others.

"It's okay," I called back through the veil of magic. "There's a path. It's just an illusion." The fog swallowed my voice. Sound didn't travel as far in the magic mists.

"Tricky," I said aloud. "No wonder we couldn't get out."

No one followed me through the illusion.

Pern, force him through! I yelled, and I heard a neigh.

Seconds later, Pern burst through the mist fighting the bit in his mouth. He danced across the ground and finally settled. A startled Liam looked around in disbelief.

"I'm alive. You're alive. I saw you plunge to your death," Liam gasped. "I even heard you scream."

"No, it's just an illusion to keep you trapped within the fog. Now we have to get the men through."

Liam tried to call through the swirling mist, but just like before, the mist deadened his voice. He spurred Pern back through the fog to bring his men to the other side.

See. Brave, Damsel added. *But stupid. Pern was the one who had to get him through the mist.*

We waited, and it took some coaxing, but soon Devin, Hayes, and others were led through the illusion.

Not far now, Damsel encouraged, leading the way. Her steps surer as she picked up her pace. The other horses followed her stride.

Not far to where? I asked.

You'll see.

I didn't like the way it was going, but I put my trust in my mare not to lead me astray.

The fog lessened, and with it, the proverbial tension that had been hanging over me lifted from my shoulders. The path became clearer, and trickles of sunlight beamed through the tops of trees. I'd never been more excited to see the sun's rays. It brought hope.

My spirits brightened, and so did everyone else's.

Devin rode by my side, and he used the distraction to test my abilities.

This is stupid. I shouldn't test her, but I need to know. Can you . . . ?

I frowned and gave him a side look. "Of course, I can hear your thoughts. You're practically shouting at me."

His grin spread across his face, and his eyes took on an impish look. He pinched his lips and looked at me expectantly.

Guess what number I'm thinking?

I sighed, having played the game with my sisters many times before. "Five."

Devin's grin became wider as he switched numbers.

"Thirteen, four hundred and two, now thirty-nine, forty. If you can't decide, this will get us nowhere."

"Amazing. Let's try something else."

"I'm not a toy."

"But this is fun, and there's nothing else to do. I'm bored. One more."

I shook my head as another image came to mind. It was a large hominid being over ten feet tall, with long gold hair that fell like waves from its entire body. Its eyes were black and beady, like polished stones, with an enormous nose that poked through the fur. It was a very detailed description.

"A basajaun. I've only ever read of them. Have you actually encountered one?" I asked, turning in my saddle toward Devin.

He sat frozen upon his horse. His mouth dropped open as a shadow fell over us.

The ground rumbled beneath our feet and Damsel shifted her weight. I felt her own dread as I looked up at the giant basajaun holding an axe that was coming down straight for my head.

"Look out!" Devin yelled.

Damsel was petrified, unable to react to the oncoming blow. My heart stopped for a split second, and I thought it was the end.

An arrow split the sky, shooting past my ear, and sinking into the basajaun's fist. The axe missed me and Devin, coming between us, sinking into the earth and spooking both our horses back into action. Damsel bolted, unprepared and not the most stable of riders, I fell from her saddle, my shoulder slamming into the ground.

The air knocked from my lungs and I gasped, unable to breathe. Stars flashed in my eyes, and I tried to gather my wits. Seconds later, air returned once more as my body remembered how to breathe.

"Aura, run," Liam yelled as he reloaded his crossbow.

Each breath was still too painful. The basajaun swung his axe, and I anticipated his strike, rolling to the side. Seconds later, Liam's crossbow struck the beast in the shoulder.

The basajaun was a guardian of the forest; a gentle giant by nature was enraged. I tried to read his thoughts and auras, but I received confused images and feelings. Flashes of red filled my vision, and I gasped with empathy for pain.

The troops surrounded the basajaun, their swords drawn, shields at the ready as they closed in to kill him.

"No!" I cried. Getting to my feet, cradling my injured shoulder. "Stop. You mustn't! You don't understand."

Hayes and Devin didn't hear my warning and moved in to attack.

"*Fiergo!*" I screamed.

A protective circle of fire, greater than any I had conjured before, erupted around the basajaun and myself cutting us off from the troops.

I surprised myself. My desperation must have fueled my magic.

Devin and Hayes retreated. The troops shouted their fear,

and Liam's worry flashed over me. I ignored them all and focused on the pain radiating from the basajaun.

My left arm hung useless at my side. I held my right hand out, pleading with the basajaun.

"I won't harm you."

The basajaun cowered before me. In my attempt to protect him from the men, I had surrounded him with his greatest enemy—fire. Terror radiated off him in waves, and he whined.

"I know it's scary, but I did it to keep us safe." The axe lay discarded on the ground, and without it, the basajaun didn't seem as intimidating. He curled in a ball and buried his head under his arm.

"Aura!" Liam cried out. I felt a pressure moving against my magic.

My head snapped toward Liam as he stood on the outside of the flames, his face intense as he tried to use his magic to smoother mine and douse the flames.

How dare he. It showed he didn't trust my intuition or abilities.

I released the spell, and the fire died down, leaving a circle of scorched earth in its wake. Liam easily crossed the circle, not fearing me or my powers. In his hand, he held a dagger, and he reached for my arm to pull me away.

"Don't you harm him," I threatened, standing between them.

"It's a monster, and it tried to kill you."

"Not on purpose." I kneeled by the golden beast and placed my hand on his soft back. The basajaun sat up and looked at me with pain-filled eyes. He didn't reach for his axe, and only let out a painful moan.

He growled and pulled the arrow out of his shoulder, leaving a bloody trail, and tossed it to the side. I placed my hand on it and closed my eyes, coaxing magic to the wound, focusing on reknitting the muscle. My hand warmed as his body began healing, all the while drawing the pain into myself. He let out a rumble of appreciation as the pain lessened and the wound closed up. I then focused on the second wound in his fist.

The basajaun kneeled and placed his large head beneath my hand, letting out another moan. He was still in pain. The creature's hair was thick with many layers and undercoats, littered and snagged with small twigs and leaves.

I made a soothing noise as gently parted the long, matted hair to reveal a large section that was hidden, the skin blackened and infected.

"This doesn't look right." I leaned forward and sniffed the infection, getting a scent of sulfur. "The wound was caused by magic." Immediately, I caught an image sent from the basajaun. An image of Aspen and four others on the edge of his vision. The dark mage sent a great fireball at him, chasing him away from what he guarded.

Liam frowned. "Come Aura, there's nothing you can do." He placed his hand on my shoulder and I pushed it off.

"No. I have to help."

He sighed and kneeled down next to me.

"I can heal it." My hands glowed, and I focused on healing the burned skin, letting it reknit. My side ached and blistered in sympathy pain. I held back the tears as I also learned what had transpired. "The basajaunak," I explained as I ran my fingers along the burn, "are the protectors of the forest, and he is protecting it—from us."

"Us? Why does he have to protect it from us?" Devin snorted, having finally crossed the fire circle to join Liam and me.

"They don't speak, at least not in a language we understand, but they can communicate." I sat and listened to the fears and emotions, putting together a story with the images the basajaun showed me. "A dark mage came several weeks ago, and he released something."

The basajaun nodded. Standing to his full height, he towered over us, and he slipped through the woods, his fur easily blending into the shadows cast by the trees. He stopped and beckoned us.

"I can only assume it was the blight," I said.

Liam gently touched my shoulder. I winced. "Your shoulder is dislocated." He reached for my arm, and with a twist and jerk, quickly popped it back into place.

I screamed in pain. "You should have warned me," I snapped.

Devin cringed and gave an apologetic answer. "No, it's worse when he gives notice because you tense up. This way was better."

"Don't take his side," I growled, rubbing my shoulder. Though, I was relieved that it felt better.

The basajaun had stopped in the shadows of the trees and waited for us. I looked up and saw the bright sunny sky, but all around us the fog swirled.

"We're close to the center of the vortex. We should follow him."

Liam frowned, looking at the large creature. "I'm not one to follow a predator into its own hunting grounds."

I shook my head. "We're the predator here. Plus, I think we will find the answers you need."

Liam turned to his men and made hand motions, and a look silenced any hesitations they had. But not for me. I heard their complaints loud and clear as we stepped into the woods and followed the basajaun. The farther we traveled, the more I noticed the signs of the fae hidden within view.

The mushroom circle, the white stones that left a trail to follow before we came to a humongous monolith of two stones. A long slab precariously balanced across a perpendicular stone, with three claw marks gouged into the piece. The men paused and remarked on the immense strength it would have taken for the beast to lift the boulders.

I smiled and answered their silent questions.

"The bigger the stone, the stronger the protector. It's a warning for those that want to hurt the fae of the forest." I pointed to the markings. "Each gouge mark symbolizes the number of basajaunak in this territory."

"Three?" Hayes spoke up. "Really, why so few? I would have expected more."

"It's his family." I hesitated, reading the basajaun's thoughts. "Was his family. He is all that's left and has been alone for many years."

Instantly, the troops' emotions changed from fear to relational. Those in our company with family dwelt on their own wives and children. Others related to the protective nature of the silent beast, and his desire to protect those within the forest.

We hadn't traveled much farther beyond the monolith before the golden beast stopped and made a great whine. He refused to travel further into the village, his aura changing to one of fear.

I slipped past him and looked down into the valley at what was once a thriving haven for fae, but now resembled a mausoleum. The firethorn tree, their source of protection—and home for the smaller sprites and fairies—was split in two, dark scorch marks were still burned into the trunk.

The surrounding hills were once home to gnomes and hobs. All that remained were the shattered and burned doors that hung from hinges. The darkness within—empty like a tomb. A crunch fell beneath my boot as I accidentally crushed a fairy chair made of thistle.

When I looked close enough at the dead trees, I could see the human faces through the burned bark, the last images of the dryads. I clutched my stomach as I tried to shield myself from the pain that was radiating from this place.

I fell to my knees before the firethorn tree. I reached out to touch one of the sharp thorns, at least two inches in diameter. Their prick was deadly to humans, but not to fae. Taking a chance, I ran my finger over the spine and pressed the fleshy pad of my finger onto the thorn, feeling it pierce my skin.

The drop of blood pooled on my fingertip, and seconds later a vision washed over me. My connection to the land was strong as the great firethorn tree shared her memories.

I saw the fae village as it once was many years ago. Fairies flitted about the sky, dancing and weaving among the branches of the willows. A young basajaun was curled up in a glade, and little sprites were busy braiding acorns and twigs into its long hair. His mother wasn't far off, watching over a small firethorn thicket. Hobs were busy gardening, and one in particular with an overgrown beard was trying to lure a mole out of a den by tying bait to the end of his beard like a fishing line.

A beautiful woman with long pale hair and a crown of flowering thorns walked along a white stone path. Hummingbirds tried to steal strands of her hair and flew alongside like a protective escort. I knew I was seeing Tatiana, Queen of the lesser fae court. When she came to a stream, one hob rushed over and held out a hand to help her cross over a slippery stream before he disappeared back into the woods.

A flaming arrow cut through the air and missed her by inches, embedding in the straw roof of a redcap's home. Tatiana looked up as the sky became littered with flaming arrows. Her face twisted into one of fear. She turned to run, dodging the onslaught. One pierced her calf, and she cried out as she quickly smothered the flame. The other arrows found their marks, the flames quickly spread from hut to hut, and the fae inside scattered. But not before the golden field of flowers turned red with the uniforms of the Rya soldiers as they stormed through on horseback, striking down anything that moved.

My heart raced as Tatiana ran, her eyes searching the glade, shoving the smaller fae into hiding. The two adult basajaunak ran to attack the soldiers. Their roar in unison caused the nearest horses to rear and drop their riders. The female basandere picked up the fallen rider and tossed him into two other riders. The male—the same one I'd just healed—swung his axe and knocked three soldiers backward into the path of the calvary.

Tatiana limped, her leg bleeding as she stumbled and fell to her knees in front of the great firethorn tree. She waved her hands. The thorns parted to reveal an empty bed of grass. Her face crumpled into grief. Her breathing picked up, she gritted her teeth, and spun to fight. The hobs ran out of their homes armed with hoes and farming equipment, the gnomes grabbed their pickaxes and charged into battle, fearless and determined. But their numbers were few and the king's army were great.

Tatiana cast a spell. The ground rumbled, but a soldier on horseback ran her down. She fell trying to avoid his horse, and she rolled into a boulder, her head slamming against the stone. Blood pooled behind her head. Her vision swam. She rolled over and tried to crawl away as the soldier dismounted, unsheathing his sword. He approached Tatiana, and I saw the look of murder on the soldier's face as he raised his sword to strike.

The young basajaun raced from the thicket, his cry less intimidating than his parents, carrying a sword too large for his smaller hands. He stood toe to toe with the soldier and struggled to raise it in defense of Tatiana.

The enemy soldier's sword arm raised to strike.

I cried out as the vision showed him swing. The blade flashed, and the young basajaun fell to the ground. Tatiana's mouth opened in a silent scream, and the world went red as fire consumed the vision.

My face was wet with tears, my heart bursting with pain for the basajaun. He lost his family to the attack.

"What did this?" Hayes murmured.

"Not what," I said sadly, wiping the tears from my eyes and patting the trunk of the dead firethorn tree, silently thanking them for the memories. "Who."

Liam moved, his royal Rya cloak fluttered. He looked exactly like the men in my vision. I felt sick.

"The king's army."

Liam's jaw tensed. "You're wrong. The king wouldn't have sent the troops to destroy a fae village."

"This was over twenty years ago." I stilled and listened to the firethorn. "A dark sorcerer attacked the basajaun and released the blight only recently."

I stood up and walked around the destroyed village. The spindle in my pocket thrummed again. I pulled it out and laid it on my palm, watching it turn in my hand like a compass. I followed as it led me to the far side of the burned-out village until I came to a never tree. The never tree's roots were giant tangles that stretched fifteen feet into the air and then sunk below the surface. They were considered hallowed ground. Approaching the tree, I saw an entrance between the roots, which led deep into the earth. The stone steps were broken and destroyed, and the earth all around the tree had been disturbed.

"Here. This is the source." I pointed down into the darkness.

"Of the blight?" Liam asked.

I nodded, feeling sick to my stomach with the feelings that were rising up to me. An echo of the past ringing into my soul. "I need to go down there. I need to see more."

"No, it's too dangerous." Liam grabbed my arm as I was about to head into the passageway.

"I'm not afraid," I said.

"You should be."

I smiled reassuringly at him. "Not when you're with me."

Liam nodded. He released my arm and pulled his sword out of his sheath, moving down the steps first. He motioned for me to stay behind. The sunlight only shone on the first few steps before he was swallowed up by the gloom.

I waited expectantly and heard him call for me. "All clear."

Bounding down the steps, I came up to his side and shook my head.

"I guess you already knew that, didn't you?"

"Yes, there's no one down here." I pushed past him and hesitated as the light didn't penetrate farther. I spotted the burned-out torches lining the walls.

Fiergo.

With a flicker, the torches came alight, and we could see that most of the tunnel was still intact, but sections had collapsed.

"Are you getting stronger?" Liam asked, taking a torch from the wall.

"I think it's because of where we are. It's boosting my magic. I've never been able to conjure more than a mere flicker of fire, but here . . . it's almost more than I can control." I tried to hide my concern.

We followed the cave. There were sections where the entire ceiling had collapsed, and the ground was illuminated by the setting sun. Other areas of the tunnel were blocked, and Liam had to clear giant rocks and boulders before we could go on.

"How much farther?"

"Not far." I could feel my stomach roiling with anticipation.

The ground leveled out, and all around us the packed dirt and walls were marked with deep grooves that ran parallel to the floor.

Running my finger along the indention, I followed it to an archway and stopped.

"There." I pointed to the arched door made of roots. "The source of the blight came from within."

The door had been destroyed and lay buried in the earth. I inspected it, reading the sigils and the warning along the door.

Liam came back outside. "What's wrong?"

"It's a curse," I said, reading the history that was embedded within the iron door. "One that had been cast on the king of Rya for a great wrong he committed."

"You're kidding."

"No, and it was a deadly curse. One that was sealed away inside this vault. But someone broke the lock, and the curse is free to run its course."

"What does the curse do?"

I shook my head. "Death and destruction."

Liam gestured for me to stay put. He held out the torch and entered the room while I studied the locks and wards placed on the door. There was something familiar about the wording and handwriting.

I was scared to investigate further, but I felt compelled to find the truth. Kneeling in front of the door, I used my magic to search for the telltale signature of the castor. My heart thudded loudly in my chest, and my hand trembled.

"It was Mother," I whispered.

"What was?" Liam stepped back out of the room.

"She was the one who bound the curse in this vault. I recognize her spell work."

Liam shifted his weight and wouldn't make eye contact. "Aura, there's something you should see."

"What?"

He ducked back into the darkened room and held the torch up high, casting a circular glow along the walls. The light caught hundreds of crystals that glittered in the wall, each in a very specific pattern.

"They're the constellations," I said in awe.

"Aura, look." Liam drew my attention away from the sparkling wall and to the object in the center of the room.

A stone dais, and upon it, a bed with a pillow and red sheet lay discarded on the floor. Scratched into the dais and all over the floor were various spells, but the one repeated over and over gave me a clue to what had really happened here.

Somnus—sleep.

"This isn't a vault. It's a prison cell," I gasped.

Looking around with fresh eyes, I took in the prison with the bed inside.

"My mother mentioned nothing about this."

"She probably didn't want you to know."

"It's a person," I cried. "Mother Eville imprisoned someone in here, casting a sleeping spell." I covered my mouth with my hands and held back my disgust as I remembered *all* of our lessons in weaving sleeping spells. "An actual person is responsible for all of this."

"We don't know Lorelai Eville's reasons, but look at the damage they've done since they've escaped. It moved across the kingdom, targeting the holdings and towns. It's only a matter of time before it chooses to go after the king. I have to believe its path of destruction was deliberate. To strike fear into the king, because where it goes"—he ran my finger along the deep gouges made by the thorns—"death and destruction follow."

"You're right." I nodded. "This was probably the reason my mother didn't want us to come here. She knew how dangerous this being was."

"What do we do now?" Liam asked.

"We know two things. One, the blight isn't a curse, so it can be defeated. And two, there's only one place left for it to go."

His mouth pinched in a determined line. "Let's go."

CHAPTER TWENTY-ONE

"It's already here." Liam pulled Pern to a stop, and we looked upon the pass completely enveloped by a giant mass of twisting thorns. Even from a distance, we could hear the creaking and crackling of the branches as they grew and twisted around each other, giving it an ominous voice as it slithered across the ground like a snake. "The blight finally reached the mountain. The next stop is the palace."

"What do we do?" Hayes removed his helm to gaze upon the blight up close.

My fingers dug moon-shaped divots in my palm as their fear washed over me.

Liam had a white-knuckle grip on his reins. "We do what we were sent to do. We stop it here, now." Liam gave me a pained smile. "We're not alone in our fight. The blight can be defeated. It has been contained before, and we will do it again."

I stared at the twisting thicket that looked very much like the same firethorn from the fae court. But it was here, growing and moving slowly across the land, concealed behind miles of thick, impassable fog. It was the fog that hid the real threat from the world, and I had a feeling that if I could get through the thorns, I would find the one responsible. It was just another barrier of protection. Refusing to show my own fear, I slipped off of the horse to study the thorns closer. Liam kept a close eye on me.

I reached out to touch a thorn, and Liam slapped my hand away. In an instant, the closest green barb shot out of the branch into a thorn larger than my spindle. Seconds later, it shifted back into a harmless thorn.

"They're poisonous," Liam warned.

"To non-fae," I added, letting my thoughts swirl with possibilities and drawing the same conclusion.

After I inspected the twisting and churning firethorns, I ended up with more questions than answers. All flora needed nutrients to grow, and to grow at the speed the firethorns were growing, they would need a constant supply of magic. Could it possibly be a ley line of power?

Imagining the maps of the ley lines Lorn had once shown me, I tried to calculate where they would be. "Get me the map of Rya. Show me everywhere the fog has moved and where the thorns have been sighted," I said.

It took a few minutes before Hayes could dig out a map, and after Liam and his men measured out the locations from their reports, they could mark the path of the thorns.

"There is a pattern," I said smugly, not able to contain my grin. "There are two separate events we are tracking. The fog is moving from city to city spreading like a disease, while the thorns are only sighted along this direct route concealed by another fog." I drew my finger in a straight line down the center of Rya, and straight through the fae court.

"What's that?" Devin asked.

"It's a ley line of power. The strongest sorcerers can tap into it to aid their magic, and that is happening with the thorns. This is the direct path that the thorns will follow straight to the palace. And what do you see between the thorns and the palace?" I tapped the lines on the map.

"The mountains," Liam said.

"Yes, it's pure stone. Harder to access the ley line, and that held up the magic user and slowed them down. I bet you they are in the middle of that thorn forest using it as protection while they head straight to the king. Remember what you said about the thorns?"

Liam's sword flew at a branch that had snuck up to them. He sliced the offending intruder clean through.

"Yeah," Liam snapped and turned to place himself in harm's way again. "They're poisonous to humans."

"Which makes navigating them successfully impossible for the men from Rya. It's the perfect defense."

After another candle mark of discussing the map, laying out all possible routes, I had come to a final decision. The men spoke in low voices, a dull mumble that Liam couldn't hear, but I could hear them loud and clear.

They found nothing.

"What do you think we should do?" Liam asked.

"I can't get your men through the firethorn safely," I said through clenched teeth. "They will surely get attacked and die. I think the best course of action would be for them to go around the mountain and come up to the palace on the south side, avoiding the ley line and thorns altogether."

"And what are you going to do?"

"I'm going to take the direct route—into the forest of thorns."

"Aura, I told you it's certain death."

"No, it's not. Because I'm part fae." I held up my finger to show him the still healing wound on my finger. "I touched the firethorn tree in the fae court."

"You are?"

"I knew I had fae blood. Lorn hinted to me long ago that empathy gifts are predominantly passed down in fae families."

"Then that settles it."

"What?" I asked.

"I will escort you through the firethorns. For where you go, I go. Even if it means certain death."

I smiled encouragingly. "You don't remember, do you?"

"Remember what?"

"When we healed you, Maeve pulled a firethorn out of you. Yes, the wound was infected from not being cleaned, but the poison didn't kill you straight away. Because you, Liam, are fae."

"I don't believe it." Liam let out a long breath.

My brows furrowed. "There's nothing wrong with being fae, or even part fae. It would explain your magic."

"It's just, I had a certain vision in my head. An idea, and I guess being fae wasn't part of it."

"Are you disappointed?" I asked.

He frowned. "No, I think this gives me a place to start. A clue I didn't have before. And for that I'm grateful." He rubbed the back of his head and turned to look at the setting sun.

"We should make camp for the night. Are we safe here? So close to the thorns."

I nodded. "We're safe tonight. The basajaun will guard us while we sleep."

Liam looked over his shoulder and searched the tree line. "You trust him?"

"I do."

"You did a good thing healing him, then."

"No, I did the right thing."

Liam silently nodded. "Get some rest. I will tell the men of our plan. Tomorrow, you and I will attempt to enter the thorn forest." Liam patted my shoulder.

I sighed, knowing that rest would not come easy.

Instead of sleeping, I spent the next candle mark walking through camp worrying about all the lives that were lost. For all lives mattered, fae, human, and even the halflings. Baist and Florin were the less accepting of the fae kind, and they avoided those kingdoms altogether. Rya, Isla, and a few others lived in a precarious balance with the fae, each their own society existing within each other. The humans obeyed the king while the fae had their own nobles in the fae courts. The only difference was that the fae courts could shift and move between realms and kingdoms.

I wandered into a grove of untouched willow trees and spread out my bedroll under the canopy of the long green branches and tried to block out the thoughts of the men.

I can't sleep. This is most definitely a trap. The beast will kill us as soon as I close my eyes.

Rolling over, I tucked my arm under my head and pressed my palm to my ear, hoping to ease the pressure.

I think the girl is in league with the fae. She's plotting to destroy us all.

After many hours, their thoughts finally settled as one by one the men fell asleep and I drifted off.

My dreams were tormented by the echo of emotions that remained in the land. The memories of the dryads and their last dying breaths. Their screams like breaking branches. The fairies as they tried to escape the smoke and flames, and the basajaunak fighting bravely, hurling rocks from the cliffs on the soldiers below, the female falling to their poisoned iron swords and arrows.

Horses, screams, blood, smoke, fire.

Tears burned in my eyes and I whimpered, feeling my own throat swell closed from breathing in the fire. I was suffocating, unable to breathe. The injured basajaun ran to a cave and rolled a rock in front, protecting whatever lay within.

"No," I whispered. "No." I flung my fist out and hit a solid wall of flesh.

A hand grasped mine and pulled me close. I fell into strong protective arms. Liam's.

"Shh," he whispered. "I'll protect you." He gathered me to him, easily moving me onto his lap, cradling me as he rested his back against the trunk of the willow.

My head rested on his chest, and the voices and haunted memories ceased. The only sound I heard was the fast rhythmic beating of Liam's heart.

Why does he have to be so gentle?

I pulled from his embrace, and he moaned into my hair. "Please, don't leave."

I froze at his words.

"I know you don't want me to chase away the darkness." It was a statement, but the next thought slipped through. *But I need you to chase away mine.*

"Liam," I began, my heart swelling with unspoken feelings.

"I know you chose Devin," he whispered. "But I can't accept it. I feel it here in my heart that you're mine." Liam leaned back. His hand cupped my face and gazed into my eyes.

Could he feel the racing of my heart? The desire to kiss him overwhelmed me. I needed him like I needed air. He was the one I was addicted too.

The wistfulness disappeared, and he became serious.

It would be so much easier if I knew how she felt about me.

Swallowing, I struggled with the truth. "I don't . . . I don't love Devin." Our eyes met, and I saw the hope rising in them.

"Really? I thought—" He shook his head. "The brothel, that night. I walked in . . . I saw—"

"A misunderstanding. We thought it was one of Esme's guards, and we pretended to be in the throes of passion."

Liam's shoulders dropped, and he let out a long sigh of relief.

It still wasn't the whole truth. I quickly added, "It started as a charade . . . and then suddenly it wasn't. The kiss became real." Heat rose to my cheeks, and I dropped my head in embarrassment. "That's the truth."

"Oh, Aura." He leaned forward and pressed his forehead to mine, his warm breath washing over me. *I really want to kiss her, but I'm scared that it will push her away again.*

"No, it won't." I inhaled and waited.

He leaned back and blinked in confusion. "What?"

"I'm giving you permission," I said impatiently.

He grinned. "Really?"

"You're losing your moment," I teased.

He pressed his lips to mine, his hand cupping my face. Unlike before, this one wasn't demanding, but sweet.

An explosion of color like fireworks lit up my mind.

I internally grinned at his response, and using his own cues, kissed him back. He broke the kiss and pulled away, but then quickly leaned in for a few more gentle pecks.

How can anyone so perfect ever love someone like me?

"I'm not perfect," I said.

He gazed at me with his eyes full of love. "You are to me. What do you see?" he asked. "Read me."

"The truth," I whispered.

He smiled. "Then believe it, and believe that I won't let anything happen to you. I'll protect you."

I looked away, out into the darkness, and shivered. Liam

tucked me into his side, letting me lean into his chest. He put his cloak around the two of us and rested his chin on my head.

I drifted off just as I caught his final thought.

Please let me be near her for just one more night. Followed by a flash of fear. He quickly shielded his thoughts from me, but he wasn't fast enough.

"Don't you dare," I said, catching his plan. As soon as I fell asleep, Liam was going to sneak away and take on the firethorns alone.

"Aura, you don't understand, I only want to protect you."

"Then you will understand when I only want to do the same." With a heavy heart, I reached up and placed my finger in the middle of Liam's forehead, cutting him off.

Somnus.

His head fell forward, and he slumped into a deep sleep.

"Forgive me. If one of us is going to go battle a vengeful sorcerer, it's me."

CHAPTER TWENTY-TWO

"I must be completely out of my mind," I muttered, facing off against the deadly looking thorns. Sneaking away from the camp, putting Liam under a sleeping spell, and attempting to take on a crazed sorcerer by myself. He had already lost so many soldiers and friends in trying to beat this blight, I didn't want him to have to go through that again.

I was protecting him and his men, or that's what I tried to tell myself.

Pulling the spindle out of my pocket, I tied one end of the golden string to a thick branch of evergreen.

"Ready, Basa?" I called out to the basajaun. He seemed keen on his new nickname. "You don't have to come with me."

From the shadows of the forest, the basajaun came out to stand by my side. My faithful companion, he kind of reminded me of farmer Brighton's old sheepdog.

His determination was strong, and I was grateful for his loyalty to me.

"Okay, let's go." I waved my hand onward and approached the first thicket of thorns. I held the spindle out in front of me, and the thorns retreated, slithering and slinking away from the spindle. Unwinding the golden thread as we walked, we made it twenty feet before they moved in again, closing around us.

I let out a deep breath and swung the spindle in another

direction and watched the thorns withdraw, as if it sensed the power within the spindle I held. Every twenty feet, I would wrap the string around a solid branch and continue our trek.

Basa let out a warning, and I turned as a sneaky branch tried to reach for me. I released my staff with the click of a button and whacked at the branch, and it retreated into the brush.

"Thanks," I breathed out. The thorns may not have been poisonous to me, but it didn't mean that they weren't dangerous.

Basa's thoughts were silent. He had a soothing, calming way about him. The two of us worked through the maze of thorns, a few times accidentally doubling back and crossing my own string.

"Well, that's the wrong way." I made the course change and headed back, trying to work my way north. The spindle hummed, and I watched as the golden string pulsed when I held it in a certain direction. "There. We must be getting close."

Our pace picked up, and I used the spindle like a compass, its golden thread pulsing faster, the spindle itself forcing the other thorns back. Until the spindle shook right out of my hands and I dropped it.

The attack was immediate and came from all sides.

Thwack! Thwack!

I swatted them away with my staff, but there were too many. Basa used his axe to clear a path while I blocked the attacks from our rear. We had made it to a clearing, and the thorns didn't seem as thick, or as mobile.

"This is crazy," I muttered, wiping the sweat from my brow. "How much farther?"

Basa pointed up the mountain. From this distance, the

palace was just a speck, but it was built into a cliff, hundreds of feet above us. The thorns inched their way up the side, but were unable to breach the mountain wall over forty or fifty feet.

"They've reached their limit and connection to the ley line. What's below us is stone, not earth," I said, feeling relieved. "Which means we're close to the source."

With renewed determination, I set out toward the thicket, hoping to fight and retrace my steps to get my spindle. A stabbing pain radiated from my ankle as a stray branch wrapped around my right foot. With its quick tug, I fell backward, and my head connected to the hard packed earth. Stars filed my vision, and the impact momentarily stunned me.

Rolling over, I dug my fingers into the earth as the vines dragged me along the ground.

"Basa," I screamed, and the basajaun ran after me. He lunged, the great golden beast flying in the air, his thick hand reaching for me. I grasped his finger, and then it slipped from mine as I was yanked deep into a deadly thicket and out of his reach.

Basa's roar filled the air as I was pulled down a hole into darkness, deep into the earth.

CHAPTER TWENTY-THREE

I landed with a thud on cold, dark soil. The hole I fell through was quickly covered by thorns, and the sunlight choked out so only the smallest ray remained. The dust particles dancing in the beam like miniscule fairies fluttering about was the only beautiful thing about the dark pit.

"You're strong," a voice whispered to me from the darkness. "I can feel power running through your veins."

The breathiness of the speaker made it impossible to tell if they were male, female, or something else entirely.

Muffled steps drew near, and a figure in a dark cloak stepped near the ray of light, their outline illuminated in the contrast.

"You made it far enough to reach me. I applaud your determination and your strength. So I will take pity on you and let you live, like I did the other one."

"You mean Liam," I breathed out.

The stranger shrugged. "I know not his name. Only that he was determined to stop me, and I can't have that. Not when I'm so close."

"So close to what?"

The person leaned forward just enough so I could see the corner of a feminine mouth lift in a smile. "Revenge," she said.

"Why do you wish to destroy the kingdom of Rya?"

A high-pitched laugh followed. "The kingdom of Rya isn't worth saving. Sometimes evil must be struck down so that hope has a chance of being reborn from the ashes."

"What do you mean?"

"Vengeance, dear girl. I am here to right the scales of justice for a wrong committed."

"What wrong?" I watched the speaker, her height, her way of walking as she moved through the small pit.

"The king of Rya took everything from me, and so I have sworn to take what is most important to him."

"His throne?" I asked, standing up and turning to keep the woman in my sights.

Her manic laugh filled the air. "No, his child."

"The king of Rya has no heirs," I stated.

"Lies. I know there was one. The king has hidden the babe from me, but I will find it. I won't stop until I've taken it from the king."

"I know of you. I know of the attack and what the king did to your people, but spilling innocent blood won't solve anything. It won't bring them back."

"You know nothing." Her voice shook with anger, her pacing became frantic. "A life for a life. They hid the child from me, but I will find it and kill it."

"Please, I beg of you, stop what you're doing. Too many innocents have died already from *your* curse."

Her pale hand reached up to cup the ray of light, its glow making it seem like her hand captured the light within. "And yet it isn't enough." Her head cocked to one side as if she were momentarily distracted. "Yes, the time has come. I've delayed long enough."

"Wait," I called out, desperately trying to delay her while I thought of a way out. "Revenge doesn't have to be the answer."

"I've been locked away for so long that my hatred consumed my dreams. All I can think about is revenge."

She sounded stark raving mad.

"What if I could help you find a better purpose? Together we can find the truth. If you would but let me—"

The woman waved her hand at me. "You're becoming a bit of a nuisance. I tire of *you*."

The ground trembled, and the earth cracked and crumbled around me. The thorns retreated, and the hole I fell through was visible again. If only I could have reached it. Limping, I raced for the wall and tried to climb, digging my fingers into the dirt and roots, pulling myself up.

"You do have fire. This will delay my plans once more, but I can't have you getting in my way."

A flash of light surrounded me, paralyzing me. Fire ran through my bones and I felt pulled and stretched. I opened my mouth to scream, but it was cut off.

∽

Sunlight burned my eyelids, the fire in my body faded to a dull ache. Opening my eyes, I was met by a clear sky full of foliage.

Groaning, I rolled over and sat up. The remains of a wax circle lay near my head. I awoke back in the fairy circle near our home. Had I really traveled hundreds of miles in an instant, or was it all a dream?

No, it couldn't be a dream. My ankle had deep puncture wounds, evidence of the firethorn attack.

Glancing around the glade, I felt the frustration build up within me. "No," I yelled, slapping my hands onto the ground. "This isn't fair!" I brushed off my skirt and was at a loss for what to do now. With a flash of a madwoman's hand, I was right back where I started. I didn't know what to do or where to go, except home.

I stood up and began the slow trek back to the tower and tried to organize my thoughts. How did I explain my sudden disappearance to Mother, or for that matter, my sudden return? She had specifically forbidden me from going to Rya, and I had done absolutely nothing to help Liam in his quest to end the blight. In fact, all I had accomplished by my presence was to delay him and cause him problems. Even when I figured out that the blight was another vengeful sorceress, I still didn't have a way to stop her. I was nowhere near powerful enough to be of help.

I had returned a failure.

When I saw the silhouette of our tower, I felt a moment of dread. I slowed my steps and took my time limping the rest of the way home. When I came to the threshold, I paused, gazing at the straw mat on our stoop, the old wood door painted with symbols of health and healing, and the iron latch that had worn down from years of use. I pushed the door open and stepped inside, the smell of home hit me: the wood oil we used on the floor, the faint smell of herbs and potions that always hung in the air from our potions room, and the faint crackling of the fire.

Time had stood still. I had been gone for weeks and discovered so much about myself. I felt different, my world had changed, and yet here it hadn't.

It was like a dream. I moved to the dining room table and picked up an apple from the bowl.

A flutter of wings followed, and a crow flew in through an open window. A trickle of power rushed over my skin as Maeve transformed and came to stand near me. Her internal questions prickled at my mind, but she was doing her best to squelch them. She moved around the table to be across from me and placed her palms on the tabletop, looking me dead in the eye.

Maeve stared at me unblinking, the corner of her mouth turned down. "You're back already. What happened?"

The back door slammed open with a thud. Rhea came in, her hair a mess, her apron covered with soot from the forge.

"You're back," Rhea breathed out, wiping her face with the back of her hand, smearing more soot across her cheek. "We've been so worried about you. Are you okay?"

That simple question snapped me back to reality, and I slumped into the wooden chair at the table. I stared at my hands and fingernails, still coated with dirt, proof that it wasn't a dream.

"I don't know," I answered truthfully, and buried my face into my hands.

Over the next few candle marks, I told my story. Neither Rhea nor Maeve judged me. They sat and listened. Rhea filling up my cup with my favorite lavender tea while the fire in the fireplace slowly died down. A chill filled the room, but no one moved to add another log, as they were so enthralled with my tale.

Maeve kept interjecting with wry comments. "Liam, is that his name?" she teased. "I would have pegged him for a Nolan."

"Not now," Rhea said. "Can't you see she's confused."

"How am I supposed to know? I'm not the one who reads minds."

"It's fine," I told Rhea. "She's only trying to lighten the mood."

"Is it working?" Maeve asked, hopefully.

"No."

"Drat." She snapped her fingers.

"What are you going to do now?" Rhea asked. "It's not like you can get back there in time to help. My spelled traveling bracelet broke, and it will take many moons to create another one."

"I don't know." I looked down at my hands cupped around my now lukewarm tea. The teacup had a pattern of thorns and roses around the edge. Another reminder of my failure to help Liam. "I don't suppose Mother would use her magic to send me back?"

Maeve shook her head. "I wouldn't mention it if I were you. She's quite in the mood right now." She looked out the window at the setting sun. "And will be back any minute."

Rhea added, "Plus, you know, using magic like that would leave her in a weakened state. She'd be vulnerable for days, and it would take quite a while to recover."

"And I doubt she will want to help me save the kingdom of Rya."

Rhea took a sip of her tea. "Mmm, that too."

"But I wonder what it is that set her off about Rya," I said.

"You should ask her right now." Maeve grinned, her eyes flicking toward the door.

Mother Eville stood in the doorway, a wicker basket filled with lavender and mandrake in her arms.

I stood, my chair scraping across the stone floor as I hastily straightened my clothes to make myself presentable. Mother eyed me from head to toe, her lips pressed together, her emotions hidden.

"You've returned . . . unharmed," she questioned, and one dark eyebrow rose.

"Y-yes," I stammered. "I'm fine, but there's a problem, a sorceress and—"

You're in so much trouble, Maeve smirked at me.

"Good. Then see to your chores," Mother ordered.

"Wait, I have to talk to you. They need help. Our help."

Mother shook her head. "No, we will discuss this no further. You will not go back to Rya . . . ever." She removed her cloak, hung it on a peg by the door, and brushed past us into her drying room, the door slamming behind her.

"That was anticlimactic." Maeve sighed, drumming her fingers on the table. "I expected yelling, death threats, and curses."

"That's a weekly occurrence for when you disobey," Rhea said. "This is Aura. She never gets in trouble."

Maeve shrugged. "Sorry, it's in my blood, mischief and mayhem."

"Now what are you going to do?" Rhea glanced at me.

I shook my head. "I don't know."

～

Sleep wouldn't come. Night after night, I struggled to rest. Each of my dreams filled with nightmares about escaping the fog, the onwae attack; thorn branches crawled up and over me, wrapping around my throat and choking me. I would wake up in a cold sweat, gasping for breath.

Worry plagued my days, and I often froze during my chores and stared north, hoping, praying that Liam was all right. Did he worry about me like I worried about him? Was Devin okay?

I lost my appetite and tried to pretend to eat, but instead stirred my dinner with my spoon.

Hack brushed against my leg under the table in solace, but I barely noticed. It was Mother who watched me closely, monitored my moods, her brows furrowing in worry, her frown growing each day.

A week went by, and I barely recognized the person in the mirror. Dark circles hung under my eyes, my face looked sallow, and my dress fit loose.

Rhea took me aside and chastised me.

"Snap out of it, Aura." She gave me a hard shake. "There's nothing you can do."

"You don't know that. I don't know that." I finally let the fear and turmoil I had been hiding rise to the surface. "The blasted mirror is only showing that cursed fog. My friends could be in danger. Liam could be hurt."

"For all you know, they could be dead," Rhea hissed. "And the kingdom already lost."

"Don't!" I yelled. "Don't you say such things." Rhea winced and grabbed her head. My mental anguish thrust upon her unwillingly. "Sorry." I reached out to touch her to remove the pain, but she avoided my touch.

"There's nothing you can do," Rhea said.

"But there is. I mean, I have to try."

"No, Aura. That's not your gifting. You can barely survive going into town without having a breakdown. I spoke with Eden. She told me how you reacted after one day in the city. And you want to walk into the middle of a war between an enraged mage and the human king of Rya? It would be your undoing. I don't care how much shield magic your knight has. It wouldn't be enough." Rhea walked forward and placed her palms on my cheeks. "I don't want to lose you."

"But Rhea," I sobbed, my heart breaking. "Without Liam in my life, I'm already lost. I feel the emptiness here." I touched my chest. "He gives me hope. Hope that I can do something great before I spiral out of control."

Rhea pulled me into a hug, her arms, reassuring. "I only hope to fall in love that hard one day." She pulled back and wiped at my tears. "Does he feel the same way about you?"

"I think so."

She gave me a sideways glance. "How can you not know what he is thinking?"

I wiped at my tears and smiled. "He is really good at hiding his thoughts from me."

"Lucky guy." She chucked me under the chin. "And lucky you. I will try to make another travelling charm. It will take a few weeks, but I will work through the night if I have to. Just don't tell Mother."

"Thank you!" I tacked Rhea in another hug.

"Maybe all will not be lost by the time you return. He could still be alive."

It was those words that gave me hope and haunted me that night.

Sitting up in bed, I stared around at my sparse bedroom and the two empty beds that once belonged to Eden and Rosalie. Fingering the threadbare blanket, I recalled how it was once a fashionable soft pink, thanks to Eden's glamour. She always knew what pleased me, but glamour was not my strength, so without Eden's warmth and magic, the room felt dark and dreary.

Slipping on my robe, I tiptoed barefoot down the steps and to the main room, and I moved to stand in front of the mirror. Imbued with magic from touching many ley lines in different kingdoms, it was a relic that had immeasurable power, and it was Mother Eville's most prized possession. Magic mirrors were charmed surfaces that with a casted spell, one could speak to someone else that had another mirror. A two-way device. Unless you were a sorceress like my sisters.

We didn't need mirrors, for any reflective surface would suffice.

Except for the mirror in our household. It was finicky, and moody. This one solely served my mother, and would often need to be coaxed. I'd frequently come downstairs to see her speaking to the mirror as if it were an actual person, begging it to cooperate and show her certain royals. We never figured out how to get the mirror to work for us like that, so we stuck to our little compacts or small handheld mirrors.

Tonight, I needed something stronger, and I would seek the help of the dark mirror.

The black framed mirror hung on the wall across from mother's high-back chair. As I passed the settee, I saw a green knitted scarf Maeve had abandoned and stuffed under the cushion. The closer I drew to the mirror, the more uncomfortable I became. I never liked the mirror or scrying. I would pick up stray feelings, and I never knew where they came from. If it was the person I was scrying, or the mirror itself.

I shuddered. That was impossible. The mirror couldn't have feelings. Could it?

Most mirror spells required a drop of blood, except for this mirror. Once again, another oddity that made the Eville mirror rare. I brushed my finger across the cold surface and felt the magic stir and wake up.

I smiled when I saw the silver metal antennae Rhea attached to the mirror had become a permanent fixture to the frame.

Unsure of what to do, I cleared my throat, and politely asked, "Mirror, can you show me Rya?"

The mirror flickered and fog filled the glass, obscuring the view, an effect of the curse or magic that was currently affecting the kingdom. Biting my bottom lip, I thought of a different command.

"Mirror, show me Liam."

The clouds parted, and I saw a little blond-haired boy about eight running around a churchyard. His clothes looked to be hand-me-downs and had been repaired and patched up multiple times. His boots were worn, and one heel had come loose from the sole, but he didn't seem to care. He found a wooden stick and pretended to slay dragons and monsters. Near to him was a woman of the church who watched over him.

A familiar man with spectacles stepped out of the church, and a towheaded boy leaped off the steps while a somber-eyed girl followed.

The brown-haired youngster immediately picked up a stick and joined the blond-haired boy in his imaginary game.

"What's your name?" the brown-haired boy asked.

"Liam."

"I'm Devin," the boy made a face and pointed to the girl. "That's Delphine."

The mirror obeyed, and I then understood just how powerful this mirror was. It not only showed the present, but it could show the past. I was watching the very first meeting of a young Liam and Devin. I never realized that Devin and Delphine were brother and sister.

"Hello, Sister," Duke Tallywood addressed the woman of the church. "I was told that you have someone *you* wanted me to meet?"

"I do, Duke Tallywood. He's been with us for years and desires nothing more than to train to be a knight in service to the kingdom. I was wondering if you could sponsor his training." She gestured with her hands, and the two adults watched the young Liam and Devin spar.

Liam was quick, his moves elegant and natural, the stick sword an extension of his arm. No matter how Devin swung his own stick, Liam was quick to deflect and charge.

"He is something. I've never seen someone move that quickly. He's a natural swordsman. Who were his parents?"

"We don't know. An old woman brought him to us about eight summers ago, and he's been in our care ever since. I thought you would help him, for his talent is like nothing I've ever seen. He is a natural protector of the younger wards of the orphanage. I can vouch for his temperament and personality."

Duke Tallywood watched Liam and Devin play. Devin over swung and fell forward, skinning his knee. Liam immediately dropped his stick and attended to his playmate.

Delphine rolled her eyes and tugged on Duke's sleeve. "Can we go home now, Papa?"

"In a minute, sweets." Duke Tallywood nodded his head. "I see what you mean. I'll do more than sponsor him. I'd like to adopt him. I think he will go far, and he may make the order of First Light proud. He'd make a fine brother to Devin and Delphine."

Rubbing my hands together, I tried to gather the courage to ask the mirror my next question.

"Mirror, please show me the missing heir of Rya."

The mists cleared and showed a dark forest. A man wearing a dark hooded robe left a swaddled bundle on a stump. The babe stirred and cried. The man didn't even look back as he left the baby in the woods.

Is that it? I wondered. A babe a few days old, abandoned to die.

A flash of lightning and the gentle patter of rain began.

The baby cried harder, and I wanted desperately to reach through the mirror and help. A shadow moved on the outskirts of the mirror and drew closer. I held my breath, hoping it wasn't a predator. But no. A woman came, her head covered in a hood. She picked up the baby and soothed its cries. Another flash of lightning revealed the hooded figure, and I recognized the woman.

Oma.

I strained my neck to search its mists when it cleared again. It was to see my own reflection, and that of Mother Eville right behind me.

I jumped, clutching my hand over my heart.

Mother stepped up to the mirror, and hissed, "What do you think you're doing? How dare you show her this?"

Confused, I looked over my shoulder as the mirror went dark.

Mother glared at the mirror, her hands on her hips, and she turned to look down at me disapprovingly.

"I'm sorry," I said.

She sighed. "No, you're not."

"You're right, I'm not. But I have to understand what is going on so I can help."

Mother moved to her high-back chair and slowly sat down. Her normally perfect hair had come undone, and there were bags under her eyes I hadn't noticed before.

"Did I just see the past?" I asked.

"Yes, the mirror is only supposed to show the present," she glared at the dark mirror, "but it does have the power to look into the past."

"And that baby is the rightful heir to the kingdom of Rya?"

"Yes," Mother breathed out.

"I didn't know if I should believe the rumors about the missing heir, but you keep hiding things from me."

Mother's fingers trembled, and she blinked.

"But I've also been to the fae court, and down the hidden tunnel. I've seen the cell and the remains of your sleeping spell," My voice was a whisper.

"So, she has been freed." Mother crumpled. Her trembling hand reached for her brow and she whispered, "I was afraid this day would come. She is one of the strongest magic wielders I had ever met. I had hoped you would never ever cross paths with her."

"Why?" I asked.

She gave me a solemn look and shook her head. "Because her grief makes her dangerous."

"Who is she?" I asked. I became impatient and picked at my mother's mind. Daring to go where I had not dared to enter before. Mother's hand rose, her eyes locking with mine in warning. "Be careful, Aura. You may not like what you learn."

She wasn't going to stop me. I felt her release her guard. The walls dropped, and she let me into her deepest parts of her mind.

I'm sorry.

Then I learned everything she had hidden from me and I cried.

Mother's lip trembled as she brushed away her own tears of shame. She cleared her throat and gave me a stare. "You can despise me later, but right now you have to make a decision."

She gave me little time to process what I had learned. "Take into account everything you know, and the vision I've foreseen. This decision must not come lightly."

"I need to go back," I said.

Two dark silhouettes hung back by the stairwell, and I felt their worry and apprehension like clouds hovering over me.

"You're not strong enough to do what needs to be done. I should be the one to go." Mother stood up from the chair and she stumbled, reaching for her head. She quickly sat down again. "Well, then again, you've grown stronger."

What about the vision? Maeve asked mentally, unable to voice her fear.

"I've accepted it and so should you." I turned and addressed both my sisters who were hiding on the steps eavesdropping.

Maeve looked uncomfortable but nodded.

Rhea patted her closed fist against her hip. "So, how do we get Aura back there in time to save the day? I won't have time to craft another item."

"Leave that to me," Mother said. "But promise me, Aura, that you'll try to understand why I did what I did."

Anger burned within me at the injustice of what I'd learned, but I held silent.

I couldn't agree. I just pinched my lips and glared up at the woman who raised me, and who had lied to me. "I make no promises."

"I understand." She turned to her other daughters. "You two, go back to bed. We'll deal with this in the morning."

"Okay," Rhea said, yawning and retreating up the stairs.

"That's not fair!" Maeve raised her voice in protest. "We should go too."

"You will obey me," Mother snapped.

Maeve dropped her head and kept silent.

I softly tiptoed up the stairs to my room and felt Maeve keep pace with me. When I went to crawl in my bed, she took her shawl and wrapped it around my shoulders and tucked me in before going and laying on Eden's empty bed.

"Maeve—"

"Hush. Just let me stay here. I promise I'll only think happy thoughts."

I snorted and rolled over and was instantly hit with Maeve's disgruntled anger.

Happy. I'll be happy for her. Going on an adventure . . . without me. Causing havoc . . . without me.

Her thoughts were not cheerful, but they were familiar, like the soothing sound of rain during a thunderstorm. Eventually, I fell asleep.

CHAPTER TWENTY-FOUR

"Come, Aura, it's time." Mother stood at the edge of my bed, a leather bag slung over her shoulder.

"It's the middle of the night?" Maeve grumbled, rolling over and looking out the window to the dark sky.

"It's magic hour. The best time to open a portal between the realms," Mother replied.

I shot up in bed and looked at my mother in awe. "A portal?"

Mother rubbed her arm and looked uncomfortable. "I am doing what I swore I'd never do."

"That's dark magic," Maeve said in wonder.

"And very dangerous. Remember what happened with Rosalie when she tried to close one. The backlash scarred her for life."

Maeve's exuberance quickly dissipated. "I forgot."

"And you should never take magic for granted." Mother turned to me. "Quickly, get dressed."

Maeve lunged off the bed and hurried for the stairs. "Not you, Maeve," she said.

Maeve halted, her momentum almost carrying her down the stairs. She gave a pleading look to Mother.

"You will stay here," she ordered.

Maeve whined and headed over to the bed. In a dramatic show, she plopped down on the bed and grumbled at us.

Faster than a fairy chasing a sunbeam, I changed into a black overdress that laced in the front over my long sleeve chemise; my hair I left long, as I didn't waste time braiding. I borrowed Rosalie's midnight blue cloak as the thorns had destroyed mine. As I was leaving the room to head downstairs, Maeve sent a parting thought.

Leave a window open . . . please.

I winked in response.

Mother was waiting for me, a lantern in her hand, and dressed in a blood-red cloak embedded with gold symbols. It gave her a foreboding aura.

Hack, who was curled by the fireplace, looked up as I moved near him. *Be careful.*

I know. I leaned down and gave him a pet behind the ears.

At first, he was standoffish, but then he lost himself to my touch and purred.

Missed you.

I missed you too.

You're not coming back, are you?

I thought back to the vision. *I don't think so.*

Hack leaned forward and gave me the most feline appreciations. A head bump. *You're my favorite.*

I could feel the tears welling up in my eyes at our last farewell. *You're my favorite too.*

A sigh of regret followed, and I glanced toward Clove, our brownie. She held out her little stubby hand and waved goodbye to me. The tears refused to stop.

Mother headed out the door, and I followed, but not before secretly cracking the kitchen window. As we crossed the threshold, mother turned and put a locking spell over the tower to seal any doors and windows that were already shut, making them impossible to open. And I knew she did that to keep Maeve inside.

We walked in silence. The lantern creating a warm glow. I followed behind her as we headed back to the glade.

"You were there that night." Now that we were out of earshot of my sisters, I wanted answers.

"Of course, I was there. I've been at the christening of every royal child in all the seven kingdoms, not as myself mind you, but in a glamour. When Tatiana appeared in the royal court, she was insane with grief, intent on destroying not only the child, but everyone in the palace and Somnielle, the town below the mountain. I have no love for the king or queen, but I care about the people. It was a devastating battle. I won . . . barely, and I did not walk away unscathed." Mother pulled at the collar of her dress and showed me a zigzag scar that I'd never seen before.

"You stole the heir."

"No. The child was taken that night, but not by me. By another's hand. But I tracked the child down to an orphanage. I did what I could to protect the child not only from Tatiana, but from the king and queen. I altered the memories of everyone in the room to forget the child ever existed."

"But why erase the king and queen's memories of their own child?"

"Because you still don't know the complete story. Sometimes those closest to us prove to be the most dangerous. Despite my spell, the rumors of an heir still spread. And by now, the king and queen surely would remember what I'd done."

"You didn't get everyone." I shook my head. "An old woman named Oma remembers."

Mother muttered under her breath. "Well, there's no use hiding what I did anymore." Mother stopped and looked around the fairy circle. "You ready?"

My stomach dropped and roiled with uncertainty. Maybe I wasn't the right person. I couldn't talk sense into the madwoman. There was no way I could save a kingdom, let alone from someone as powerful as Tatiana. Just the thought of her sending me away, and this time potentially getting ripped into shreds, had me feeling sick.

Mother must have seen my expression, for her hard face softened. "We all have a destiny. We have to make hard choices. Just remember that Tatiana isn't the villain."

"She's not?" I asked.

"No, we are."

I swallowed and remembered all the years of fear and hate directed at us. The misunderstandings, the stones and mud thrown at me by the villagers in town.

She placed her hands on my shoulders and gave a squeeze. "You're my daughter, who I raised to bring vengeance upon the kingdoms. Vengeance earned because of their wickedness. Remember the reason Tatiana went mad. It was because of the death of the fae. Hundreds of fae mercilessly slaughtered by a cruel king."

I sucked in my breath and nodded. "It wasn't her fault."

"Whose fault is it?"

"The King of Rya," I said sharply.

She patted my cheek. "There you go. Maybe you will do better than I did. I always wondered what would have happened if I chose differently back then. If I had cursed the king or heir with the sleeping spell instead." Mother raised her dark eyebrow up at me. "You never told me why you left.

Maeve has been ever quiet as of late. I know she contacted you in the mirror."

I felt my cheeks grow warm.

Mother frowned. "Don't tell me you're falling for the stranger?"

"I am."

Her voice dripped with disapproval. "Love will only cloud your judgement. You must do what I could not. Don't repeat my mistakes."

"I won't," I promised.

"Good." Mother took out a piece of chalk and drew symbols on the ground. "The veil between realms is already thin here. It hasn't had time to heal. It will be easier to send you back from the same spot in the fairy circle and will require less magic from me."

"Where are you going to send me? It has to be somewhere you've already been in Rya."

"Don't worry, it will be somewhere close," she hedged. Her hands glowed, and she wove a spell in the air. Magic filled the surrounding space, the scent strong and heady. I watched as a portal appeared. A vortex of magic, and on the other side, a dark blur. Too early in the morning in the kingdom of Rya to make out exactly where I was going to land. There was a good chance that she would be knocked out, or have her magic exhausted by doing this because she wasn't fae.

A glowing circle rising up like a column of white light appeared in front of me.

"Goodbye, my daughter," she said. "Stay safe."

I raised my hand to wave goodbye and stepped forward, feeling the pull of magic. A dark shape flew toward me just as the portal closed. A stabbing pain ripped through my chest, and I cried out.

CHAPTER TWENTY-FIVE

It hurt to breathe. The pain radiated from the black crow that had barreled into my chest at the last second of the spell. Now, I lay sprawled on the ground, my back sore from the impact with the stone walkway.

"Maeve," I moaned, releasing my sister. "That was reckless. You could have ended up split in two."

The crow flew to the ground, and I watched her shift, something that I never got tired of seeing. Her body elongated, the beady eyes becoming sparkling pools of mischief, her black feathers becoming long, waist length hair.

"Really? Had I known that I might have rethought my plan," she said, tossing her hair over her shoulder. She reached out a hand and pulled me to my feet. "Thanks for leaving the window open. I knew mother would spell the windows and doors."

"Your plan?" I moaned and swung my arm around, feeling the stiffness in the muscles.

"Yes, I'm here to protect you."

I winced when I found a sore spot. "And who is going to protect me from your daring exploits?"

"Bah, you know I needed to come."

"Wrong. You're just here to stir up trouble." I turned in a slow circle to gauge our surroundings.

Maeve's eyes twinkled mischievously. "Maybe."

It was then I realized just where Mother Eville had spelled me. We were on the battlement on the outer wall of the palace. I leaned over, looking down the cliff and saw that the thorns had made progress up the mountain. They'd scaled hundreds of feet, but they had stopped for the moment and were no longer trying to climb the wall. What happened? Did Tatiana give up, or had she already been defeated? No. She was probably weakened from using the traveling spell and had to withdraw until she regained her strength.

Over here. I saw a flash.

We're under attack.

"Uh oh," I moaned.

"What?" Maeve frowned.

"We're about to be arrested," I answered.

"Not me, you." Maeve gave me a wink and then shifted back into the larger of her chosen bird forms, the raven. She flew off into the air, leaving me alone.

"So much for protecting me," I shouted after her and heard a loud kraa in response. "Dumb bird," I muttered.

Soldiers in golden helms and red cloaks trimmed in fur came from the guard towers, swords and shields drawn. I held my hands up in surrender and turned as the lead guard slowed, his sword lowering.

"Aura?" a familiar voice called.

The guard removed his helm, and I stared into Liam's disbelieving green eyes.

"Liam? You're okay?" I gasped excitedly.

The sword quickly raised and pressed near my neck. His green eyes hardened. "Take her to the king."

"What?" I stepped back, surprised at the sudden change in Liam's temperament. I didn't struggle as firm hands grasped my upper arms and pulled me along. I tried to keep pace and spoke loudly to Liam's back. "I'm sorry for what I did. I thought I could take on the blight by myself. Is everyone okay? What about Devin and Hayes?"

Liam ignored me, and I could only hope that they were safe.

The procession of hope didn't last long as we passed through the palace gates and they closed behind us. Three epic towers pierced the sky, and the royal flag battered the air, whipping into a frenzy. I stared up at the closest tower and saw a shadow of a figure back away from the window.

The courtyard was round with a fountain in the middle. Like a wheel, each spike headed toward a different area: the largest spike headed toward the palace gates, another went to the gardens, one toward the stables and another toward the barracks, and one toward the outer wall. The courtyard was packed with makeshift tents and shelters as hundreds of figures huddled together and slept by the fire.

I gestured toward the group. For now, most were asleep, but those that weren't, were awake and scared. "Are they refugees?"

Liam's eyes glowed with displeasure. "They have nowhere else to go. They've come here to escape the blight, but we have little time. The thorns have stopped their attack, but they will resume their climb at first light. Each day they make it further up the wall." He turned, his cloak billowing out behind him as he raced up the steps and into the palace.

The guards pulled me after Liam. I felt insignificant as I looked up through the glass ceilings in the main hall, to the spiral towers throughout the palace. There was so much glass it gave the impression of walking through a greenhouse.

Liam turned and gave me a once over, inspecting my

clothing as if I were one of his soldiers. He must have seen something that displeased him because he rushed over to me and flung my hood up, hiding my hair as he whispered a warning to me. "I wish you had never come back."

"I came here to help."

He looked away, and I clasped my hands under my cloak.

We passed through colorful glass doors and into the throne room, where I was unprepared for the introductions we were about to make.

A man with dark inset eyes and a brown beard spotted with gray sat with a stony glare upon his throne, the smaller feminine seat next to him was empty. The king of Rya sat, his legs crossed, his fingers steepled together, and he didn't move an inch when Commander Liam came and kneeled on the floor, bowing. I wasn't sure what to do, so I kneeled as well, keeping my eyes on the floor, my hood sinking even farther over my face. A curtsey may have been enough if I was a lady of the court, but knowing that I wasn't of noble blood, it was my safest option.

"You wake me in the middle of the night. Have you come to bring more disappointing news?" King Pharell drawled out lazily. He sighed and leaned deeper into the cushion of his throne. "I'm not even sure why I still tolerate you as commander of my guard."

"I've done nothing but serve your kingdom. I've fought for years to protect your borders, and will continue to do so with my life," Liam answered nobly.

"But not when the threat comes from within my kingdom. What have you done against this blight, except lose men to it? I suffer under the burden of both your annoying presence and your failures."

My body trembled in anger, and I could hold my tongue no longer.

I stood, and yelled, "That's not true."

King Pharell's legs uncrossed, and he leaned forward on his gold throne expectantly. "And who, pray tell, are you?"

Liam gave a slight shake of his head, but I ignored him. If I could save him, I would. "I am Aurora Eville, daughter of Lady Eville."

The king was not impressed. He sneered at the mention of my mother's name. "Lorelai, the very one who brought down this curse upon my kingdom out of jealousy?"

"Jealousy?" I stammered and felt my heart thud against my rib cage. "She did no such thing. She saved this kingdom from the person who tried to destroy you," I yelled.

"More like ruined," King Pharell said. The king stood and stepped down off the throne, stopping on the golden wheel etched in the marble floor in the center of the room.

"Lady Eville is the one who kept the blight away from your doorstep. The fact that it wreaks revenge is no one's fault but your own. If you want to stop the blight, then you need not look further than yourself and your own sins."

"How *dare* you speak to me so bluntly. I should have you punished."

Frustrated I pulled back my hood, revealing my white-blonde hair.

The king's nostrils flared, and I saw the hint of wild fear in his eyes before he looked down at the once again kneeling commander. "The resemblance is uncanny. Do you think she could be . . .?" the king trailed off as he became lost in thought.

I could tell from his expression that Liam was angry, frustrated with my outburst, and even more so at the king's reaction to me. But I didn't understand why my hair would be an issue. I focused on the king and felt nothing, heard nothing, and realized that Liam was shielding me, hiding his and the king's thoughts from my magic.

"Interesting. This changes things greatly. Have her prepared for tonight," he said to Liam. "If the curse wants an heir, I will give it an heir." His voice was quiet, barely a whisper, as he spoke his last thought. The king ran his fingers across his mouth in thought and then looked over to an alcove.

I followed the king's glance and only saw a shadow move and a curtain fall back in place.

"Liam, take her to the southern tower. Keep her comfortable. After all, she is a royalty." He beckoned and Liam drew close, kneeling on bended knee. The king whispering into his ear instructions while those keen eyes never left me.

"Yes, your majesty," Liam said, his voice low.

King Pharell clapped his hands, and two female servants slipped out of another alcove. They were clad in gray dresses with white aprons, their hair similarly styled in buns under a white mop cap. The taller one beckoned gently.

I was hesitant at first and turned to Liam for instruction. Liam was stoically silent. I couldn't help but wonder if I had wandered willingly into a trap. Led here by the noble intentions of Liam.

Liam grasped my upper arm and pulled me after him, my feet barely making purchase along the ground. I was running on tiptoes to keep up when we passed Devin in the hall.

"Devin," I cried and dug my heels into the ground. "You're okay."

"Aura?" Devin replied. He raised his arms for a hug, but got a surprise when Liam pulled me away.

"What in the world, Liam?" He moved to confront his friend. "Release her."

Liam's eyes darkened. His hand never left my arm. "You would do well to not question my authority, or do you forget I'm the Commander of the Guard?"

"And you would do well to remember, brother," Devin challenged, "that I'm no longer one of your men. I don't answer to you."

The two of them squared off, neither backing down.

I don't want to fight him, but I will. Devin's thoughts made my decision for me.

"Devin, it's fine." I gently pulled my arm and felt Liam release me. "I'm safe."

"I'm not so sure," Devin answered, but stepped back and let us pass. "Something odd is going on here."

I moved to follow the two servants up a flight of stairs to the southern tower.

After a few moments, Liam whispered. "You had no right to interfere."

"I did it because he didn't want to fight you."

"No, I mean interfere with me," Liam said.

He reached forward and pulled me against the wall. I was a few steps above him and now we were at the same height.

"You tricked me." His voice filled with anguish, and I knew then I had deeply hurt him. "Put a spell on me and abandoned us amid our greatest need." He laid his palm against the stone wall above my head, looking deep into my eyes for an answer.

"I did it to protect you. I was going to stop the blight by myself," I said.

The muscle in his jaw tensed and he wouldn't meet my gaze. He beckoned me forward. "You failed at both," he said.

The stairs leveled out, and as we came to the top floor and stopped in front of our destination, the shorter servant pushed a door with a heavy iron handle, and it swung inward with a creak. She waited for me to be escorted in, and I crossed the threshold and stood on the plush carpet near the bed.

"But you made it here safely," I said.

"None of the men could wake me from your spell. By the time it wore off, it was midday. I left them behind, raced after you, and found the golden thread. Fighting off the thorns, following your trail until I found this." Liam pulled the spindle from under his cloak and tossed it onto the bed. "I thought you were dead." His head dropped, and he took a deep breath. "I wanted to give up. Right then and there. If it weren't for the stupid basajaun. He dragged me back to the men and then retreated into the woods." He wiped at the corner of his eyes. "What were you thinking?"

"I was only thinking about you."

"There you go, all self-sacrificing again."

"I'm fine, really."

He grabbed my shoulders and whispered. "But *she* could have killed you."

"She?" I glanced up at Liam in realization. I felt betrayed, fooled, duped. I was a complete moron. "Liam, I never said the gender of the person imprisoned within the cell. That it was a *woman* responsible for the blight."

He looked away, and I knew.

"You know about Tatiana."

Liam nodded. "I told the king about what we found in the fog's vortex, what was in the lesser fae court. He told me the tale of the crazed queen, intent on destroying his kingdom. He knew it must be her, here for revenge."

"There's more to the story, Liam. More than you know."

"What does she want?" Liam asked. "Other than to destroy the king."

"She wants to kill his heir."

Liam blinked in confusion. "There is no heir."

"No, there is. Just like the spell I weaved on you to forget about me, Lady Eville weaved one over everyone to make them forget there *was* one. Obviously, hers was a lot stronger than mine because it lasted years."

"That poor child . . . forgotten, alone, unwanted. Why would anyone do that?" Liam asked.

"Why does my mother do anything? She had her reasons, and I have to trust her judgement that it was for the best."

Liam shook his head, and I knew now wasn't the time. I quickly changed the subject. "What's the king going to do?"

It took Liam a few seconds to respond, still upset by the news of an heir.

"He's going to open the doors and invite her in."

"What?" I gasped. "She's too powerful. She could once again destroy the court, and my mother isn't here to stop her."

"Then you better pray, because you're the only one who can." He pointed to my hair. "And now the king knows you're fae. He's going to use it against her."

We stood quietly, inches apart in the tower, letting the silence fill the air. I turned to look out at the window.

"Those in the palace will wake up soon. I will do my best to return quickly so I can shield you. But until then, stay here . . . please," Liam begged.

He pulled the door closed, and I heard the key turn in the lock.

I stared at the locked door, and a feeling of perpetual numbness overcame me.

The lock on the door meant nothing to me. There were no wards preventing me from using magic on it. I could easily unlock it with magic or blow it up, but then that would create more chaos and fear against me and my family. Even bring guards down upon me, and I would hate to injure or hurt them.

The trickling thoughts of the people on the grounds crept into my thoughts. Their fear. Their terror. Their worry. The strongest emotions washed over me.

I don't want to die.

It's going to get us. Isn't it?

I paced the room, pressing my palms to my ears.

I can't get the baby to stop crying.

My home. Destroyed by the fog.

We're going to starve if we can't bring our crops in.

I sprawled on the bed and used the pillow to cover and smother my head, trying to focus on the sound of the blood rushing in my ears instead. But it did little to drown out the sounds.

My stomach hurts.

This is because of the cursed fae.

"Stop," I whispered, but they couldn't hear me. "Go away." I sat up and flung the pillow across the room and it hit the stone wall.

I ran to the window with every intent to close the shutters in another attempt to silence the sounds. I leaned out the window, seeking a cool breeze across my skin as a distraction. My eyes glued to the battlement wall and the forest of thorns beyond, knowing that creeping toward us every second was a woman mad with grief, and she was stronger than me.

I looked down hundreds of feet below and could feel the ground moving beneath my feet. My mother's warning. A daughter will fall. My vision swam, and I felt myself get dizzy as my body pitched forward.

"What are you doing?" Hands grasped my waist and hauled me back over the sill, and I landed on the floor. "Are you crazy?" Devin cried out as he finally released me. He got to his feet and offered his hands to help me up.

I slapped his hands away and pushed myself up off the floor. "I wasn't going to jump. But after being locked inside all morning, I may contemplate it."

I eyed the tray of food he brought that now lay discarded in a messy pile on the floor, dropped as he tried valiantly to save me. My mouth watered at the delicious scents that wafted up to my nose. I smelled eggs and beef. If I was a prisoner, at least they were feeding me well.

"Are you a servant now?"

Devin blushed as he picked the tray and the cracked plate off the floor. He did his best to clean up the mess. "No, I may have bribed a servant to let me bring this up."

Devin stood with the tray in his hands. He shifted his weight from foot to foot. "It was wrong of you to leave us and take on the blight alone. Liam didn't take it well. He really cares about you."

"I know."

"No, I don't think you do. Liam is always rational, steady as a rock and the perfect commander, able to think things through. When you're around, he's a different person. He struggles, he's distracted, loses his temper if there's even a hint of threat to you."

Heat warmed my cheeks.

"All signs he's in love. And I've never seen him so protective of someone, and I've known him forever."

"Ever since Duke Tallywood adopted him and he became your brother."

"Who told you? It's a sore spot with Liam, being adopted. He doesn't talk about it."

"Oh, you must have."

Devin shook his head. "It's best if you stay put—for now."

"Fine." I agreed and sat on the bed, politely clasping my hands in my lap, giving him a pleasant but forced smile.

It must have been too forced because he gave me an odd look.

"You have no plans to stay here and obey, do you?"

"No." My smile grew wider, but my hands shook, and I squeezed them together tighter.

"Do I want to know how you're going to leave?"

"It's best if you don't, then you can claim ignorance."

"Okay, but there's two guards outside the door, and one at the bottom of the stairs," Devin muttered under his breath. "They're my friends, so try not to kill them."

My smile waned. I didn't even think of having to incapacitate guards.

The door shut, and I heard the lock click.

A dark shape landed on my sill, and Maeve cocked her head at me.

"Took you long enough," I chastised. "I need you to watch the thorns for when Tatiana leaves their protection and heads to the palace."

Why? she thought to me.

"Because the king's going to kill her, and she's going to kill the king."

Maeve's eyes glittered with mischief.

This will be fun.

CHAPTER TWENTY-SIX

"*Lochni*," I whispered the unlocking spell under my breath.

The door unlocked and swung inward a few inches.

I flung it open and surprised the two guards.

This is the witch?

She doesn't seem that dangerous.

I frowned, and quickly touched my fingers to both their foreheads, making the spell stronger by doing so.

Somnus.

They slumped, their armor clanging together as they collided and fell asleep on the floor. Their thoughts suddenly became silent as they slept.

"Oh, that's a relief." I touched my head and thought of a plan.

I crept down the stairs and sure enough, there was another guard at the bottom. Tapping his shoulder, he turned, and I did the same to him.

Somnus.

He crumpled into a pile, his helm clanging loudly against the stone wall. I winced at the sound and wondered if I injured him. Then he let out a long snore and I sighed in relief.

Passing near the throne room, a strong aura washed over me. I stumbled as a flash of red flickered in my mind.

Slowing, I found a space in a dark alcove and hid within the shadows. I tried to block out the unnecessary feelings and focus on the anger coming from the corridor.

When can we go home?

Mary won't share.

I can't pay that price for flour.

"Not now," I muttered. Pressing my palms to my ears, I tried to ignore them and focus on what was going on right in front of me. But there wasn't any way to do it surrounded by thousands of people. Walking up and down the halls, I tried to narrow down from which room I was getting the anger and heightened emotions.

A flash of green and red lit up my mind—greed and anger —as my hand settled around a golden doorknob. I leaned in, pressing my ear to the door.

"Do you have enough?" a muffled voice said.

"I have plenty for what you need," a female speaker answered.

"If this does what you say it does, then we have a deal."

The voices became distant, as if they were moving away from the door.

Turning the handle, I opened the door an inch and peeked into the room. A fire blazed in the fireplace, two oversized chairs faced the low burning embers. A round table with two glasses sat abandoned. I heard the far door closing and swung open the door to enter the study. I must have just missed the occupants leaving out the side door.

A cloying scent reached my nose, and I covered my mouth and almost gagged when I recognized the familiar smell, one that a certain brothel owner used. Madam Esme. Keeping my sleeve over my mouth and nose, my knees went weak. The scent was growing stronger, making me sick. I could feel my terror rise, my stomach doing flips. Someone grabbed my elbow, and I cried out in surprise.

"What are you doing here?" Liam whispered.

"She's here," I cried out and felt myself lose control. My entire body trembled.

"Who's here?"

"Madam Esme, I can smell the devil's breath."

Liam looked around the room and took a deep breath. "I smell nothing, except the smoke from the fireplace."

"I'm telling you she's here in the palace. You have to find her. She's planning something. Alert the king."

"Aura, it's fine. You're just overwhelmed with everyone's emotions. You probably imagined it."

"No, I'm not. I didn't imagine it." I couldn't keep the terror out of my voice.

Liam pulled me into a hug, and I crumpled. The fear disappeared, along with the voices. I relaxed and let him shield and comfort me.

His head snapped up, and his eyes filled with sorrow. "I need you to stay strong. Filter through the fear and focus on me. Or no one will survive this meeting. Come. It's time for you to get dressed and meet the queen of the fae."

∼

I didn't recognize the young woman staring at me in the mirror. The servants, Hermine and Herla, had outdone themselves styling my hair. The sides were pulled back and braided into a crown. They left the rest long, cascading down my backless dress. Delicate silk and pearls adorned the long sleeves of my white gown, which felt as though it were made for a wedding. It was too extravagant. I feared it brought out my pale skin and eyes and made me look ethereal and wane, not beautiful. But then I had never worn such a dress as this before.

Hermine beckoned, and I leaned down for her to place little pearl drop earrings as a finishing touch. Herla brought me white satin slippers with no soles. On the cold stone floor, they did little to insulate my feet. They left me to await my summons. Liam said he would return to escort me to the main hall where he would protect me.

The sky had turned to a dark pink, and the sun set. A knock came to my door, and I opened it, expecting to see Liam.

The smile fell from my face when King Pharell greeted me.

"Well, if it isn't my own personal slave."

"What—?"

He stepped back and a familiar woman raised her hand and blew a fine powder in my face. Instinctively, I inhaled. The powerful drug filled my nose, and I felt my senses dull as the devil's breath entered my body.

Madam Esme leaned forward. "You will obey the king's every command. Do you understand?"

My limbs were heavy, my brain a fog, and I could not do anything but obey. "Yes, Madam Esme."

King Pharell had retreated to a safe distance and came forward to test out my loyalty. "Stand on one leg."

Fighting the compulsion, I cried out as my body balanced on one silk slipper. His eyes took on a mischievous glint. "Slap yourself."

I did. My cheek stung and my palm burned.

"Good. You will do me no harm, protect me with your life if need be, and obey only my commands." The king stepped further into the tower. "How long will it last?"

Madam Esme followed. No longer dressed in silks, she wore a deep red velvet dress, making her pale pink eyes seem even more sinister. Her pale hair was pinned back by a simple comb.

Madam tested the weight of the bag of powder. "A few hours at the strongest, then she will gain more control, unless you give her a second dose."

"You didn't give me enough last time. I could only control her for a few months before she wanted to go home."

Contempt flickered briefly across Madam Esme's face before it was replaced with a small smile. But I had seen the anger she had for the king.

"If I had known you were planning to start your own permanent personal harem of one, I would have given you more. Plus, she was fae. You knew you couldn't keep her."

My stomach dropped as I pieced the story together. The fae woman in the story wasn't King Pharell's true love, but his prisoner.

"Stop whining. I looked the other way for you for years. Now you owe me." King Pharell held out his hand expectantly. "Give me enough this time."

The king took the bag, and Madam added, "There's enough to keep her compliant for years."

Her? Was he referring to me, his wife, or Tatiana?

"Excellent." King Pharell tucked the purple bag into his pocket and handed Madam an even bigger bag filled with coin.

Madam Esme stepped back, her eyes glittered with greed as she pulled open the string and counted her gold.

"This is more than enough to get my business going again," she preened, and I felt sick to my stomach. Then the queasiness turned into a burning hatred. She had to be stopped. I had to stop her. I vowed she wouldn't leave here and hurt another woman again.

Obey me! I thought loudly at her.

Her hand clutched the gold coins, and I saw her freeze. Her brow furrowed as she heard my internal command.

She was an empath—like me—and she hid behind the fog of her own drug to not feel anything. But that also meant she could also be compelled. I wasn't cut off from using my empath powers like before. Her command was for me to obey the king.

Silence! You will not speak a word.

Her open mouth clenched closed as I saw her about to make an attempt to compel me.

Her eyes went wide with terror, and she turned to warn the king. I had little time and little choice. My eyes flickered to my open window, and I knew I was going to go down a path of no redemption. I was going to destroy my soul, but by doing so, I would save hundreds, if not thousands of others.

Jump.

She fought my compulsion, fought the command, but my powers were honed, and I was desperate.

Madam Esme couldn't drop the gold coins, but she clutched them even closer to her belly as she moved to the window ledge.

"What are you doing, you daft woman?" King Pharell bellowed.

Madam Esme didn't look back as she jumped from the window. Silence followed her descent as she couldn't even cry out. But I felt her terror as she fell.

I heard the greenhouse roof shatter, and the thoughts silenced.

I buckled, falling to my knees. I cried and felt my soul

shatter like the glass of the greenhouse. My body and mind felt broken, for I had sinned. I had taken a life and felt her die.

King Pharell looked over the windowsill and cringed before looking at me in awe.

"You did that, didn't you?"

I faced him, expressionless.

"Answer me."

"Yes, I did."

He cupped his hands over his mouth and laughed. "Extraordinary. So powerful, so young, and all mine." He trailed a finger under my chin, forcing me to look into his cold, cruel eyes, and I saw myself.

My eyes became glassy as the weight of Madam's death weighed heavily on me.

"Come, Aura, I know the kind of woman she was. I know she had kidnapped you for her brothel."

It took effort, but I muttered. "How?"

"Do you really think I don't know about the dealings that go on in my kingdom? I had almost bought you for myself." He pulled out the paper advertisement and read out loud. "Milky white skin, hair like moonlight, eyes like pearls."

I sucked in my breath.

"You should thank me."

"Th-ank you," I said under command, but my body recoiled at the king's nearness, wishing I could rid the world of the horrid person standing in front of me.

He beckoned a finger, and the king's personal attendant came forward, bowing his head. The king whispered instructions, and they exchanged the purple bag between them. "You know what to do?"

The servant nodded and slipped away into the shadows.

King Pharell held out his elbow to me, and I noticed the dagger he hid under his blood red velvet jacket.

"Come," he commanded. "The night is only beginning, and there is more blood to be shed."

I shuddered as my hand touched the velvet, my eyes never leaving the weapon, wondering who the instrument of death would be . . . the king's dagger, or me.

CHAPTER TWENTY-SEVEN

Music and lights filled the banquet hall. The melodious singing of violins and cellos grated on my nerves. Instead of calm, I was becoming increasingly stressed. They decorated the hall with red paper lanterns, their glow casting a red sheen on the floor that looked like spilled blood.

Like a puppet, I followed behind the king, obeying his every command, internally screaming and waging war against the drugs flowing through my system. I counted down each second, waiting for them to wear off, all while testing the limits of my compulsion.

"Sit here," the king commanded, pointing to a padded stool to the left of his chair on the dais. Like a dog, I sat, my back straight, focused forward on the hall and the meager guests. I'd only ever watched a banquet through the magic mirror, and this one felt staged.

Below us was the head table, and on each side was another table with placards designating seats for the guests. A quick look at those within the room gave it away. It was easy to see they were not nobles, lords or ladies, but soldiers and servants disguised as guests.

I recognized Hermine dressed as a lady, her dress not nearly as fine or ornate as the others. But her fear poured off of her in waves. Her hand never strayed far from her clutch and the weapons I knew to be hidden inside.

All an elaborate plot to hide their forces and numbers to deceive Tatiana into thinking she was a welcomed guest and not walking into the obvious trap that it was.

A dark aura clouded my mind, and I looked up as a beautiful woman stepped into the room, her hair hidden beneath draped gold silk, pinned up with rubies. Her golden dress had long flowing sleeves that fell to the floor. I couldn't pull my eyes away from the beauty that was Maris, Queen of Rya. Tall, elegant, and with sharp, predatory eyes, she reminded me of a golden eagle with winged sleeves as she zeroed in on me and approached. I knew if I were worried about King Pharell's madness, the real danger had only just arrived.

It was the darkness of her aura that gave me grief.

"I thought I told you to stay in your rooms tonight, dear?" King Pharell's voice was strained as he stepped in front of me.

"Nonsense, we have two very special guests. What kind of host would I be if I weren't here to greet them?"

Anger flashed in my mind, and I had a vision of two tigers circling each other, sizing up their opponent.

Blood will be shed tonight.

My neck snapped toward the royals in shock. That same mantra came from the Queen's mind.

A noble with long dark hair caught the king's attention, and I could feel his reluctance to move away from me. He turned to me, and whispered, "Don't move," before heading off.

The mood changed as Queen Maris turned those rapacious eyes on me. She took in my short stool, my hands clasped in my lap, and then she taunted me.

"So, it's true. A daughter of Eville has entered my home." I turned and looked at the thin, frail woman standing before me. Her lips, stained the shade of blood, pulled back into a fake smile.

I moved to stand and curtsy, but could not, my body firmly stuck to the seat at the king's command to not move.

"Who do you think you are that you don't address me properly?"

I will break her, the Queen thought.

A hand drew back, and she slapped me in the face. I could do nothing but take it, and I felt the sting and then a warm trickle as blood ran down my cheek. The queen smirked as she rotated her giant diamond ring around to sit on top of her finger. A diamond stained with my blood.

She leaned close and stared at my face. Her hand reached for my hair, she gave it a yank, forcing my face forward so she could stare at the bloody mark she left on my face.

"What a passive little thing you are. And to think I had thought you a threat." Her eyes strayed past me to her husband, the king, who was oblivious to our discussion.

I hate him. He destroyed everything I love.

"W-why," I asked. "do you hate him?"

She blinked at me and released my hair, and my scalp stopped burning.

"What did you say?" she hissed.

"What did he take from you?"

Those dark eyes filled with pain. Her mouth turned down, and she raised her hand to strike me again.

No, I mentally commanded and felt her falter.

The hand stilled, her eyes filled with fear.

A trumpet peal cut us off, and they announced dancing. It angered me, the great lengths they were going to create this charade. This trap. The king returned to my side, and the queen retreated to her smaller throne a few feet away. As the noble with dark hair passed below the dais, the candlelight reflected along his hair, giving it a strange green hue. Guests moved toward the dance floor, but there were few females present. One noble moved toward me, he bowed, and I only saw the dark top of his head as he requested a dance, his voice muffled.

Frozen in my seat, my eyes craned to look toward the king.

He smirked and seemed to enjoy the power he had over me.

"You may dance, but you will not leave this room."

I nodded again and stood up. My muscles ached. I had only been seated for a few minutes, but I had been tense, fighting the compulsion the whole time. I took a step down the stairs and stumbled down.

Idiot. The king's stray thought was not missed.

A warm hand grabbed mine and pulled me into the crowd of swirling bodies. My face pressed against his fine suit, his hand on the small of my back, he guided me farther away from the dais until we were behind a column—out of the sight of the crowd.

"I felt I owed you a second dance," a familiar voice murmured into my ear.

Aspen's grip around my waist tightened, and I looked up at his cold eyes. I struggled, and he released me. Instead of his robe, he wore a dark suit, the collar tight against his throat, his hair impeccably styled. The grace with which he moved showed his nobility. "Relax. I'm not here to harm you. We're here to watch the chaos."

"We?"

He gave me a wicked smile, bowed, and slipped back into the crowd.

We. He had said *we*. Panicked, I scanned the throng of people for the noble I had seen speaking with the king. Why hadn't I caught it earlier? There was only one person I knew with hair the color of a deep sea, and he had died months ago.

"Vasili," I breathed out, searching.

My heart thrummed against my rib cage as the trumpets bleated for the second time, announcing our awaited guest. The palace attendees stood at attention, the double doors opened, and the crowd parted down the middle as a woman in a white hooded cloak walked through.

"Announcing Tatiana, Queen of the lesser fae court," the crier called.

Tatiana stepped into the room and removed her hood. Her pale hair billowed down her back like a cloud, and her long-sleeved dress draped her in the color of the night sky.

I couldn't help but see the resemblance between us.

Come to me, the king commanded.

Pulled by compulsion, I moved across the floor, keeping to the sides as I made a beeline for the king.

"Aura, wait." Liam rushed into the room from the hall. His hand went to the sword at his side as he glared at the fae queen, but he dared not draw it.

As Tatiana walked down the center of the room, I was parallel with her moving toward the king, but I was keeping to the shadows.

"Welcome, Tatiana Morningstar, to my court. It's been years since you last graced us with your presence." The king's smile didn't reach his eyes.

"I think you know why that is, Your Majesty," she said coolly, her eyes a steely blue. She stopped before the dais, her chin raised in defiance—but the auras coming from her were not the ones I had encountered earlier. There was no anger, rage, or hatred. Only amusement.

Something was off.

The king moved down the steps and offered her a bow. "The circumstances by which you were imprisoned were not by my command, but by those of another," King Pharell answered cryptically.

"Nevertheless, you destroyed everything I hold dear when you destroyed the fae court," she answered as if reciting a line.

"And you stole my child," the king roared.

The court gasped, and the room fell silent as their dark secrets finally came to light. Mother was right. He had finally remembered.

Tatiana's lips pursed in amusement. "That I did not. Though, I tried."

The king's face paled, and he became flustered. "Then who did?"

Tatiana laughed; a high-pitched tinkle filled the air. "For that answer, I would look closer to home."

Enthralled to have the upper hand, Tatiana twirled and looked at the tables laid with golden plates and gold-rimmed glass goblets. "Come, now. It's been years since I've been here for one of your illustrious banquets. What was the last occasion? The christening of your child. The one I supposedly stole."

"It seems that we have both erred and are in the wrong. Please accept my humble apologies." The king's response was dry and insincere. "Sit, and we will discuss business after dinner." He snapped his fingers to announce it was time. The servants appeared from behind curtains and moved to stand behind each chair. The king and queen moved to the head table, and they kept me in the shadows, near enough to heard but not be seen. They pulled the chairs out, and the guests sat, only after the king and queen had first.

This was wrong. I could feel it in my bones. The way Tatiana moved, spoke, and even teased—this was not the same crazed woman I had met in the forest of thorns. But someone else. An imposter.

Tatiana sat right below the king and queen's head table in a spot reserved for the guest of honor.

There. Down a few seats from the fae queen was the one that I had seen die in Isla. Vasili. But there was something off about him. If only my head wasn't foggy, I could hear their thoughts.

The servants filled the guest's goblets with dark red wine and handed one to each of the guards. Liam was only a few chairs down from the queen and he looked uncomfortable. His eyes found mine, and I could read the sadness within. He knew something was wrong.

Almost time.

"A toast." The king lifted his goblet. "To Tatiana of the Lesser Fae Court, may we find the answers we seek."

He drank first, followed by the queen. Glasses raised, and the room followed suit, one by one, each taking a sip. Liam caught my eye, and I carefully shook my head. He brought the glass to his lips but did not drink.

Neither did the fae queen, I noticed.

Dinner began with the soup course. Light chatter and the scrape of spoons across the bowls filled the air. Then came the salad course. I refilled glasses multiple times, but I watched as Tatiana only brought the spoon to her lip, but never drank, or she moved food around on her plate, but never took a bite.

Not having been commanded to eat, I stared at the closest

candelabra on the table and fixated my gaze upon it. One wick had fluttered out, and I focused my power.

Fiergo, I whispered under my breath.

The candlewick relit, and no one noticed. I breathed a sigh of relief. I was getting easier to use magic.

Drink, darn you! The king was becoming impatient, which only confirmed my suspicion that he had drugged Tatiana's food and drink with the devil's breath.

Dessert came, and it was more of the same. She never ate or drank a bit.

Clever, the king thought, *but not clever enough.*

The king nodded, and each servant moved to a red lantern. They pulled a silk ribbon, releasing a hidden compartment within. The lantern shifted, a flume of powder fell onto the flame and burned. Immediately an overpowering aroma filled the air.

Devil's breath.

I covered my mouth and nose with the sleeve of my dress and tried my best to not breathe in anymore. All around the hall, silverware clattered to the table as the drug took its victims one by one. First their limbs became heavy, then their minds would begin to cloud over. Liam staggered and fell back into the wall before drawing his sword and attacking the closest paper lantern, knocking it from the hook and stomping on the flame. Other soldiers followed suit, but it was too late. The damage had been done.

Tatiana slumped forward in her chair, her chin dropping toward her chest.

The king stood, his hands held open, and he bellowed, "All that hear my voice must obey me."

Wide, blank eyes stared back at him. Over a hundred

guests were now in a drugged state, easily controlled by the king of Rya.

The king stepped down from the high table and moved to stand over Tatiana. He withdrew a knife and held it to her throat.

"Now that you're under my command, tell me how you murdered my child, or I will kill you now," he said, seething.

"I don't know what you are talking about." Tatiana looked ill. She stood up. The chair tipped and fell to the floor with a thud. Her dress flickered in and out. The lace disappeared and was replaced by a dark blue wool. Tatiana's white hair turned lavender as the glamour wore off, and the mermaid known as Velora stood before the king.

"A glamour. What is this?" the king bellowed, his finger pointing at the betrayer. "That's not Tatiana."

The double doors burst open, and a powerful voice filled the room.

"No, Your Majesty. It's but a decoy." The real Tatiana entered, wearing head to toe black, her pale eyes glowed with power. "I knew you. This talk of peace was nothing more than a trap. The one who calls himself Allemar said you would betray me." She pointed to Vasili and Aspen, who hadn't been affected by the devil's breath. Aspen moved to scoop up the drugged Velora, and he gave me a wink before heading out the side door.

"Allemar. No, it can't be!" King Pharell paced back and forth, distressed that his plan had backfired.

Allemar in Vasili's body came forward. "In the flesh, or rather someone else's flesh." He gestured to his taller, leaner new body he now inhabited.

"What are you doing here?" King Pharell asked.

"Well, since I was never paid for the deal I struck, I

released the curse upon your land." He gestured with his head toward Tatiana.

"I never made a deal with you." King Pharell seethed between clenched teeth.

"No, you didn't." Allemar bowed his head toward the queen. "She did."

Queen Maris stood up and pointed a finger at him. "He lies. I did *no* such thing."

"What did you do, Maris?" the king yelled, and the two argued loudly.

"Oh dear, this is going to get messy." Allemar grinned and walked over to me. He placed his hand upon my forehead and whispered.

I screamed in pain as the blood in my body felt like it was boiling.

"W-what are you doing?" I cried out.

"I'm evening the odds by burning the devil's breath out of your system." A few agonizing seconds later, it was over. I fell to my knees—in pain, but clear-headed—no longer under the influence of the hated devil's breath. He backed away. "Good luck, and may the craziest person win." He waved his hand and disappeared in a cloud of fog.

"Here!" King Pharell pointed at me. "There's my heir. Take her and be done with it."

Tatiana laughed. "Fool, I am past the point of wanting your heir. Now I just want you dead."

"You will pay for your betrayal."

Neither of them seemed to have noticed the exchange between Allemar and me.

Tatiana's head fell back, her eyes glowed, and she flung her fingers toward the air. The earth rumbled, and the white marble floor cracked and split as giant thorns erupted from the ground and rushed toward the king.

Liam jumped in front of the king, his sword drawn. Faster than I had seen him attack before, he took out every barb that aimed for the king.

One barb scraped across Liam's face, creating a streak of red.

King Pharell spun to me, and ordered the crowd, "Kill her. Kill the witch." Liam and Devin stepped in front of the king, each one of them fighting back Tatiana's deadly thorns.

One by one, the compelled guests, armed with knives, spoons and whatever cutlery was available to them, stalked Tatiana.

"No," I said, my voice cracking. Getting to my feet, I stumbled as I heard hundreds of thoughts at once. I winced as I tried to focus, tried to sort the lies from the truth.

Tatiana's attacks turned to defense, the thorns swiping under people's feet, the bladed barbs retracted as she focused on keeping them at a distance and not killing them. It seemed she was saving murder for the king.

"Well, stop her," King Pharell stormed over to me.

"No," I snapped. "I'm done being a puppet. You have no power over me."

"Is that so?" he sneered. "Well, then what about your precious Liam?"

"Liam!" King Pharell screamed. "Draw your dagger."

Liam, his eyes dull, pulled the dagger from his belt.

"Kill her."

"No!" I cried, and with a flick of my wrist, I flung the dagger across the room, and Liam fell to the floor without being injured.

King Pharell snarled. "I'll take care of you myself." He

OF THORN AND THREAD

reached for his closest guard and yanked the sword from his hand. He raised it to strike me down, but a branch wrapped around his legs, yanking him to the ground. The sword clattered to the floor.

An attack on all fronts, one soldier made it through and slashed at Tatiana, slicing her arm. She cried out in pain and I screamed. Feeling every emotion.

"Now, I will kill you all," Tatiana cried out. Her hand flicked, and one thorn transfigured into a blade, and it pressed against the king's throat.

Yes! Do it.

A flash of yellow. Intense joy filled my mind, and it was coming from the queen.

A blur of black streaked through the door. Shifting magic hit me and Maeve appeared before me, her eyes wild with fear.

"Stop her," Maeve yelled. "Stop the witch before she brings the palace down on us."

The thorns had gone out of control, growing in size, busting through the windows, crawling up the side of the walls and ripping through the roof.

Screams filled the courtyard, and I felt their terror. Part of an exterior wall collapsed outside, crushing innocents. I felt their pain, their grief and death, and I tried to block it out.

Clutching my head, I agonized over the mental pain that was thrashing about in my mind.

"I can't. It hurts too much."

"Then I will." Maeve turned on the crazed fae woman. "If it's one thing I don't back down from, it's a fight." Maeve cracked her knuckles and lifted her hands.

"*Ignis Fiergo.*" Green flames shot from Maeve's hands as she attacked Tatiana with mage fire.

Sensing the attack, Tatiana pulled the surrounding thorns,

creating a green shield. The thorns immune to normal fire burned under the mage's fire.

I felt her fear as the thorns burned. She fought back by sending more magic into the growing vines. I felt the pressure build and roll under my feet, and even more thorns ripped up from the ground. But mage fire was not easily conjured or controlled. It was made of magic, and therefore part alive. It wafted and moved like a snake and struck out at a passerby, missing, and lighting the curtain on fire.

The mage fire didn't stop, shifting into a fiery dragon that ripped through the main hall. It crashed through a window and came in through the north side, sweeping up to the rafters. The banners, flags, and roof caught on fire.

"Run," Liam cried, waving at me to go for the door.

"We have to get the people out," I yelled, terrified they were still under the influence of the king's command to attack Tatiana.

A young woman, her face streaked with soot and tears, armed with a knife, ran straight into the burning flames toward Tatiana.

I felt her death, and I gasped.

"No more," I whispered. Turning, I searched for the king who was cowering behind his throne. Queen Maris had disappeared, presumably running for her life. I grabbed him by the collar and hauled him to his feet.

"Command them to run for their lives."

"Not until she's dead," King Pharell said through gritted teeth, spit falling from his mouth.

"Aura, I need help!" Maeve cried as she struggled to control the flames and fight off Tatiana.

I let my anger take over. Reaching out, I touched King Pharell on the forehead, and I ripped from him his memories, his thoughts, and I dug for the truth. He screamed in pain, but I didn't care. I dug further, not at all concerned if I destroyed his mind while doing so. What I found made me despise him all the more. What I left of him was a whimpering king, crawling on his knees, begging me to kill him.

I took a step, and a burning beam fell, cutting off my path to Tatiana and Maeve.

"Call back your mage fire," I yelled.

"I would if I could," Maeve replied. She brushed her hand, and with a blast of wind, pushed five people out of the room, just as more of the ceiling came down. "Aura, do it. Lose control!"

"Aura?" Tatiana heard my name, and she looked at me as if truly seeing me for the first time. "It can't be," she breathed. Her hand touched her heart. "You're alive?"

The fire dragon made a figure eight in the air and then rushed toward me.

"No!" Tatiana cried out. She waved her hands in my direction, and a wall of thorns erupted out of the ground, flinging me out of the way. My body went through the window, colored glass shattered around me like snow. I fell onto the balcony that overlooked the cliff, my body rolling until I hit the outer wall with a crack, and everything went black.

CHAPTER TWENTY-EIGHT

The world was on fire. When I came to, I saw the green fire dragon burst through the roof. Spinning in an arc, it passed above me and flew over the battlement wall and down, burning the forest of thorns surrounding the castle.

A loud groan filled the air as another section of the main hall roof collapsed. I could feel the people trapped inside, feel their pain, their terror, and it became my own.

My fingers dug into the stone as I tried to pull myself to my feet. As I did, I looked over the outer wall and saw that not only was the castle on fire, but so was the entire forest below. Green flames flickered, creating a sickening glow across the night sky.

This was all wrong. This wasn't supposed to happen. I had come to Rya to help the kingdom, but I realized the problems started with the king and queen, and the hatred and evilness had gone on for generations before them. I understood why Lorelai had chosen the path she did. Because sometimes the only way to save a kingdom from a villain was to become a villain yourself.

"This is all your fault," a manic voice called out to me.

I looked up as Queen Maris stood over me. Her hair pulled from her pins, her dress ripped, and soot covered her face.

"All I had to do was to bear a child and all would be well,

but no. Even that was denied to me. Your mother cursed my womb."

"A barren womb means you or someone close to you has taken another life. And in return, one has been taken from you."

Her eyes glittered with unshed tears. "You *lie*."

"I do not." I stood my ground. "A curse isn't always meant as punishment but can right a wrong. It's a means of justice, and sometimes to avenge evil, you need a greater Eville. Sometimes that evil is my mother, and sometimes it's me."

The queen paled at my warning, but I had to play my cards and keep her at bay, for there was a madness behind her eyes, and one hand still buried deep within her skirts.

"I know your sins," I said. "I know what you did."

Queen Maris' hand shook, and she took a tentative step toward me. I felt that the queen was close to breaking. She crumpled, folding in on herself, her hand clutching her stomach.

"You don't know the truth. The pain that I suffered when that woman came here," she said, seething. "I was his favorite. Until he met *her*. She did not belong here, just as you do not belong here."

"You killed Ophelia."

"She was a pregnant whore," Queen Maris spat.

"She was a prisoner of your husband's desire, bound by drugs. You could have helped her, freed her. Instead, you poisoned her."

"He was obsessed with that woman," she whined, running her free hand down her face. "I couldn't stand it. Being number two to her. A nobody fae without an inch of noble blood. She had to go, by any means possible. But then I didn't know about the brat."

"The king made you keep the child, pretend it was your own."

Maris cried out, her fingernails raking down her own arms in distress. "I couldn't allow that child to live, let alone pretend it was mine. So I made a deal with a sorcerer to steal the child the night of its christening, but then Lorelai showed up. Since then, I've been barren, and it's her fault."

She raised from the folds of her skirt a silver dagger. Queen Maris drew the dagger closer to her chest, the tip pointed toward me.

The queen's lips pulled into an ungainly smile. "I knew what was best for our kingdom then, as I do now. Allemar told me that once I've killed you, I will no longer be barren. Your death will lift the curse from my womb."

She lunged, swinging the dagger toward my throat. I easily knocked it from her hand, but a mad woman was strong. She flung herself at me and I fell backward, her weight pushing me over the ledge of the outer wall. My back bent over the wall as she clawed at my face and ripped at my hair.

I grabbed hold of both wrists, but I could feel my hip sliding further over the ledge.

"Get off!" I screamed, as I felt myself falling.

She leaned back, and I grasped at the stonework and pulled myself back up. But she hadn't retreated, only regained her footing to charge at me. She jumped, pushing me over the ledge. We both fell, and I screamed.

My hands clawed at the air and latched onto a hanging banner, bringing it with me as I fell. I grasped at the fabric, and I caught it inches before it ran out. Queen Maris grabbed my dress, holding onto me as I hung onto the banner.

"No! You were supposed to fall." She clawed at my back.

Our combined weight was too much, and the banner ripped further from the ring.

"Crawl up," I demanded, still trying to save us both.

"Never. My blood will atone for that I spilled, and yours will break the curse over the kingdom."

The cloth ripped further, and we plummeted another few inches. I looked up. It was a few feet before I could reach the ledge while we hung suspended in the air.

I watched the banner give way, felt the tension lesson, and we fell.

"Aura!" Liam appeared, catching the banner at the last second as the end slipped over the wall. I cried out as my body slammed into the stone.

"Liam," I cried, but could feel my fingers giving way. The queen was too heavy for me, and he was struggling to pull us both up.

I could hear him straining and grunting through gritted teeth as he tried to drag us up slowly, inch by inch. He lost his grip and fell forward, his stomach slamming into the wall. We fell again, losing the precious few inches we had gained. I saw the inevitable.

I looked down below me, toward the burning forest, and remembered my mother's warning. One of the daughters will fall. I closed my eyes and felt the tears burn as I realized this was the end. I was out of strength.

I met Liam's gaze, and he read my thoughts. "No, Aura. It's not the end. I won't let you fall." With renewed strength, hand over hand, he pulled us up. But I could feel my strength waning and knew it would be too late.

"Why won't you *die?*" Queen Maris cried out, and I felt a painful stab in my side.

I gasped in shock and felt my fingers lose their grip.

"Aura, no!" Liam cried out and dove for my wrist, catching me at the last second.

A raven appeared and dive-bombed the queen.

Queen Maris withdrew the dagger from my side. The bird wouldn't give up and clawed at the queen's face, causing her grip to lesson. Maris lunged and waved the weapon wildly at the air, making contact and slicing the raven. I heard Maeve's mental scream, felt her pain, and watched as her black form plummeted. The queen lost her grip, falling with the bird into the burning mage fire, her scream echoing into the night.

CHAPTER TWENTY-NINE

"Maeve!" I cried. I heard nothing in response. My world swam. Pain radiated from the wound in my side. I was so tired. I wanted to let go and join my sister in death.

"Don't let go, Aura," Liam yelled, pulling on my wrist until my ribs rammed against the ledge. With a last tug, he pulled me up to safety. Liam's arms wrapped around me, his lips brushing across my brow as he whispered promises. "It's okay, Aura. I've got you. I won't let you go."

Tears streamed down my face and I felt numb. I looked back over the ledge, searching the burning forest below with my eyes and reaching for her with my mind.

I yelled her name over and over with no response until my voice was hoarse. Everything was silent, and then I knew why. I spun on Liam.

"Stop it!" Liam was shielding me with his magic. He was trying to block out the pain and the emotions.

"Aura, she's gone. She couldn't have survived that far of a fall, and into the fire."

I flung his arm away. "Don't touch me! I have to find her." I raced for the stairs that led toward the palace exit. Liam gripped my elbow, stopping me.

"No, help them." He pointed at the burning palace, the

courtyard filled with people as they tried to escape the mayhem. Fire blocked every exit while a battle raged on between Maeve's fire dragon and Tatiana's magical thorns.

"I don't care. Let them die," I snarled. "I need to find my sister."

"You don't mean that." Liam backed away from me, his eyes filled with sorrow.

"I do. I hate this kingdom. I hate this place and wish I had never come. I wish I'd never met you. Then . . . then she would still be alive. She wouldn't have followed me here."

"Aura," Liam coaxed. "I have to shield you. There's too much death. As an empath, you can't handle it."

I was being smothered. The intense pressure was moving in and I could see he was trying to help me.

"Stop shielding me!" I screamed. "If you want me to save your kingdom, Your Highness, then you will stop shielding me right now."

Liam blanched, and he stepped back in surprise. "What do you mean? I thought you were the heir?"

"You are King Pharell's and Ophelia's child."

"I don't understand . . ."

"The night of your christening, Allemar took you into the forest and left you to die. It was Oma, Ophelia's maidservant, who rescued you and took you to the Order of the First Light, the orphanage that Duke Tallywood adopted you from."

"How do you know that?"

"I saw their memories, and their sins. He drugged and imprisoned your mother, and the queen poisoned her and paid Allemar to get rid of you. I saw your rescue and adoption."

"I don't know why, but this explains it . . ." He backed away, and I instantly felt his shield magic fall. "I feel it here. I've always felt it. A love and loyalty for this kingdom."

"Believe me." My hands trembled, and I felt the madness and the anger roll through my body.

He looked at me with tears in his eyes, and I felt his fear. "Aura, if you love me, save my people."

"I'm not strong enough to fight her," I whispered. "I can't do it." He handed me the spindle.

"I believe in you." He reached down and kissed me on the forehead. "You will save them."

I pulled away and nodded, looking up at the castle, my body shaking as I went to do the impossible.

But who will save me?

Holding the spindle, I ran toward the flaming hall. Liam tried to follow me, but I waved my hand, cementing his feet to the stone walkway.

He cried out my name in protest, but I knew this battle would end in death. I couldn't save everyone, but I could try to save him.

When I entered the destroyed hall, King Pharell had Tatiana pinned against the wall, a blade to her throat. Her eyes met mine across the room, and I picked from her thoughts how the battle ended. She wasn't completely heartless as I'd first believed. When she had tried to protect me, she had let her guard down. She lost her advantage, and the thorns retreated.

"I did it," King Pharell crowed. "I defeated the fae queen. Now you will bow to me, or die."

Tatiana's chin raised. "I would rather die than bow to you."

"So be it." The knife pulled back.

"Stop it," I screamed, and the king faltered. Lifting the spindle high into the air, I stabbed it into the ground and reached deep into the earth for the ley line, searching for it, but finding it too far out of my reach. I wasn't strong enough to reach it through a mountain of stone.

The king smirked. "Is that it? That's the extent of your power? I knew you were worthless."

Tatiana's eyes, glassy with tears, met mine from across the room. "My magic comes from the earth. Your magic comes from emotions. Use it, Daughter, to destroy him."

King Pharell sneered. "Daughter? What are you talking about?"

I opened myself to the feelings and thoughts of those in the room. A kaleidoscope of reds, blues, and grays flickered across my mind. Hundreds of voices spoke at once inside my head and I heard them all. I felt their pain, and I took it into myself. As an empath, I desired to take pain away from others. I wanted to heal the mind, but in doing so, I had to endure it.

This time I didn't. I siphoned emotions and feelings until my knees shook, my back felt like it would break, and my mind split into two. Then I directed all of it into the spindle. The string fell from the spindle as the firethorn took shape and sprouted new golden branches. With the sheer amount of pent-up emotions I'd directed into it, it grew faster than Tatiana's. Racing across the floor, twisting brambles of gold shot out and went right for the king, wrapping around his legs and working up his body.

The king cried out, desperately swiping with his blade across the thorns. "Help me," he commanded. "Kill her. Kill the girl."

The guards and those left in the main hall moved as one unit, raising their weapons against me.

You will not attack me.

With a flick of my wrist, I sent the brambles after every one of the attackers and watched with a smile as the thorns pricked the nearest guard. He ran two feet and then collapsed. One by one, the thorns attacked until there was no one left standing except the king who was wrapped in my thorns up to his neck.

"You killed them," he cried out, glaring at Tatiana. "You're just like her."

"I should hope so," I said smugly. "She is, after all, my mother."

"Impossible."

I waved my hand, and a branch rolled up my arm, its leaves stroking my skin like a cat. The thorns did not dare to prick my skin, but glided across it gently.

"Kill him," Tatiana seethed. "Kill him now, then drive his head on a spike and put it outside the castle as a warning for others."

"You have to let the anger and bitterness go," I said.

"Never. I still hear their dying screams. Hundreds of fae, and I was unable to protect them. Only blood will stop their ghosts from plaguing me." Spit fell from her lips, and I saw the crazed look in her dilated pupils. I knew she couldn't be brought back. Her mind was too far gone.

"I'm sorry, Mother, please forgive me." I raised my hand and touched her forehead.

Somnus.

Tatiana sighed and fell to the ground.

King Pharell realizing his defeat, begged and bargained. "Now, if you just let me go, we can talk about your future. I mean, our future. What do you think about an alliance?"

"I would never align myself with the likes of you." I grinned evilly as the branch that was wrapped around my arm rose up like a snake and pricked the king in the neck. His eyes rolled back in his head before he went limp.

CHAPTER THIRTY

"Well, I never expected this from you." Mother Eville walked among the destroyed main hall, stepping carefully over a sleeping woman. "Maeve, yes, but not you, Aura."

"It had to be done," I said numbly. "I had no other choice. They would have continued to attack under the influence of the king's compulsion until no one was left standing."

Mother moved toward a golden branch that was wrapped around King Pharell. The king's mouth was slack, and drool dribbled down his chin.

"It's a shame that you'd altered the poison within the firethorn. You could have rid the world of another corrupt king."

I knew it was a jest, but I was beyond caring. I rubbed my arms and stared across the destroyed hall and the hundreds of people in various positions of sleep. Feet poked from under a table, some had collapsed on the floor, weapons still in hand.

I kneeled by the thorn that had once been the spindle and lifted the golden string, showing the unique knots I had tied and wrapped around it.

"A sleeping spell."

"It is what I'm best at," I said.

When I cast it, I had only meant to keep them asleep until

the devil's breath had run its course through their system. I had already discarded the pouch and destroyed the remains. But that was over a month ago, and they had not yet woken up.

"When do you plan on releasing them?" Rhea asked.

"I don't know," I answered, moving to sit upon the king's throne, my fingers running along the wood, feeling the warmth.

Mother watched me warily.

"You don't?" Rhea asked.

"I like it," I said, giving them a half smile. "My head doesn't hurt anymore. It's quiet and yet"—I got up from the throne and walked over to a sleeping Devin propped up against a wall, his head slumped forward. I fixed a section of his hair that was out of place—"I'm not lonely."

Rhea sucked in her breath. *This isn't right.*

"Who asked you?" I snapped, spinning and knocking a goblet from the closest table. "I didn't ask either of you to come here. I'm fine on my own."

Rhea's bottom lip trembled, her eyes filling with tears. "No, you're not, Aura. You can't hold them hostage. They aren't to blame for Maeve's death."

"No, just him." I pointed to the sleeping king before gesturing across the room to the sleeping Tatiana. "And her."

"No," Mother said. "It was Maeve who chose to disobey and come here against my wishes. You did as well, and now you both have suffered the consequences."

"I did what you didn't have the strength to do. What she should have done years ago. Instead of imprisoning Tatiana, you should have killed the king and queen, and then none of this would have happened. Now there's peace in Rya. I did that." I pointed out across the kingdom, to the fog that was no more. Tatiana's thick forest of thorns was still present, a wall of protection around the palace that was currently keeping unwanted intruders out. But the rest of the kingdom had slowly begun to rebuild. Refugees returned to their homes, their crops, and their families.

"It wasn't time," Mother whispered. "Events had to occur in a certain order to get the outcome that would do the most good."

"Oh come now, Mother," I teased. "Isn't this what you wanted. Revenge on the kingdoms? I finally did it, and I now rule a peaceful and sleepy kingdom. You should be proud."

She's gone mad. Rhea let her thought slip.

I snarled. "I hate that word."

"Why do you hate the truth?" Mother moved to stand over me. She was still an intimidating figure. "You are an empath. It's your destiny to heal, not harm—and yes, that destiny leads down the path toward madness, but not always. When you use your gifts for good, you can live a full, long life, but when you harm others"—she gestured toward my crazed mother—"it brings nothing good."

"You should talk," I said bitterly. "I can't believe you didn't tell me about her. You told me my mother was dead." I pointed to Tatiana, who I had moved to the table. Her head propped on a red pillow, her petite hands crossed across her chest, her long white hair carefully covering the burns and scars that covered her arms.

Lorelai shook her head. "The sleeping spell *is* called the sleeping death."

Rhea kneeled by the spindle and began to sweep back the dried leaves. When it was free of debris, she broke off the original spindle from the thicket. With a wave of her fingers, she easily transfigured it back into a spindle and wound the remaining gold thread around it, tucking it into her apron pocket.

"Plus," Lorelai continued. "It wouldn't have done you any good to know about your mother too soon."

"You said she went mad."

She pointed at the missing roof and the destruction of the main hall. "She did."

"I guess I will never understand your motives, or why you took me," I said, as angry tears threatened to fall.

"When I brought Tatiana back to the fae court to imprison her, an injured basajaun approached me, holding out an infant. Your mother believed you were dead, but the basajaun must have protected you during the attack. It was that grief, losing you, that sent her spiraling out of control. I had already sealed the vault, or I would have placed you inside with her to sleep until the spell wore off in a hundred years."

"I wish you had," I said sadly, wiping away tears that had fallen, my rage waning.

"Nonsense. If I had, you wouldn't have been able to save the day here. Although, someone will need to stay and clean up this mess." Mother Eville frowned and looked around at the destroyed palace as we headed up the stairs to the tower.

"Not me," Rhea piped up.

I sighed as we passed the stairwell window, and I looked out at the empty courtyard. Those sleeping there had been moved to the closest shelters, inside their tents, or inside archways so they were out of the elements. It was slow work, but I did it.

We walked into the same tower room where I had stayed, and I stared at Liam sleeping peacefully on the bed. His aura drew me to him, and I'd spent many hours sitting by his bedside watching his dreams. I rested my hand on his forehead, and I caught the glimpses of his thoughts and dreams.

And they were always about me.

Heat rose to my cheeks as I blushed. He was dreaming of kissing me.

"Aura, are you listening to me?" Mother chastised and moved to the other side of the bed.

"Hmm?" I dreamily looked up at her.

"I said, what are you going to do now?"

Glancing down at Liam, I dropped my hand and felt my throat constrict. "I'm going to leave, and then I want Rhea to release the castle from the sleeping spell."

"I can do that." Rhea nodded, her brain already working on the counterspell needed. Then, she pointed to Liam. "What about him? He will be mad when he wakes up to find you gone."

"He won't remember I ever existed." I leaned forward and brushed a kiss across his forehead, whispering the words of the forgetting spell.

His breathing changed, and as I closed my eyes and touched his forehead, I watched his dream change. Liam and I were standing in a field surrounded by yellow flowers. He was watching the sunset, and he lifted my chin to kiss me.

It was only a dream, but it felt real. I could feel the brush of his lips across mine. I could see myself through Liam's eyes, and the forgetting spell took hold. The setting sun behind me blinded him, and he couldn't focus on me. Then my face and features faded and became less descript. My image blurred, and like a wind catching the seeds of a dandelion—I was gone.

I felt a tear of regret slip down my face.

His confusion hit me first. Gray filled my mind, and he searched for the nameless person. My brows furrowed as he was fighting the spell. So I had to go deeper into his mind, further back, and I erased every memory that included me, until the gray faded away.

"It is done." I wiped at my tears.

Rhea clutched her dress and wiped away a few of her own. "Why did you do that?"

Mother watched the entire exchange, her face void of emotion. "Because he is the prince and must rule the kingdom of Rya, and Aura cannot survive in his world."

"Oh," Rhea said sadly, as she realized what I had known my whole life.

I wiped my hand across my face and stood to face my mother, smoothing my dress, feeling the nervousness wash over me.

"Now, there is something I will need your assistance with. Do you think you can help me?"

"I will help you," Mother said softly.

CHAPTER THIRTY-ONE

I checked the wards. They remained undisturbed since my last trek below the fae court. Placing my hand on the stone surface, I let my magic unlock the door, and I slipped into the cell where my mother slept.

Like I had done with Liam, I listened to her dreams. They were restless, filled with pain and anguish as she relived the night of the attack and my presumed death over and over. I sent a sliver of magic her way, spelled on a whispered breath, soothing her turmoil. With a touch, I took her pain as my own, easing her dreams, gently reminding her I was here. That hope was not lost, and that her fae court was coming to life again under my care.

Her breathing evened, and the nightmare faded. I relaxed. Twice a day, I came to check on her and spent time healing her broken and scattered mind.

"What is broken can be fixed," Mother Eville had said when she helped me create new vaults deep below the never wood trees.

"I can repair her mind," I promised.

"I believe you. You are more than capable and strong enough to do so. But it will take time. Years, even."

"Then it will take years."

Mother Eville nodded, her face solemn as she looked over

the new archways built out of stone, and she tested each of the wards along the base of the doors. "I wasn't referring to the fae queen." She pointed to the roots of the never tree that hung from the dirt ceiling. "You can rebuild the fae court."

"Who says I want to? I like the quiet of living alone."

She shrugged. "Suit yourself; but just remember, as an empath, life is inevitably drawn to you. You won't be alone for long."

Mother Eville's words stuck in my mind as I touched the strange woman before me. For that is what she was: a stranger, and not my mother. I focused on a particularly devastating memory and tempered it. Repairing the mind took a delicate hand. Tatiana's mind was like a vase whose varnish had crackled. Each day, I would mend another crack, but there were thousands of fissures. It really would take me years. But I believed she would be queen of her court again, and I would bring them back to life.

As I left the vault, I turned to the one covered in black sigils and I shivered. I did not check on the dreams of the soul sleeping behind the door, nor would I ever. If I had my way, I would have killed him, but just like Mother Eville, I was not strong enough to follow through. Killing the queen had been an accident, and I could still feel the heavy weight upon my soul from her death, and that of Madam Esme's. I would not be the instrument of death when it came to King Pharell. So as much as I hated it, I followed in Mother Eville's footsteps, and wove the strongest sleeping curse I could upon him. A hundred years.

He would be preserved, protected behind the door, and I would guard it, keeping the evil deep inside where that tainted soul could not harm another person.

I walked up the stone steps and came above ground, raising my hands to block out the sun. The never trees had indeed grown under my care, and with the help of a little magic, most of the willow groves had sprung up almost overnight. The streams were already filled with undines as well.

"Dah!" Sneezewort called out in greeting as he waddled over to me, a shovel over his shoulder. Sneezewort and another had made the journey to Rya to help me rebuild the lesser fae court.

"Dah!" I waved back.

Sneezewort pointed at the old hob hill and the home he had just repaired.

"It looks wonderful," I commended.

"Already occupied." Sneezewort rubbed the back of his neck awkwardly.

"Really?" I placed my hands on my hips and studied the closest hob home.

A female hob with a pile of scraggly red hair, in a dress made of leaves, walked out the front door and shook out an old rug.

"Durn women," Sneezewort bemoaned woefully, a contrary reaction compared to the rosy color that bloomed along his cheeks.

His murmuring didn't last long before something caught his eye and he went charging, screaming at the air, swinging his shovel.

"More Pixieees," Sneezewort howled, taking off after the little pixie who dodged the whack of the shovel and pulled his moss hat over his eyes.

"PFFFFttttt," the pixie blew his tongue and then flew up

to the top of the never tree and hid among the branches of their new home.

"Stupid pixie." Sneezewort thumbed his nose toward his arch nemesis. He turned back to the hob homes, and his waddle became a little wider as he headed to greet the new occupant.

I couldn't hold back my own grin as I headed deeper into the firethorn thickets to check on the fairy circles. The firethorns parted, allowing me to pass unharmed, and a blur of gold darted past me, making a beeline straight for the circle of mushrooms.

Hack was my second visitor that traveled all the way north in Sneezewort's bag. Hack gave me plenty of grief when he arrived and demanded treats. He seemed to settle into life at a faerie court. He rolled around in a patch of dark grass and then strolled over and made a show of chomping on a cowslip. He gave me a perturbed look.

Tastes bad.

"Of course it does. Not everything that grows near a fairy circle is edible, nor does it taste good."

He glared at me, and his tail gave one flick before he turned away.

Stupid pixie lied.

I held back laughter and tried to hide my amusement.

"Did she?"

She said if I roll in a fairy circle, everything you eat tastes good.

I sighed. All pixies were mischievous. I was going to have a long talk with the pixie after I sorted out the new guardians that had moved to our court. Across the glade, I could hear the three new basajaunak pushing more giant stones toward the entrance with Basa. He was the one who had saved me as a child, and in doing so, his own family had perished. Basa was alone, guarding the fae queen for years. Until I came along. He was thrilled to add the basajaunak to his family, and their marks on his stone.

Mother was right. As an empath, my presence seemed to attract new life to the courts, and fae thoughts didn't plague me as much as those of the human variety. Maybe because their thoughts were simple or purer of intent.

Hack flicked his tail at me and squinted his eyes.

Hungry.

"You're a hunter." I waved my hands at the air. "Go catch something."

Hack coughed, showing his disdain before he stretched, showing off his feline claws.

Fine. I'll go catch something. He sauntered off into the brush. *And then leave it on your pillow.*

"Hack!" I yelled out in feigned irritation, realizing that I was so close to my future of living alone and becoming a crazy cat lady. Except, instead of cats, I collected mischievous fae.

I felt a featherlight tickle poke at my thoughts, and I turned, searching the glade.

There was nothing there but the fields of daylilies I had planted in honor of my mother, and beyond the glade was a wall of firethorns—my own added protection against non-fae, in case they ever thought to attack again.

The feeling didn't pass, and so I crossed over the fairy circle and walked to the edge of the glade, staring at the wall of thorns.

"I told you I would always find you."

My heart fluttered in my chest, but I knew I had to be imagining his voice. Slowly, I turned and cupped my hand over my mouth to hold back my sobs.

Liam's golden hair had grown longer, touching the collar of his shirt. A brown traveling cloak had replaced his red cloak. His tan was more gold, and there were dark circles under his eyes, and scratches from the firethorns across his cheeks and arms.

"What are you doing here?" My voice was barely above a whisper.

"Why . . ." He swallowed, struggling to form his words. "Why did you make me forget you?"

"I had to, Liam, because of who you are."

He shook his head in disbelief. "I'm still the same person."

"No, you're the heir to the throne of Rya. A prince. A king."

"What difference does that make?"

"I'm not like my sisters. I can't live in a palace surrounded by hundreds of people. I will go mad."

"I can shield you." He grasped my hands and rubbed his thumb over the back of them.

"You can't shield me constantly without blocking my power. That's not fair to you, or me. And I can't go back there. Because that's where Maeve . . . I lost my sister."

"I'm so sorry, Aura." Liam pulled me into a hug and let me grieve. I'd been bottling it in for so long, that once I let it loose, I wasn't able to contain my sorrow.

He didn't shield me, instead letting me cry. When I could cry no more, he wiped away my tears with his fingers.

"I only wish I could take away your pain like you do for everyone else."

"The pain helps me to remember her," I whispered.

"Then I promise you will never have to step foot in the palace again. I'll build you a different palace if needed."

"Thank you. But I found where I belong." I smiled and

gestured to the forest and the fae that were spying on us from the trees and flowers.

"You belong with me." Liam's voice was husky as he leaned forward, pressing his forehead to mine. The feel of him touching my skin made me dizzy.

"I can't live my life surrounded by stone walls and thousands of people. It will be a mental prison," I said.

"Then I don't want that life either."

I pulled back in surprise. "What do you mean?"

"As an orphan, I searched my entire life to find my purpose. I thought it was to protect the kingdom of Rya, and I spent years training to do just that. But my purpose is to protect you."

"But you're the missing heir. You have to take the throne."

He grinned. "And who's to say the heir's been found? He's been missing for decades, and no one believes there is an heir, anyway. Let the heir stay a mystery."

"Then who will repair the palace, run the kingdom?"

"I'm the commander of the guard. The running of the palace falls to me, and I've already put someone in charge."

"Who?" I asked.

"Devin."

"No," I gasped.

"He's ready to kill me. Threatens to every single day. He's champing at the bit to run away, but I told him he will stay there until I say otherwise. Besides, he is Duke Tallywood's oldest adopted son by only a few weeks. He's next in line for the throne."

"Oh, he is really going to hate you."

Liam tossed his head back and laughed. "Devin has already whined about not hitting the taverns, and how all the ladies must miss his shining personality and jokes." Liam's smile faltered. "Actually, Devin is the reason that I'm here."

I realized my folly. "I didn't erase Devin's memories."

"No, you didn't. He kept asking about you, and I had no clue who he was talking about. I had enormous gaps in my memory and had to conclude that someone tampered with them."

"I'm sorry." I turned away, feeling the shame of what I had done wash over me.

Liam grabbed my elbow. "No, you're only sorry because you got caught. But I don't even care because you haunted my dreams."

"That's not possible. I erased myself from your dreams."

"Not your voice. I remembered the sound, how the pitch would get higher when you were nervous. I could hear your laugh. I listened until I recalled the shape of your eyes, then the color came, then your lips. Until I remembered everything. I remembered you."

"I was a fool—" I began and stepped away.

"Yes, you are. I swore to protect you, but how can I if you erase yourself from my life?" He closed the distance between us and pulled me against his chest.

I gasped in surprise. My hands pressed against his muscles, and I could feel the beating of his heart matching my own frantic pace.

"Run away, erase yourself from my mind a hundred times over—I will always find you. My heart will lead me back to you. You are unforgettable, Aura."

He brushed his knuckles down the side of my cheek, his eyes following and lingering on my lips.

My lips parted in excitement.

"Can I kiss you, Aura?"

"Yes," I whispered and leaned up on my tiptoes, closing the distance.

"Can I kiss you forever?" he asked, pulling away at the last second.

"Only if you marry me," I teased.

"Are you proposing?" Liam asked, his green eyes suddenly serious.

"No, I . . . uh." The question rattled me. Heat rushed to my cheeks in embarrassment.

"I accept," he said firmly.

"Wait, I don't think that's how it's supposed to work?"

"So, you don't want to get married?" Liam's brows furrowed in confusion. Then I saw his lip twitch as he held back his smile.

She's so cute when she's flustered, he thought.

"Am not." I playfully hit his arm.

"Are you going to kiss me? I'm still waiting." Liam grinned.

Not letting anything or anyone interrupt us, I wrapped my arms around his neck, and we kissed. My heart that had once broken apart was slowly being repaired.

I love you, Aura. His unshielded thoughts drifted to me.

And I you.

When we broke apart, he wasn't ready to let me go. Nuzzling the top of my head, he breathed into my ear. "Look."

I turned and looked at the setting sun and how it cast a halo around us, making the yellow daylilies look like fields of molten gold.

It was just like Liam's dream. He'd imagined this very moment before it even happened.

"You saw the future?" I whispered in awe.

"No, I see *our* future." He left a trail of butterfly kisses across my cheek and threaded his fingers through mine. We turned to face the many fairies, pixies, and hobs that had gathered around to watch our reunion.

Sneezewort was wiping his eyes, and the pixie brought him a large leaf and he loudly blew his nose. The pixie patted his back awkwardly before Sneezewort bowed his head in respect. The female hob and pixies followed. The trees moved as I saw the dryads bend low; the grass shifted as the cù sìth dogs bowed. I even heard Hack cough in response.

"What's going on?" I asked, confused.

"I may not be able to give you a kingdom, but that doesn't mean you're any less a queen to the fae."

"But I don't want to be queen," I whispered.

He chuckled. "You're the missing heir," he repeated back to me.

"I'm not ready." I panicked. "What if I make mistakes?"

"Don't worry, you will." Liam wrapped his hand around my waist giving it a squeeze, and I felt his calmness wash over me. "And I'll be by your side for each one of them. You can't live in my world, but I can live in yours."

EPILOGUE

I couldn't move. Something trapped me, and I could feel the heat racing across my body. I coughed, my lungs filled with hot air, and I knew I would either bleed out or be killed by the encroaching mage fire. Even now I could feel the fire singe my feathers.

Kraa!

My voice was too weak as I tried to call out to Aura. She had to hear me. She would come after me. I moved my wing, and pain ripped down my side. I saw it was bent at an odd angle which meant it was broken—and that made it dangerous to shift. If I did, there was no telling if I would survive the transformation.

"Well, if this isn't a surprise?" a deep voice spoke from the darkness. A young man with dark hair and eyes leaned over me, his back silhouetted by the green mage fire.

Kraa! Kraa! I screamed until my voice went hoarse and I could no longer cry out. My vision filled with smoke as two more hooded figures drew near and lifted the body of the dead queen off of me.

I shuddered. Once I was free, I tried to stand, but only collapsed to the ground, unable to rise. I lay there, my heart beating wildly as I waited for them to kill me.

"Is this the one you had the vision of?" the young man asked.

"Yes, Aspen, she is the key. The one whose anger burns like a never-ending fire," a man with dark green hair said. "She's the one who called down the mage fire and killed the innocents when the roof collapsed."

No, I thought weakly. *I didn't mean for anyone to get hurt.*

"She's the one I want. Bind her and bring her with," the man with dark green hair ordered.

"We must hurry. The fire is spreading fast, and our way will be blocked."

The one called Aspen leaned forward and clipped a band to my leg. As soon as the cold metal touched my clawed foot, I could feel my power drain with its spell.

No!

I knew it was wrong, and I knew it was risky, but I had to shift.

I closed my eyes and imagined my feathers shrinking back into my skin, the crown of feathers on my head becoming my hair, but when I did, I cried in pain.

"It's useless," a soft voice spoke to me. A young woman with lavender hair leaned down and gently picked me up from the ground, placing me on the floor of a black iron cage. "The band binds you in that form and keeps you from shifting."

No...

I flapped my wings, rage filling my mind. I attacked and pecked at the girl's hand, drawing blood.

She hissed, pulling back and slamming the cage door shut, turning the key in the lock. I heard the click and felt my hope fade away. She pulled the key from the lock and there was a thin silver chain attached. She handed it to the one called Aspen, who put it around his neck.

"It's done, Allemar," the girl said, holding the cage up.

Allemar leaned forward, his lips pulling up into a creepy smile, exposing his slightly pointed canines.

"Good, Velora, then let us leave this place. We have work to do, and a new apprentice to break in."

His laugh was bitter—dead inside—and it echoed into the night air. Even though the forest burned, and the air around us was a hundred degrees, I shuddered.

Note from the Author:

When I was researching the original Sleeping Beauty story, I forgot how many variants of the tale there were—from Giambattista Basile's earliest printed version called *Sun, Moon, and Talia,* that was adapted by Charles Perrault into *Sleeping Beauty,* and by the Brothers Grimm into the *Briar Rose.* I knew I wanted to make sure that Aura had a more active part in the story, which is why I love to write antiheroes.

But when I read Basile's *Sun, Moon, and Talia,* the message really bothered me. Where the king rapes the sleeping Talia, and from their non-consensual union are born twins named Sun and Moon. The king, already married, brings Talia and the twins to his court, where his queen tries to murder them. The story progresses, the evil queen is killed, and the king marries Talia, and they live happily ever after.

Stop . . . right there. No! No! No!

I knew right then how I was going to have to write this story in a way that I've not written others by touching on subjects that might make readers uncomfortable: sex trafficking, mental health, and abusive relationships. We should be uncomfortable when confronted with these topics. Mental health should be discussed and not stigmatized. Sex trafficking and abusive relationships shouldn't be normalized.

I've seen it popping up all over the internet, social media platforms, and TV shows normalizing this kind of behavior. Books promoting bully romances, shows whose plot revolves around kidnapping and rape while the victim falls in love with her abuser, and more. But most of all, they all have the same

AUTHOR'S NOTE

message: they promise that if the victim sticks it out, there will be true love.

Dear Reader,

Love is gentle, love is kind, love is patient.

Love does not raise a hand or hurt others.

The world has a problem, and that's turning a blind eye to the victims of mental, physical, and sexual abuse. And it was important for me to write a story where Aura struggles with mental issues, becomes a victim of abuse, and then speaks her mind. Consent is a powerful part of the storyline. Where Liam asks permission for a kiss. There are Liam's out there in the world. I married one.

We live in a society where 1 in 5 women have been sexually abused. I will make my voice heard loud and clear, and the only way I can is through writing.

I'm 1 in 5. I'm speaking from experience, and from the heart, when I talk about healing and finding hope after.

If you have ever been a victim of any kind of abuse, you have a voice. You are not ignored. You are not forgotten. Because I see you. I'm listening.

Please, if you need help, reach out to a family member, pastor, counselor, or one of the below resources for help.

- National Sexual Assault Telephone Hotline.
- If you would like more information on getting counseling for sexual abuse, please visit https://rainn.org
- Or call 800.656.HOPE (4673)
- National Suicide Prevention Lifeline

AUTHOR'S NOTE

- If you or someone you know is suicidal, please call 800-273-8255. They are available 24/7.
- Or visit https://suicidepreventionlifeline.org for support and prevention and crisis resources
- If you would like more information about mental health, including depression, suicide substance abuse, please visit
- Mental Health Gov at https://mentalhealth.gov
- Or call 800-273-8255

CONTINUE THE DAUGHTERS OF EVILLE SERIES WITH

Of Mist and Murder

COMING 2021

ABOUT THE AUTHOR

Chanda Hahn is a NYT & USA Today Bestselling author of The Unfortunate Fairy Tale series. She uses her experience as a children's pastor, children's librarian and bookseller to write compelling and popular fiction for teens. She was born in Seattle, WA, grew up in Nebraska, and currently resides in Waukesha, WI, with her husband and their twin children; Aiden and Ashley.

Visit Chanda Hahn's website to learn more about her other forthcoming books.
www.chandahahn.com

Printed in Great Britain
by Amazon